Artificial sweethearts

a North Pole, Minnesota novel

JULIE HAMMERLE

Entangled Publishing, LLC
2614 South Timberline Road
Suite 109
Fort Collins, CO 80525
Visit our website at www.entangledpublishing.com.

Crush is an imprint of Entangled Publishing, LLC.

Edited by Kate Brauning
Cover design by Erin Dameron-Hill
Cover art from Depositphotos

Manufactured in the United States of America

First Edition July 2017

For Augie, my summer baby
For Erin and Kate and all our happy summer memories

Chapter One

They look…different.

That was Tinka Foster's first thought as she entered the baggage claim area and caught sight of her parents at carousel number seven.

They looked like themselves, but slightly off. They looked like aliens attempting to impersonate her mom and dad, but not doing a great job of it.

Her boarding school roommate, Jane Packer, who was staying with Tinka in Minnesota for the next four weeks, stopped next to her. "Are those your parents?"

Tinka snuck a quick glance at Jane, as guilt and regret nagged at her again. This was how it would be for the next month. Their last night at school would haunt her every time she caught a whiff of Jane's rosewater perfume. Shaking away the guilty feelings, she focused on her parents instead. "I… think that's them." Tinka squinted. "What the hell did they do to themselves?" The people standing next to the baggage carousel were not the same couple she'd seen six months ago during winter break.

"They're adorable!" Jane took off running, rolling her pristine, raspberry Louis Vuitton carry-on behind her. A weight lifted from Tinka's shoulders as Jane left her side.

Tinka trailed Jane, delaying the reunion with her parents by a few seconds. Her dad was wearing shorts and an untucked collared shirt. And sandals. His phone was nowhere to be seen, which was maybe the most alarming part of all. He had his arm around his wife's shoulders and he was, incredibly, 100 percent present in this moment. Tinka had to rub her puffy, bloodshot eyes to make sure she was actually seeing what she thought she saw.

Her mom had dropped a couple clothing sizes over the past few months and had traded her usual polyester Old Navy dress and flip-flops for a perfectly fitted wrap dress and a pair of stylish strappy sandals. Her previously straggly, un-dyed hair was now cut in a chic, long bob and was streaked with highlights, making her now more blond than either brown or gray.

Tinka's parents hugged Jane, then, once her mom finally caught sight of Tinka, she started bouncing on her toes and clapping her hands with glee. Tinka's dad joined in the celebration and full-on waved to his daughter with a gigantic beam of delight and pride on his face. He shouted, "Tinka! Tinka, over here!"

Pretty sure she'd somehow entered *The Twilight Zone*, Tinka raised her eyebrows and let her aviator sunglasses fall from her forehead onto her nose. Though she'd missed her mom and dad while she was away at school, Tinka was simply too hungover to process their metamorphoses at the moment.

She hunched her shoulders, trying to appear smaller, almost invisible, as she slunk over to her parents. When she was close enough, her mother leaped the chasm of space between them and swept Tinka into a bear hug. Mrs. Foster kissed her daughter's cheek, and when Tinka was finally given room to breathe, she reflexively wiped her face to rid herself of any errant hot pink lipstick. That, too, was one of her mother's new features.

Her dad stood back, observing. He nodded when Tinka looked at him. She gripped the nylon straps of her backpack, waiting for her father to take the first step, not wanting to spook him with any sudden movements. Then he, still smiling like a fool, clutched his daughter to his chest and nearly squeezed the life out of her. "Welcome home, sweetie."

Her eyes watering from this unexpected display of affection, Tinka stiffened under his grip. "Sweetie" was not and never had been in her father's vernacular.

"Your mom and dad have a big surprise for us." Jane hugged Tinka's mom's arm. "I love surprises."

Tinka didn't love surprises, and neither did her parents, usually. They weren't surprise people. They were "we need at least six weeks of notice on absolutely everything" people.

The three Fosters stood in size order at the carousel — mama bear, papa bear, and baby bear, while Jane danced around them, taking in all the sights the Minneapolis-St. Paul International Airport baggage claim had to offer. "How was your last night at school?" asked her dad.

"Great," Tinka lied. She snuck a peek at Jane, who was chatting with a random three-year-old and his parents. It'd only been one of the worst nights of Tinka's life, no big deal.

Her mom was still doing the thing where she filled Tinka in on gossip no one in their right mind would ever care about, so, at least that hadn't changed. "Tinka, honey, you won't believe what I heard from Mrs. Tucker. She told me that Colleen Sullivan's son Conor *is gay*." She whispered the last two words.

"I don't know any of those people, and *so*?" Tinka looked to her father for help, but he was now staring at the baggage carousel like it was his job to do so. The luggage from her flight was starting to emerge. Jane found her massive raspberry suitcase right away. Some middle-aged man helped her hoist it off the conveyor belt.

Tinka's lack of interest in neighborhood gossip did not dissuade her mother. "Sure you do. Karen used to babysit for the Sullivans all the time. Or maybe that was Genevieve Torres. I don't remember…" Her mother trailed off, trying to mentally reconstruct the tangled web of which of Tinka's childhood friends used to babysit for whom.

"I don't know, Mom," Tinka said.

"But you've heard about Karen's parents, right?"

Tinka shook her head.

Ah, now her mom had a bombshell to drop. "They're getting divorced. It's official."

Tinka frowned. "That came out of nowhere."

"They've been separated for months."

A chill snaking up her spine, Tinka stared hard at the baggage carousel. Karen's parents were getting divorced, and this was the first Tinka had heard about it. Once Tinka had started forging a new identity for herself at boarding school, she'd let her relationship with Karen, her oldest and best friend in the world, fizzle out. Tinka'd had no idea Karen's family was going through so much. She should've known. She should've asked.

She was an awful friend. That was a fact. She was literally the worst. And Jane would be here for the next four weeks as a constant reminder.

Tinka's father's eyes were glued to the little door through which piles of luggage were now tumbling out. When he saw what he'd been waiting for, he dove past a family of four blocking his way and heaved Tinka's golf clubs over his head. "Got 'em!" he shouted in triumph, still grinning. "That's all of it, right?"

She shook her head. "I haven't gotten my suitcase yet."

Her dad was no longer paying attention. He'd removed the cover from Tinka's golf bag and was inspecting each club as a jeweler might inspect a diamond. He held up the three wood and squinted into the light. "Are the scratches from you, or are they new? I should've gotten insurance for these before the flight. You can't trust the airlines."

"They're from me." Possibly. Or Jane, who'd been using them in a last-ditch effort to reconnect with her golfer boyfriend, Colin, who had been in the process of dumping her.

Colin. Tinka shuddered involuntarily again. *Colin. Tequila. His dorm room…*

Tinka's dad peered into her eyes, and she knew she was in for a shot of Old Dad, Stern Dad. She braced herself for the lecture that was about to come her way: *These are Callaways, Christina. Special edition. They cost more than your tuition.* She'd welcome his return to form.

But that's not what happened. Instead her father, still beaming, tossed the clubs back into the bag and zipped up the cover. "No big deal. Scratches happen."

Tinka stared at him, open-mouthed. *Scratches happen?* Not in the world of Tinka's father, Mr. James A. Foster.

He plopped the clubs onto the floor and put his arm around his wife again. Tinka's mom gazed into her husband's eyes like she was seeing him for the first time and it was true love. Jane watched the pair wistfully as if they were the most beautiful sight she'd ever witnessed.

Tinka was about to vomit. She wasn't sure if it was because of her lingering hangover or because the events from last night kept steamrolling through her mind or because of the Karen news or because her parents were being so touchy-feely—it was probably a combination of everything. Out of self-preservation, she kept her focus on the little door at the end of the baggage area, through which bag after bag kept spewing. Brown, green, blue, black…

Finally, she spotted her own luggage. "My suitcase is here." She nearly took out the family of four herself as she hurled her bag off the carousel and rolled it in the direction of the exit.

. . .

In the car, Tinka leaned back and closed her eyes, already regretting inviting Jane home for the month. Tinka had crossed the streams of her life. At Florian's Academy, she was the good time party girl. In Minneapolis, she was the homebody whose parents kept close tabs on her and dragged her to golf lesson after golf lesson. Jane expected her to behave one way, and her parents another. She was going to twist herself into knots juggling her two personae for the next four weeks.

"You seem tired, Tinka." Her mother turned around, practically kneeling on the passenger's seat. They had purchased a new car while Tinka was gone, a silver luxury SUV. ("Liquid Platinum," her dad had called it.)

Though it was late in the evening and the road was pitch-black save for the street lamps and the headlights from other vehicles, Tinka was able to make out her mother's surgically whitened grin in the darkness. *So this is what she's been doing instead of calling me every five minutes*. Tinka had been replaced by new clothes and cosmetic dentistry.

"Tinka's tired from the dark party last night," Jane said.

Tinka shuddered and rubbed her bare arms. She couldn't tell if the goose bumps were from the air conditioning or the conversation.

"Dark party? What's that?" There was a teasing glint in her mom's eye.

Jane opened her window a crack and flicked a bug off the glass. "At the end of the school year, the students throw this big bash out on the football field, but it has to be completely dark — no lights, no phones — because it happens in the middle of turtle mating season and the lights mess with them."

Mrs. Foster frowned. "What do you do at the party if it's pitch black out?"

"We can still have music going, so there's dancing and stuff." Jane shrugged.

Tinka shivered again. That was a loaded word, "stuff." Everyone needed to get off this topic before she either threw up or had a heart attack. Fortunately, this was when Tinka realized that her dad was driving in the wrong direction.

"Uh, where are we going?" she asked. "Minneapolis is back that way."

"That's the surprise, honey." Tinka's mom blinked, staring at her daughter for a few beats, waiting for some kind of response.

Jane clapped her hands. "Ooh. Yay!"

"I kinda just want to go home," Tinka said, after a moment. "And home is the other way."

Her mom grinned cryptically. "No, honey. Home is this way."

A lump formed in Tinka's throat, a lump of despair she should get used to. This lump, along with the guilt in her gut, would probably stick around for most of the summer.

Her father chimed in. "Maybe you should tell the girls what the surprise is, Eleanor."

"Well, honey, you know how your dad's business has been doing so well lately and how we've always wanted to buy a place in the country?"

"You bought a place in the country," Tinka deadpanned.

"That's right!"

"Yay!" squealed Jane. "A country house!"

Tinka blinked back tears that threatened to spill over. This was nothing new. She always had to go along with her parents' whims and wishes — like boarding school and the golf team and absolutely every other thing in her life. She forced a smile. Looking happy was half the battle. The rest of her would catch up eventually. "Exciting. And on Monday we'll go back home."

Mrs. Foster glanced at her husband. "No, we're going for the whole summer. This is where we live now. Your father and I sold the house in Minneapolis. Surprise!" She grinned again at Tinka, but this time her smile didn't seem so sure of itself.

Well, now, this was on-brand for her parents—making huge, life-altering decisions without her input.

She sensed Jane's eyes on her, waiting for her reaction. Tinka widened her grin, really playing up the feigned excitement. She probably looked like a clown. "Wow. You sold our house. That *is* a big surprise." Tinka pictured the living room, the formal dining room, the entire upstairs all her own. The kitchen. Now someone else was living there. They'd probably ripped down her pastel balloon wallpaper. They'd probably painted over the crayon drawings on the living room wall, the dinosaur she talked to like it was her guardian angel.

There'd be time to mourn later, in private, away from her parents. For now, at least, she had to keep up the appearance of being all right with this situation. This was how things worked. Her parents made the decisions. Tinka went along with them. It was her job to keep them happy, and she took that job very seriously. "Where's my stuff?" she whispered, still smiling like everything was cool.

"At the new place, honey," her mom said. "We think you'll love it. There's a lake and running paths and some great new neighbors."

"And you can golf all summer long." Her dad grinned at her in the rearview mirror.

"But what about Jane?" Tinka asked. "Her parents think she's going to be in Minneapolis this summer, not…where's the new house?"

"North Pole," her mom said.

"The North Pole?" What the hell was going on?

"No, silly." Her mom patted Tinka's hand. "North Pole, Minnesota. It's a quaint resort town, Christmas-themed, about three hours from the cities."

This did not compute. "A Christmas-themed town…in the summertime."

"Exactly," her mom said. "Christmas three hundred and sixty five days a year. That's the motto. You're going to love it."

"But Jane—"

"My parents dropped me off at school and left me to fend for myself while they're in Dubai. Minneapolis, North Pole, Cleveland—it's all the same to them."

Jane didn't get it. She'd never get it. Sure, Jane had to scramble to find people to stay with over breaks, and her parents weren't around if she got sick or hurt or whatever (though her grandmother was available in an emergency), but she had so much autonomy. Jane was seventeen years old and her parents saw her as an adult.

Tinka's parents saw her as a baby who happily went along with whatever they wanted.

"So, we won't be going back to Minneapolis at all?" Tinka's voice wavered, but she focused on the back of her mom's chair, trying to distract herself, to find something positive in all this. The negatives were winning out. She was homeless now, basically. She lived in a rented dorm room in South Carolina, and she was about to spend the summer in some strange house her parents had bought without even telling her they were moving.

She pinched the skin between her thumb and forefinger and focused on that physical pain instead of the sadness. Jane reached over and squeezed Tinka's hand, which only made Tinka feel worse. She, of all people, did not deserve Jane's sympathy.

"I don't know if we'll have time, honey," her mom said. "There's a lot to do in the new place. You're going to love it. Trust me. Why don't you lie back and rest and we'll be there before you know it."

. . .

Sam Anderson picked a chocolate chip off his muffin and popped it into his mouth.

"What about Marley Ho?" asked Harper. "You like her."

Sam frowned at his sister. "Isn't she dating Kevin Snow?"

"They're just casually dealing with each other." Harper played with the straw in her iced mocha with whipped, her summertime drink of choice at Santabucks, North Pole's resident coffeehouse. The A/C was on full blast, and reindeer wallpaper covered the walls. The baristas wore Santa hats, no matter the season. It was December in here all year round. "Kevin's vile," Harper made sure to add.

"What about your friend Elena?" asked their brother Matthew.

"She has a boyfriend now, duh-doy," said Harper. "How do you not know that? Oliver. *Prince*." She raised her eyebrows.

So did Matthew. "One of the *Prince* Princes? You never mentioned that. Were they together when I saw her in Florida over spring break?" Matthew lived in New York and missed out on the most salacious North Pole gossip. Whenever he came back to visit, he relished catching up on all the happenings around town.

"Yes, but it was new, and you know how Elena is about her privacy, plus you were all up your own butt about wedding planning."

Sam tapped Matthew's wedding binder on the table, trying to call his siblings back to order. "Yes," he said. "Elena

Chestnut is dating Oliver Prince and their families aren't fighting anymore, and it's all a big whoopee-dee-do. Can we drop this, please? We have bigger things to worry about."

"Bigger than the end of the Prince-Chestnut feud?" Harper asked.

"Bigger than you bringing a date to my wedding?" Matthew smirked.

Sam groaned. "Much bigger. We've got, like, today to get this stuff done before you two ditch me until the rehearsal dinner." Harper was working all summer as a camp counselor, and Matthew was going back home to New York until the wedding.

"Hakeem and I are coming back the week before," Matthew said.

Harper grabbed the binder and flipped through. "Me, too. Besides, you've got Matty's meticulous notes to keep you on course."

"Still." Sam snatched the binder back from his sister. "It's not like I'm a wedding planner. I'm an eighteen-year-old guy who has never even come close to getting married."

"Understatement." Harper nudged Matthew.

Matthew patted Sam's hand. "You only need to be here to answer vendor questions, collect the RSVPs…"

"Make the wedding favors," Harper added.

"You were going to do that!" Sam said.

She shook her head. "I have no idea what you're talking about."

Matthew pulled out his phone and tapped on the screen. "Other than those few things, everything else is taken care of."

"Not true." Sam opened the binder to the third page and pointed to the second line item. "What about tuxedos?"

"We should probably order those." Matthew laughed at the text on his screen.

"You think? Your wedding is in a month." Sam's brother was getting hitched on Independence Day, ironically. Matthew and Hakeem thought that was hilarious.

"I've got the fireworks all squared away," Matthew said.

"Good." Sam checked off "fireworks" on the list. "Because that's what's important. If the fireworks are distracting enough, your guests might not notice that there's no cake and you're walking down the aisle naked."

"We're finalizing the cake order today." Harper patted Sam's hand. "Relax. It's all going to be fine."

"Says the girl who's skipping town for the next three weeks."

She sipped her drink.

Matthew put his phone away and got serious for a moment. Sam loved his brother, but they were very different, in almost every way. Matthew was conservative—fiscally, politically, sartorially. He was very neat. That was the word that always came to mind for Sam. He looked neat. His hair was always perfect, and so were his clothes. He was blond, fit, and trim.

Sam was a good three inches taller than his older brother; and his physique was more "defensive lineman" than "quarterback." If Matthew was a greyhound, Sam was a Rottweiler.

"Sam, I don't say it enough, or okay, ever, but thank you for taking the reins on this. I knew the wedding stuff was going to be tough…emotionally…and I'm so grateful to you for handling everything." Matthew cleared his throat. "Mom—"

Harper waved him off, furiously. "Stop. We get it." Harper was all about keeping things light.

"No." Matthew shook his head. "I'm saying it. It needs to be said. It sucks that Mom's not here for this."

Harper stared out the front window of Santabucks, biting her lip.

It had been five years since their mom died, and Sam still thought about her usual order every time he came into the coffee shop. Earl grey with lemon. But he didn't tell his siblings that. He never let on how much he missed her. He tamped down his emotions, as always, for his family. It was his job. He placed his hand on Harper's forearm, which only made her bite her lip harder. Sam was shocked she didn't draw blood.

Matthew squeezed Sam's other hand. "You're the one who keeps this family afloat. You're the rock, Sammy."

Sam smiled. "I'm the rock? Who keeps us afloat? Talk about a mixed metaphor."

Harper snorted. "Besides, Matty, Sam's not The Rock. He's not Dwayne Johnson. He's more like the Pillsbury Dough Boy. Or The Rock's before picture."

"Ha-ha." Sam didn't remind her that he'd lost ten pounds over the past few months and had started to tone up, thanks to helping out with the landscaping at home. Facts never mattered to his siblings. He'd always be the fat one to them. Besides, Sam had done his duty. He'd let himself be the butt of the joke. Again. Reliably, his physique had rescued his family from their funk.

Harper checked the time on her phone. "Shall we?" She grabbed her cup and stood up.

Sam and Matthew did the same. On the way out the door, Matthew nudged Sam in the ribs. "You know what would've made Mom really happy? If you could somehow manage to find yourself a date for this wedding."

Sam groaned, and his brother and sister spent the entire walk down the block to Sugarplum Sweets naming a litany of North Pole girls Sam could ask to Matthew's wedding.

The words "Old Mrs. Page" had just crossed Harper's lips when she pulled open the door to the bakery and the girl behind the counter greeted the trio of Andersons. "Hi, Sam.

Harper," she added with a slight sneer.

Sam didn't recognize her. She was a bit younger than him, but definitely in high school. Maybe a sophomore or something. She had big glasses that made her eyes bug out like an insect, and she was wearing her dyed, electric blue hair up in two tight buns on top of her head.

"What's up, Dottie?" Harper leaned against the counter.

"Oh, Dottie." Now Sam remembered. "You changed your hair."

She touched her buns. "As one does from time to time." Her voice was inflection-free, bored, almost robotic.

Matthew reached across the counter and shook Dottie's hand. "I'm Matthew Anderson. We're here to test cakes for my wedding." He handed her a paper shopping bag. "We want the cake to look like my fiancé's parents' from the 1970s."

"Fountain and all," Harper said.

"Yes, fountain and all." Matthew pointed to the bag. "There's a photo in the bag for reference, along with all the decorations for the cake—the groom figures, the plastic stairs, et cetera."

Rolling her eyes, Dottie wrote "Anderson wedding" on the front of the bag before shoving it under the counter.

"Dottie's going to be a junior next year," Harper said. "She's super smart. We had what class together last year? Science?"

"Biology." Dottie pushed her glasses back up to the bridge of her nose as she stood from her crouch and narrowed her eyes at Harper.

"Oh yeah," Harper said. "You really got a kick out of dissecting stuff."

Dottie, with a curl of the lip and a curtsey, said pointedly to Harper, "My aunt left some samples for you. I'll get them, *my liege.*"

When Dottie was safely behind the door leading toward

the back of the store, Harper jabbed Sam in the side. "Maybe you should ask Dottie to the wedding."

"Shut up," he said.

"I think you should," Matthew said. "She seems like tons of fun with all the sneering and sarcasm. You two could perform experiments on the calamari."

"Dude," Harper hissed at Matthew. "You have no idea. She got pissed at her lab partner and left a dissected worm in his locker. I'm not even kidding."

Their cattiness irked Sam. It was one thing to make fun of him—he was family. Sam couldn't deny that Dottie seemed a bit strange and surly, but still. She could be the girl in the movie who was hiding a stellar personality behind the brightly patterned clothing and the sarcasm. As far as Sam knew, she really hadn't done anything to either Harper or Matthew that warranted an attack.

Her lab partner, on the other hand. He might have a beef.

Dottie came out carrying a tray with four different kinds of cake on it. She pointed to each one, reading the crib notes her aunt had pasted on the tray in what was, presumably, her normal flat voice, like each word out of her mouth exhausted her to no end. "This is almond cake with a cherry filling and amaretto buttercream. Here's chocolate cake with a chocolate Italian buttercream. There's a carrot cake with cream cheese frosting. And caramel cake with caramel icing."

"Mom's favorite." Matthew took the teensiest bite of that one. He mostly ate Paleo, so that one nibble was probably torture for him.

Sam, the foodie of the group, dug his fork into the almond cake. He wrinkled his nose. A little too much almond. "Can we put a vanilla buttercream on that layer? The almond is oppressive."

Dottie made the note on her pad of paper.

He tried the caramel. "This is a little too sweet. And

burnt."

"Hey, Dottie." Harper dipped her finger in the chocolate frosting. "What are you doing on the Fourth of July?"

Dottie folded her arms and cocked her jaw. "Uh…let me check my calendar. Nothing."

"That's when Matthew's wedding is, but you knew that." Harper licked her finger. "Sam doesn't have a date."

Dottie blushed to her electric blue hairline. It was the first time she'd shown any emotion beyond ennui. "And? So?"

Sam stomped on his sister's foot.

"Ow!" she squealed, hopping around. "That's my bad foot, you jerk." She had broken her ankle back in February, and she'd been using it as an excuse to get out of…well, basically everything.

Sam kept his eyes down on the tray as he gave Dottie their final order. The cake was his domain, and the only part of wedding planning he was actually excited about. "Top layer, carrot cake. Then the almond, the caramel, and the chocolate. Does that work?" Now he looked at her. She was staring at him with the big bug eyes. He focused on the cakes again.

"I'll tell my aunt," said Dottie. "And I'll give her your notes."

Matthew leaned closer to Dottie, resting his elbows on the counter and his chin in his hands. "Hey, Dottie, can we get your phone number, just in case we—and by 'we' I mean 'Sam,' because he's the one handling my wedding details— need to contact you with any questions or concerns?"

Dottie's face got even redder, like it could burst into flames at any moment. She wrote her number on the notepad and handed Sam the paper.

He glanced down and ripped it in half, giving Dottie back the part with the notes for her aunt on it. "You're going to need these."

Before the door closed behind the trio of Andersons,

Sam heard Dottie yell from inside the shop, "Call me, Sam! Anytime!"

"I'm going to murder you two," he muttered. "That was really rude."

"Oh, she's fine." Harper skipped down the street. "You just made her day."

"And when I don't call her?"

"Why wouldn't you call her? She likes you." Harper stopped and turned to face him. "Besides, what other options do you have?"

• • •

Sam's brother and sister kept teasing him all day; and when they returned home, they even got their eight-year-old sister, Maddie, in on it. She kept bouncing around the family room, screeching, "Dottie Go-old. Dottie Go-old."

The truth hurt. Sam didn't have options. He'd always been the doughy, goofy, friendly guy. He wasn't someone girls fawned over and dreamed about. In a movie, he'd be the best friend character, the comic relief. Losing some weight and getting fit was supposed to have been his silver bullet, his ticket to romance, but that hadn't panned out yet.

Maybe it wasn't how he looked. Maybe it was him.

By the end of the night, during a heated—they were always heated—family game of *Trivial Pursuit*, Sam reached his final straw. It started when their dad asked how wedding planning had gone that day. "Did you get everything you needed done?" He rolled the die and moved his pie to an orange space.

"We did." Harper pulled a question out of the box and asked their dad something about the 1986 Boston Red Sox, which he answered correctly. "Sammy may have found a date for the wedding."

Sam stared at the condensation on his lemonade. She was teasing him, which was nothing new. But her words were hitting him extra hard today.

"Who's the girl, Sam?" Mr. Anderson looked like the other kids, not Sam—or, well, they looked like him—blond and trim. Sam was the outlier.

"She's no one," he said. "There's no girl. I don't want to take anyone to the wedding. I just want to have fun with my family. Is that so hard to comprehend?"

After his dad finished his run by giving the wrong answer to a question about some random 1990s TV show, it was Sam's turn. He picked up the die and shook it.

"Come on, Sam," said Matthew. "Roll a big one for Dottie."

Instead, Sam chucked the die right at Matthew's chest. "You do it."

To a chorus of "Come on, Sam!" and "We were just messing with you," Sam stormed out to the back deck, where he ran his hands along the slick, varnished railing and stared up at the stars in the cloudless sky. If this were a movie, now would be the part where Sam met the gorgeous girl next door. She'd see right through Sam's physique to his big heart and better-than-average sense of humor.

He glanced over at the Fosters' house, his new neighbors' place. It was dark, as usual. Life wasn't a movie. Life was life.

Sam sighed and checked his phone. He opened up his contacts and found the name Harper had entered earlier today—Dottie Gold, heart emoji.

"You texting Dottie?" came a voice from behind him.

Sam turned toward Harper, hiding his phone behind his back. His sister was either a wizard or she had X-ray vision. "Nope."

"You should." She stood next to him and placed her hands on the deck railing, facing the Fosters'. "You're going to college soon, Sam. Get some experience before you leave."

"I have experience." He did. Ish.

"Kissing a random sophomore during a school play is not 'experience.'"

She had him there. "I don't want to start anything now. I'm leaving in a few weeks, and it'll be hard enough leaving this town and you assholes." He nudged his sister in the ribs.

"You'll have no problem leaving Dottie, believe me." She held out her hand. "Give me your phone."

He hid it behind his back. "No." Bringing Dottie into this wouldn't solve anything.

"Suit yourself, but think about it." Harper turned to leave, but stopped. "Make sure you're honest, though, about what you want. Hooking up is fine, great even, as long as everyone's on the same page. Don't give her the wrong idea. I speak from experience." Harper had run into a similar situation a few months ago with her friend Regina.

Alone again on the deck, Sam flicked on his phone and turned toward his neighbors' house. He rested his elbows on the railing and stared at the screen. *Hi, Dottie*, he typed.

And he was stuck. He lifted his eyes to the Fosters' second floor balcony again and was so lost in composing his message to Dottie that he almost didn't notice the person standing there, a girl, resting her hands on the railing. Her long, blond hair curled around her shoulders, and it seemed like she was doing the same thing Sam had been—breathing, escaping.

The girl peered over at him, and he tentatively raised his hand in greeting. She, the actual girl next door, did the same for one brief second, then scurried into the house and slid the door shut.

Sam stared at the balcony for a moment, waiting for her to reappear. He put his hand to his chest, where his heart hammered against his sternum.

This right here was his problem, always had been. He

was too caught up in the movie version of his life. That girl showing up on the balcony was a coincidence, nothing more. There was no deeper meaning. They weren't destined to be together. There was a very strong likelihood they'd never even speak to each other. Sam couldn't keep putting his life on hold, waiting for something amazing to happen.

Without another thought, he finished his message to Dottie and pressed send.

Chapter Two

"You girls are going to love Mark and Trish," Tinka's mom said as the family loaded itself into the car.

Tinka wasn't so sure about that. She couldn't shake the sense of dread she'd had since her mom had announced during lunch that the Fosters (and Jane) had been invited for dinner at their new friends' house. There was something sinister going on. Tinka could tell by the way her mom had ordered her to borrow fresh clothes from Jane when Tinka'd come upstairs wearing a wrinkled maxi dress she'd found at the bottom of her suitcase.

The only positive was that going out meant leaving her parents' new house for a few hours. The place was a disaster. It was like that movie, *The Money Pit*, but times a million.

First of all, the house wasn't on a regular street in a neighborhood or anything. It was inside a golf resort, very secluded. The place was a horror movie setting. The house itself currently had only one fully functioning bathroom (which was in the basement and hadn't been updated since 1979; both the sink and toilet were avocado green), no air conditioning, and no appliances in the kitchen — the fridge, the stove, and the dishwasher had all been removed. There was no TV and no internet. Tinka and Jane had to share a leaky air mattress on the dusty shag carpeting in the basement. Tinka didn't even want to think about what kinds of bugs were living and breeding within those fibers.

Her mother called the place a "work in progress," and the Fosters were using Tinka and Jane as cheap labor. Jane saw no problem with this. But, for Tinka, the house wasn't the only issue. There was also the golf.

Today her dad had woken her up at six o'clock and driven her immediately to the resort course for a round of eighteen. When they returned, she'd barely had time to wolf down a room-temperature sandwich (the perils of having no fridge), before her mom handed her a roller and ordered her to start painting the guest bedroom on the second floor.

"We can do this every day." Her dad had cheerfully hauled a new vanity up to the guest room. "We'll golf in the morning and then fix this house the way we want it in the afternoon. It's going to be a great summer."

Tinka nearly drowned herself in a gallon of dove gray latex paint right then and there. She was on a hamster wheel of torture, yet she kept smiling. Twenty-four hours down; so, so, so, *so* many more to go.

She did have to give her parents credit for one thing: they hadn't put out any Christmas decorations. At least not yet. Outside the resort, the town of North Pole was a year-round winter wonderland. Grown adults had painted their fairytale cottage-esque homes with an array of candy-colored paint. Though it was June and fry-an-egg-on-the-sidewalk hot, most of the houses still boasted holiday decorations on their lawns. Tinka was fairly certain she'd wandered into a cult.

Even the infamous Mark and Trish were in on this nonsense. They had a plastic Santa with his reindeer on the roof and a gigantic, illuminated blowup menorah on the lawn in front of their blue and green Victorian home.

When Tinka stepped inside, the sweat on her arms evaporated immediately. She'd never take air conditioning for granted again.

Jane hugged Trish like an old friend and said, "Your house is beautiful. I love the Christmas decorations in June. So edgy."

"They're for Christmas in July. We don't keep this stuff out all year." She turned to Tinka with a wink. "Don't judge us. Please."

Trish didn't seem so bad, but maybe Tinka was just feeling charitable because of the A/C.

In the living room, Trish introduced the girls to her husband, Mark, who immediately handed Tinka's dad a beer and her mom a glass of wine.

Tinka sat on the couch, which, unlike the ones at her parents' house, was soft and velvety and not covered by a plastic drop cloth. She observed her mom and dad like she was watching a play and they were the actors. Her parents didn't drink, really, other than the occasional beverage at a wedding or whatever. Maybe that was because back in Minneapolis they didn't have many friends. But now they had Mark and Trish, apparently.

Her parents clinked glasses and took swigs of their drinks. They weren't pretending. They were actually consuming the alcohol. Tinka got the sense that they'd done this before, possibly more than once.

The house smelled overwhelmingly like lavender, which was coming from one of those flameless candle warmers her friend Karen's mom used to have around the house. "What's for dinner tonight?" Tinka asked, making sure to smile pleasantly.

"Burgers and brats." Trish beckoned them to follow her.

"But not 'til way later. Right now it's happy hour on the deck."

"Fun!" Jane said.

Tinka started sweating despite the air conditioning. Dinner was merely a concept at this point. The Fosters were at Mark and Trish's for the long haul.

"We're so glad to have you all over." Trish lit a citronella candle on the table outside as her guests grabbed seats. It was needed. Tinka had already swatted away three mosquitoes. "Your mom and dad come for dinner all the time."

"Whenever we need a home-cooked meal, which is pretty much every night." Her dad touched glasses with Trish.

Tinka stared at him like he'd grown a second head.

"So, you girls go to boarding school?" Trish sipped her wine.

"We do," Jane said. "In South Carolina. I'm from Charleston originally."

"But your parents' live in Dubai?"

Jane accepted a glass of pop from Mark. "For now. My dad's opening a hotel there. They come home to the states for the summer, but they're going back again in the fall."

"It's so nice that you have Tinka's family to stay with while they're gone."

"Very." Jane squeezed Tinka's knee. "She's a great friend."

Tinka nearly choked on her pop. "Great friend" was so not an apt description.

Mark plopped an unmarked bottle in the middle of the table. The entire party so far was just glasses clinking and liquids sloshing. There was one tiny bowl of guacamole and blue corn chips as an appetizer, but that was it in the way of sustenance.

"Homemade Limoncello. Moonshine." Trish poured four shots. Moonshine, shots, and very little food. Mark and Trish were living in a frat house.

Tinka's dad waved Trish off. "None for me. I'm driving."

"I can drive," Jane offered.

He tossed back the moonshine. "Well, okay then."

Tinka jumped up. Though she was outside, claustrophobia hit her and she scanned the yard, looking for an out. She needed to walk, to escape this scene of her parents doing shots with Mark and Trish. "Bathroom," she said, already making her way toward the house.

"Just off the kitchen!" Trish shouted.

Inside, Tinka booked it right to the powder room, where she splashed cold water on her face and rested her hands on the sink, letting the water drip down her cheeks and into the bowl.

She was in a parallel universe where her parents were happy and liked to drink moonshine with their friends. She'd spent the past six months worried sick about them. Her mom had gone from calling Tinka five times a day to calling her two times a week. Tinka had assumed they'd been lost while she'd been at school, that they'd drifted into despair without her there to reel them in. But no. They'd been fine without her. Better than fine. They had *Mark* and *Trish*.

Tinka wiped the last of the water from her face and returned to the patio. She'd fake an illness. She'd say she needed to go home, so could they please stop doing shots for a minute and let Jane drive them all back to the house?

As she stepped out the sliding glass door to the patio, she heard Jane asking, "I have to know. Why did you decide to move here?"

Tinka paused at the door, waiting for the answer. Her parents stared at each other with tilted heads and faint grins. Eventually, Tinka's mother pulled her eyes away from her husband's and said, "We used to talk about moving here years ago."

Tinka said, "Here? North Pole?" All eyes swung to her. "I never knew that. Not once in seventeen years have I ever heard you even mention this place."

Her mom's eyes turned glassy. She smiled. "We used to come here all the time before you were born."

Tinka knew what that meant—they used to come here with *Jake*, back when life was perfect and they were happy. Tinka prepared herself for an emotional breakdown, but it didn't come. Her mom tickled her dad's arm, and he rested his head on her shoulder.

Mark and Trish grinned at them like they were all in on this together, and wasn't that just fantastic?

Jane gazed at the Fosters with a dreamy, satisfied expression. "That's so sweet."

It wasn't sweet. It was weird. These were not Tinka's parents. "Really, though. Why now?" What she didn't ask about was the catalyst for this emotional breakthrough. Did it have something to do with her being gone all year? Maybe Tinka's presence really had been the thing keeping them in life limbo for sixteen years. She ran her fingers along the rough, warm brick behind her.

"Right house, right time," her dad said. End of story.

So, he didn't think she deserved a straight answer, not even after she'd spent her entire existence bending over backward to keep them happy and make their lives easier. She opened her mouth to tell them she needed to leave, but she didn't get the chance.

"Excuse me."

Tinka stepped out of the way on instinct, and turned to see a guy maybe a few years older than her stepping through the door.

Trish jumped up and ran to hug him. "Dylan!" She grabbed his arm and led him over to the patio table. "Everyone, this is our son, Dylan. Dylan, these are the Fosters. And Jane."

Still hovering near the door, ready to escape at any time, Tinka sensed Dylan's eyes on her. He was cute in an obvious, preppy, rich boy kind of way, and she suspected he knew it. She wouldn't give him the satisfaction of letting him know she'd noticed him even the teensiest bit. He was nothing special. Her boarding school was full of Dylan Greenes.

Tinka's dad stood and shook Dylan's hand. "Eleanor and I have heard so much about you." He glanced over at Tinka and nodded toward Dylan. "Duke golf team."

"Good for Dylan." Tinka folded her arms across her chest and leaned against the sun-baked brick wall.

Jane couldn't take her eyes off this guy, but Tinka gave her a pass. Jane had only recently broken up with her boyfriend of three years (shudder, *Colin*) and was new to the dating scene. She didn't know that Dylan, Colin, and half the other guys like them at Florian's were avoid-at-all-costs kinds of guys. "Tinka's on the golf team at our school."

"She's there to work with Gregor Kiln," Tinka's dad said.

"The golf coach?" Dylan's jaw dropped as he turned toward Tinka. "Impressive."

Tinka's dad pulled out the chair next to him and urged Dylan to sit. "You know, Duke is on our college shortlist."

Tinka gawked at her dad. *What?* They—she and her father—had a college short list? Since when?

"We'll have to get together for a round sometime." Tinka's dad glanced over at her. "Wouldn't that be fun, Tinka?"

"Wonderful." Great. Now not just more golf, but golf with a skeevy guy who couldn't take his eyes off her. This summer was going to be aces.

Trish took another pull on her wine. "You know, Eleanor and I were talking, maybe you two should hang out together sometime—"

"Get to know each other," Tinka's mom added. "You might wind up at the same college, after all."

This was a setup. Tinka's gut had been right. Dread had been the appropriate emotion for this occasion. Her survival instincts had been doing their job.

A knowing smile played on Dylan's lips. "I'd definitely be up for that, if Tinka is." He really had the preppy god bit down pat. Well, he was barking up the wrong tree. Tinka ate guys like him for lunch, and she had lost her appetite.

She reached behind her and pulled open the sliding glass door.

"Where are you going, hon?" Her mom patted the chair next to her. "Come on over. Get to know the Greenes."

Tinka's claustrophobia was back. She was suffocating here, not just in this house, but in this town. She'd spent the day golfing and doing hard labor because she was the good daughter, because she'd always been expected to go along with whatever her parents asked of her. She'd never questioned them, ever.

But now they were messing with her love life. They were asking her to throw herself at their new BFFs' son, whom they'd handpicked for her. The way her mom was looking at her right now, it was like she'd thrown all her hopes and dreams into this potential relationship.

Of course they'd expect her to go along with it, no questions asked. She'd never, ever pushed back on anything, and she couldn't start now. She was only going to be here for a few months. Tinka shut the door, dragged herself back to the patio, and sat next to her mother. She'd give Dylan a shot, for her parents' sake.

• • •

"It has been decided, Craig. The people have spoken. It's Christopher Guest night, and we're showing *Waiting for Guffman*." Sam was manning the register at the shop where he worked. Every Saturday night, Maurice's Video Store showed a different movie in the back room. It had been a

North Pole tradition for decades and the hot date spot for high school students—watching old movies in a dark room on saggy couches and old beanbag chairs.

Craig Cooper, however, was not in high school, nor was he here on a date. He was here to bully Sam into showing the movie he wanted to see. The twenty-something DJ/sporting goods store employee hiked up his mom jeans. "*For Your Consideration* is better."

"You know it's not." Sam handed Craig his complimentary popcorn and pop of his choosing—in Craig's case, a can of Mellow Yellow. "You only like *For Your Consideration* because literally no one else does."

"This attitude is not a good look on you, Sam." Craig stepped away from the counter.

"Take it up with the manager." Sam nodded to the back room, where the owner of the video store, Maurice Gibbons, was setting up the movie.

Sam peered into the screening room as Craig opened the door. There were only a few people there so far, but it was still early. He checked the popcorn machine and restocked the fridge. Then he resumed his place behind the register and watched people file past the shop.

North Pole changed identities with the seasons. At Christmastime, there were constant crowds. Visitors merrily skipped through the snow, stopping to chat with elves and check out festive window decorations. The locals pushed past tourists, avoiding Main Street, patronizing the few places frequented only by those who lived here—Mags's Diner, the library, and, yes, this movie shop.

After the holidays, things slowed to a crawl, which Sam loved. January was an exhale. Suddenly the streets weren't as crowded, and the people who remained were familiar faces—the locals—who'd come out of hiding. This year had been especially fun because the Princes had run a contest that had everyone running around town in parkas and hats, interacting with one another.

In summer there was more intermingling between the guests and the townies—local girls and guys falling for people who were here for the summer. Maybe it was simply because everyone happened to be wearing much less clothing.

Sam perked up as the door swung open and in came his friend, Brian Garland, who, like Sam, had recently graduated from North Pole High. Brian held the door for a small brunette.

"Hey, buddy." Brian put a few bills on the counter. "How's it going?"

"It's going." Sam nodded to the girl. "New friend?"

"That's Abby. She's from Canada."

Sam tucked Brian's money inside the register.

As Abby wandered off to check out the horror section, Brian whispered, "She's a gymnast. Maybe she has a friend for you."

Sam's siblings weren't the only ones trying to pair him off. "I'm good, thanks." His mind went right to the girl on the Fosters' balcony, something that had been happening all day, despite the fact that Dottie had been texting him non-stop over the past twenty-four hours. "Hey. Do you know anything about the family who moved in next door to me?"

Brian took the popcorn and shoved a handful into his mouth. "The Fosters."

Sam nodded.

"The guy comes into Santabucks once in a while, but that's it. He likes non-fat cappuccinos." Brian's mom owned the coffee shop.

"Nothing about a daughter?"

Brian made sure Abby wasn't listening in before he whispered, "Daughter?"

"She kind of…showed up. I was wondering."

Brian grinned. "You were 'wondering.'" He put the "wondering" in air quotes.

Blushing, Sam waved him off. "In a neighborly way."

"Sure, Sam," said Brian. "I'll let you know if I hear anything."

Brian and Abby headed into the screening room as a group of high school students filed in. Sam was so busy taking their money and slinging popcorn, that he hadn't noticed Dottie Gold was among them. After everyone else headed toward the back, Dottie remained up front. Sam busied himself wiping down the counter.

He'd regretted texting Dottie as soon as he'd pressed "send" last night. She'd responded seconds later, saying she was happy to hear from him and that she'd love to hang out sometime. Then she started sending him diatribes about all the people she hated at North Pole High and what they had done to slight her. Sam was starting to think that maybe she wasn't so much the misunderstood nerd as she was the girl in the horror flick who vows to destroy her enemies.

"Is the movie any good?" Dottie still had her hair up in the blue buns, and she was wearing a dress with a movie ticket print, as if it was her uniform for nights like this.

Sam handed her a bag of popcorn. "It is good. A classic. And it's about to start."

"That's okay." She leaned against the counter. "I'll wait for you."

"You don't have to." Shit. This was her cashing in on his offer to "hang out."

Sam cast about for something, *anything* to do that would give him the appearance of being busy. The look on Dottie's face was one Sam was familiar with, though it was not a look normally directed at him.

Brian's brother, Danny, came in with his girlfriend, Star, and Sam sent the pair into the screening room armed with popcorn and two cans of ice cold Diet Sunkist.

Dottie sneered. "Star Lyons."

"What's wrong with Star?" He asked the question, even though he knew the answer was Star had somehow done something rude to Dottie at some point.

Dottie turned to Sam with a sly grin on her face. "I was in charge of the cake for her sweet sixteen last year. I swapped flour for the powdered sugar in the frosting."

Sam wrinkled his nose. "Ew."

"It was ew." Her eyebrow twitched. "Star had been planning that party for months, and she even came in several different times to taste the cake. Such a bummer it didn't turn out well." She brushed something invisible off her shoulder. "Aunt Nancy changed the locks on me after that, but it was worth it. Besides, there are other ways in."

"Your aunt's the baker, though. Didn't she get in trouble?"

Dottie waved him off. "She gave Star store credit or something. No big."

"Kind of big," Sam said. "That's your aunt's livelihood."

Dottie shrugged.

"Do you even like your job?"

"My parents say it builds character. Whatever."

Maurice exited the screening room and shut the door behind him. "You can go in, Sam. Movie's started."

Dottie eyed him expectantly. This was turning into a date, something that had been unappealing before, but seemed unfathomable now that he'd heard Dottie's story about ruining Star's birthday cake for vengeance. That was a dick move. "You go on in. I'll be there in a minute." Sam was never texting anyone ever again. That much was for certain. His thumbs were retired.

Taking his time, he grabbed his own drink and some popcorn and trudged toward the back room. When he pulled open the door, he was greeted by Dottie's voice. "Sam! Over here."

Sam's eyes swung around the dark room. The only open seat was right next to Dottie on a small couch set up along the left wall. She waved him over.

He made his way toward the front. "I'm gonna sit on the floor," he whispered as the movie started.

"Don't be silly, Sam!" Dottie shouted.

"Shhh!" hissed Craig.

"I have a seat right here! Come on!"

"Go sit by Dottie, Sam," one of her friends said.

"Yeah, Sam," said another. "Why won't you sit by Dottie?"

To shut them all up, Sam took the open spot next to Dottie, keeping his body as close to the armrest and as far away from Dottie as possible. He placed his bag of popcorn between them.

As his eyes adjusted, he started to make out people scattered around the room, well, making out. Brian and Abby were on the couch across from him. Other people were similarly entangled. It appeared only Craig in the front row was focused on the film. Sam had never figured *Waiting For Guffman* for an aphrodisiac.

Dottie moved Sam's popcorn to the floor and scooted closer to him. He tried to shift away, but he was already at the end of the couch. He started to stand, but Dottie placed her hand on his knee and Sam froze. This—something—was really happening. Dottie was actually making a move on him. He adjusted his leg and she lifted her hand, thankfully.

"Dottie, I—" He was going to tell her right then and there that this couldn't happen, it wouldn't happen. Texting her was a mistake. He wasn't interested in her—or anyone. His focus was on the wedding and hanging out with his friends—the people he actually wanted to spend time with—before leaving for college.

But Dottie cut him off. "You're the only good one in this

town."

"Thanks?" Was he, though? Maybe he was too good. A less "good" guy would've left Dottie several scenes ago. In fact, a less "good" guy never would've sat next to her in the first place, putting himself in this precarious position.

Sam tried to focus on the film, but Dottie wasn't making that easy, either. Every time something happened on screen, she'd say, "That's so funny," instead of laughing.

The tenth time she did it, Sam finished her sentence for her. She said, "That's—"

And he responded with a "So funny."

She took that as a green light and fully pivoted toward Sam. She put her hands on his cheeks and kissed him. Again, Sam froze, too shocked to shut this down.

His friends did this kind of thing all the time. To them, it was no big deal. But it was a big deal to Sam. Kissing Dottie wasn't right. It wasn't what he wanted. He ended it, backing away and hugging the hard, scratchy armrest.

Dottie licked her lips and leaned in again.

Sam put his hand up, heading her off. "Dottie, we can't."

"Sure we can. You texted me. You said you wanted to 'hang out.' I know what that means."

He searched the room for divine intervention—a skipping DVD or a smoking popcorn machine. A fire would be great right now. "I…" He spotted Danny Garland and Star Lyons—as solid a North Pole couple as ever there was—cuddling on a couch across the way. "I already have a girlfriend."

Dottie backed away, affronted. "No, you don't. Who?" She forgot to whisper.

"Shhh!" hissed Craig.

"Um…no one," Sam muttered.

"No one? Your girlfriend is *no one*?" Dottie's voice had, thankfully, come down to Sam's level.

Sam shook his head. "No one you know."

Dottie narrowed her eyes.

Sam shut his eyes for a second, thinking of the blond girl from the Fosters' balcony, not believing what he was about to do. This was not wise. This was not a good guy thing to do, but these were desperate times. "She—she just moved here. She's my neighbor." He hoped this would never get back to her... whoever she was. He'd be devastated. She'd be creeped out. And she'd have every right to be.

"You texted me."

Sam shook his head. "Harper did. She took my phone." This was all Harper's fault anyway. Besides, she was leaving for camp tomorrow. She'd be far from the heat.

"Harper. Of course." Dottie narrowed her eyes. "But I've never seen you out with any girl."

"We're keeping it on the down low for now." Forever, if possible. Or at least until Sam left town in August.

"Why?"

"Reasons." Man, he was terrible at lying.

"I don't believe you."

"I swear." He held up his hand, Scout's honor. He was really in it now.

"You kissed me," Dottie said.

"*You* kissed *me*," Sam countered.

"And you didn't stop it right away." Dottie shook her head in disgust. "I should've known better than to trust Harper Anderson's brother. You're all alike." Dottie leaned toward him. "If you are even messing with me right now..." She got that look in her eyes, the same one she'd had when she'd talked about putting flour in Star's frosting.

Sam pictured Matthew and Hakeem's wedding cake crashing to the ground and bursting into a million pieces. "I'm not. I swear."

Dottie stood up and drained the rest of her pop. "You better not be."

Chapter Three

On Wednesday afternoon, Jane grabbed Tinka the second she returned from yet another round of golf with her father.

"We're going running!" chirped Jane.

Tinka wiped sweat from her brow. With no A/C in this house, she was in a perpetual state of perspiration. Golf had been a disaster, and her dad had kept questioning Tinka about her practice regimen at Florian's and whether her coach at school (the *great* Gregor Kiln) had been messing with her swing. At least her poor golfing had distracted him from trying to set her up with Dylan Greene for the time being.

"Go running with Jane or help me fix this bannister," yelled Tinka's mom from the spiral staircase to the second floor. She was using wood glue to fix the broken spokes.

Tinka glanced around. The living room couch and chairs were covered with drop cloths. Paint samples and balled up paper towels littered the ground. The kitchen was a staging area for every other project. Her parents' new bathroom vanity sat where the refrigerator should be. They'd been working in this house for days and there seemed to be no improvement. Tinka sighed and dragged herself toward the basement stairs to change. "Running it is, I guess."

In moments like these, Tinka missed her old friend Karen. Karen never would've made Tinka go running, especially not on a hot day like this. Tinka would've made them some kind of no-bake cookies that didn't require use of the oven, and they'd have lounged around watching movies and doing crossword puzzles all afternoon.

But Jane was Tinka's guest, and Jane wanted to run.

In the scorching afternoon sun, Tinka's already sweating brow became a waterfall as she and Jane scampered along the asphalt path that jogged through the entire resort, up and down hills, through the woods, along the golf courses, next to the main thoroughfare. Tinka's parents now lived in a place where other people vacationed. How bizarre was that? They'd spent sixteen years ignoring reality and now they were dwelling in an actual fantasy world.

The girls ran about two miles out and walk-jogged the rest of the way home. As they approached Tinka's house, Jane slowed down, gazing with mischief at the mansion next door.

"Let's keep going. We're almost home." Tinka needed a cold shower—even if it had to be in a low-flow, avocado bathtub that was never lacking for spiders. Resting her hands on her knees, she checked out the house. It was beautiful, magazine-ready. A circular drive, flanked by colorful blooms, went from one end of the property to the other. Jane stepped onto the driveway and tiptoed toward the house.

Tinka glanced around. "What are you doing?"

Jane flipped her long black braid over her shoulder. "A quick detour. I want to see this place up close."

"Jane, no."

But Jane kept traipsing along a path to the back of the house. Groaning, Tinka followed her into the backyard.

Their neighbors' place was everything Tinka's parents'

new house was not. It was sparkling, pristine. There was a vibe of joy here. The huge, glossy deck glistened in the sunlight. The lawn shone bright green, and the flowers were every color of the rainbow. Even the sandy beach at the edge of their property was cheerier than the rocky one over at the Fosters' new house.

Tinka glanced over at her parents' money pit. It was the house on the block that little kids might dare each other to walk past, all dark wood and cobwebs. The dock at the end of their property was practically falling into the lake. Even the bench on the shore was decrepit and sad and looked like it was about to throw itself into the water to end it all.

"Um…" came a voice from behind Tinka.

She swung around and found herself face-to-face with a tall guy in long basketball shorts and no shirt. His brown hair curled out from under a Twins cap. He was holding a pair of hedge clippers and he seemed as shocked to see Tinka as she was to see him.

"I'm sorry," she stammered. He'd caught her trespassing and gazing at this house like a common weirdo. She tripped over a rock as she tried to simultaneously walk and flag down Jane, who was standing on the dock, shading her eyes from the sun as she peered out at the shimmering lake. "My friend and I will leave right away. Don't tell the owners we were snooping around."

The guy laughed. He had a friendly, robust laugh. "The owners don't care."

Tinka wished he'd put down the hedge clippers already. "Jane! Let's go. We're trespassing."

Jane waved and ran from the pier, but her eyes went right past Tinka. She affixed a flirty smile to her face and held out her hand. "Hi. I'm Jane."

The guy dropped his clippers and accepted Jane's hand. Then he turned to Tinka. "And you are?"

"Tinka. I live next door." He wasn't unattractive. He wasn't normally the type of guy she'd notice, but the way his biceps rippled under his tanned skin, well, it was hard to miss that.

"Okay, Tinka-I-Live-Next-Door, what kind of name is that?" He grinned down at her, and, against her better judgment, she found herself smiling back at him. He had these cute dimples she kind of wanted to press with her finger. She shook her head. *Not productive, Tinka.*

"It's short for Christina." She kept looking squarely at the ground, actively avoiding the appealing features of this (potential) hedge clipper murderer.

"I was just about to take a break." He stretched his tanned, muscular arms, pulling Tinka's focus back to them. "Would you girls like some water?" He gave Tinka a side glance, like he knew this decision was up to her.

Jane, however, took a step toward the house. "We'd love some. Gotta stay hydrated."

As the guy led them up to the deck, Tinka glared at Jane and mouthed, "What the *hell*?"

Jane skipped cheerfully and flopped onto a bench that ran along the perimeter of the deck.

"Is anybody home?" Tinka asked.

"Ain't nobody here but us chickens." The guy opened the sliding glass door and disappeared into the house.

When the door had shut behind him, Tinka said, "We need to get out of here."

"What are you talking about?" Jane draped her arm luxuriously over the side of the railing, looking every bit like she belonged here. She was the picture of summertime decadence.

"We're trespassing, and this guy could murder us. He has hedge clippers." She blushed at the thought of his arms holding various gardening implements.

"He's not going to murder us." Jane closed her eyes and soaked in the warm rays.

"You don't know that."

"True," Jane said, "but I tend to assume people are innocent until proven murderous. Plus, he's nice. He's getting us water."

"He's shirtless and—"

The sliding glass door *whooshed* open behind them. Their opportunity for escape was lost. Tinka spun around as the guy headed toward them. He was carrying three bottles of water and had put on a T-shirt, a faded movie tee, over his mesh shorts. *Jaws*. A story about a terrifying shark that kills people. The guy handed a bottle to Tinka. "Take a seat."

Ready to flee at any moment, she perched next to Jane on the bench, where the hot, sticky varnish stuck to her legs immediately. Tinka unscrewed the cap, which gave off the familiar rip-pop sound that proved the bottle had not been tampered with. Tinka tilted it back; and as the cold water coated her parched throat, she forgot for a moment she was about to be murdered.

"This is a gorgeous house," Jane said.

The guy knocked back his water, then screwed the cap back on. "Thanks. I like it."

Tinka decided to play civil. "Do you do all the landscaping yourself or do you have a crew that helps you?"

He smirked at Tinka, like she was the most curious thing he had seen in a while. "We have a crew, but I noticed a few spots on the bushes that needed trimming."

She nodded. "If you need to get back to work, don't let us stop you. We wouldn't want you to get in trouble with your boss."

"My boss?" He was still grinning at Tinka with those dimples as he kneaded the plastic on his water bottle. "You mean my father?"

"Your father owns the landscaping business?"

"My father owns the house. I'm Sam. Anderson," he added for good measure. "I live here." He gestured toward the back door.

Jane dropped her face into her hands. "Oh my God, Tinka."

Tinka spun toward her, pointing. "Oh my God nothing, Jane. You didn't know he lived here, either."

"I did so."

"How?"

Jane waved her hand to indicate Sam and the flirty smile reappeared on her face. "He has a way about him."

"He has no way about anything. No offense." She nodded to Sam.

"None taken." Knitting his brow, Sam lifted his hat and ran his fingers through his curly brown hair. He had hazel eyes with friendly crinkles on the corners that didn't disappear even when he frowned.

"And, I mean," Tinka said, "I assumed this place had people to take care of the landscaping."

"We do," Sam said. "But I like gardening. It's relaxing."

"What else do you do for fun, Sam?" Jane said.

He beamed at her, and Tinka figured he'd finally noticed her much more attractive running clothes and gorgeous, silky black hair. It was bound to happen. "I work at the video store in town. I'm kind of a film geek. Or…not kind of. I am a film geek."

"Do you go to school?" Jane asked.

"I'll be starting college in the fall. What about you ladies?"

Jane spoke for both of them. "We go to boarding school in South Carolina. We'll be seniors next year."

But Sam was back on Tinka. "Boarding school, eh? Fancy business."

Jane kept on talking. "My mother went there. Tinka's

parents wanted to get rid of her, so they sent her away last year." She had a joking smile on her face, but Tinka winced.

Sam frowned, and Tinka, sensing that he was about to ask her some personal question she had no desire to answer, stood, ripping her bare thighs from the tacky wood bench. "We should get going."

"Already?" Jane peeled the label off her water bottle.

"We have to help my parents."

"Ugh." Jane hoisted herself from the bench. "When I agreed to visit Tinka this summer, I thought I'd be in for an entire month of cakes and cookies. Instead, it's constant construction."

"You said you didn't mind helping." Jane had been nothing but cooperative since they'd arrived in North Pole, which hadn't reduced Tinka's bad friend guilt level, not one bit. Jane was the ideal pal. Tinka was the girl who got drunk and kissed her roommate's ex-boyfriend.

"I don't mind. But a mint chocolate brownie would be nice once in a while. I mean, what's the point of living with Tinka Foster if she can't whip you up a batch of peanut butter cookies?"

Sam, still watching Tinka with those crinkled hazel eyes, asked, "You bake?"

"Does she bake?" Jane said. "You don't even know, Sam. She's a wizard. At school, all we had was this tiny little kitchenette across the hall with an itty-bitty oven. Tinka worked literal miracles in there."

Tinka blushed. She'd spent some of the money her dad sent her for golf on baking equipment and ingredients. Jane was right. She had worked wonders in the tiny dorm kitchen.

Jane ticked off a list. "Cherry streusel bars. Lemon Bundt cakes. Brown sugar cookies. Blueberry boy bait. You name it, she made it. Our friend Violet gained fifteen pounds this year, just because of Tinka."

"That's overstating things." Tinka handed her empty bottle to Sam. "Thank you for the water."

"Why haven't you baked anything this summer?" he asked.

Tinka laughed. "Have you been to my parents' house? It's a disaster. The kitchen is like the opening scene of *Saving Private Ryan*."

Sam grinned. "Nice."

She'd dropped in that movie reference on purpose, because she knew he'd appreciate it. What was she doing? Flirting? That had gotten her nothing but trouble. "My parents have left the kitchen for last. They're more worried about having enough working bathrooms, I guess."

"Then they've got their priorities screwed up," Sam said. "You should stick it to them by refusing to work on any other room in the house until the kitchen's done."

"You're totally right. I should do that." Except her parents didn't even know how much baking meant to her. Even though she'd loved reading cookbooks and watching cooking shows since she was a kid, baking wasn't something she did in their presence—only while away at school or when she used to hang out at Karen's house back in Minneapolis. Her mom hadn't been big on letting Tinka play around with the oven and other appliances. Too unsafe. Too much opportunity for injury. Too much sugar.

"You know you're welcome to bake anything here any time. We have a fantastic kitchen no one uses," Sam said,

"I might take you up on that," she said.

"I mean it. Come over whenever. Door's open." He nodded toward the house.

Without warning, Jane wrapped her arms around Sam's neck and pulled him close. "It was so nice to meet you."

He patted her back, but his eyes bugged out at Tinka, like, *What is going on?*

Tinka shrugged. "Jane's a hugger." And Tinka was not, no matter how huggable someone's arms appeared to be. She folded her arms across her chest.

Sam did the same after Jane let him go. "See you around, neighbor?"

Tinka nodded, sneaking one last glimpse of Sam's delicious forearms. "See you around."

. . .

Tinka's mom met the girls at the door as soon as they returned home. Tinka caught the smell of paint and sweat mixed with her mom's perfume. "Jane!" Her mom seized Jane's arm. "I need you."

Yanking off her stinky running shoes, Tinka hopped into the front hallway, basically unnoticed.

"I finished painting the upstairs bathroom. We need to go find a shower curtain. Immediately." Breathless, Tinka's mom grabbed her purse and her keys.

"You want me to come?" Tinka asked. She'd never seen anyone so frazzled over a guest suite before.

"No. Just Jane. You're…" Her mom paused and took a moment to look at Tinka. "It's a surprise." *Goodie. Another surprise.* "Dad's working at the coffee shop in town." Tinka's mom and Jane dashed out the front door.

"I'll take a shower and…" She trailed off. No one was around to hear her. Back in Minneapolis, she would've killed for some alone time. Her parents usually had her entire life scheduled. But there was absolutely nothing to do in this house, no way to relax, nothing to take her mind off the fact that her family and roommate had abandoned her this afternoon without a moment's hesitation. She couldn't bake. She couldn't mess around online. She couldn't watch TV. She hadn't even brought any books with her because she'd had no idea they were coming here and not going to Minneapolis. There was a bookshelf packed with old Sidney Sheldon paperbacks in the basement, but Tinka wasn't in the mood for sexy intrigue.

The dilapidated kitchen caught her eye. Dust-covered and neglected, it was full of tools and supplies for other parts of the house. The plan was to demolish the whole thing, break it down to the studs after every other room had been finished. But at this rate, with the ancient cabinets still stuck to the walls and the grotesque, mustard yellow vinyl tile still clutching the floor, that wouldn't happen until Tinka was back in South Carolina.

Unless...

Glancing around casually as if to make sure she was alone in the house, Tinka stepped into the kitchen. Groaning, she hoisted up a sledgehammer that was propped against the sink. She sucked in a breath, then rammed the hammer into one of the cabinets above the counter. Tinka smiled to herself as the ringing in her ears subsided. Then she wound up and hit the cabinet again. And again. She dropped the hammer with a thud and reached up, grabbing a handful of wood, which she tore down with her bare hand. A large splinter dug into her palm, ripping her skin from one end to the other.

"Ow!" Tinka clutched her hand, stinging eyes darting around for a rag. She dashed into the powder room and grabbed one of her mom's new hand towels, which wouldn't buy her any friends, but these were desperate times. Tinka pressed hard on the wound for a full minute, then lifted up the towel. The blood wasn't stopping. She needed stitches. The cut was no joke.

This right here was why she always followed her parents' rules, because when she didn't, she got hurt. And then she had to string together a web of lies, like the time she burned herself trying to make caramel, even though she'd been expressly forbidden to use the stove. She'd run upstairs to her bathroom—her hand radiating pain up and down her arm—and straightened half her hair, just so she could tell the lie that she'd burned herself on the straightening iron.

She had no clue how she was going to explain away a bashed-in kitchen cabinet, something she would've had to justify anyway even if she hadn't hurt herself. She had not thought this through. Not one bit, which was so not like her.

Tinka tied the towel around her palm as best she could, then, with her other hand, she reached into her pocket and extracted her phone. "Damn it." Her battery was dead, and both parents were at least a half hour away. She couldn't stand here bleeding for that long.

Turning toward the window, she caught sight of the Andersons' house. She knew at least one person who was home right now.

With a deep breath, she marched back over to Sam's.

• • •

"This is all your fault anyway." Tinka strapped herself into the front seat of Sam's ancient pickup truck, which he wished he'd had time to clean out before she got in it. There were empty Santabucks cups all over the cab and it smelled faintly of sour milk. Tinka hadn't seemed to notice though. She was too focused on her hand, which she had wrapped in a lacy white towel, through which a growing patch of blood had soaked.

Sam backed out of the driveway without resting his arm across the back of the passenger's seat, which is what he normally would've done. He didn't want to give Tinka the impression he was hitting on her right now. Especially not after he'd recently used her—before he'd ever met her, assuming he'd never meet her—as his excuse not to hook up with Dottie. "How's your injury my fault? I wasn't in the room when you decided to become a one-woman wrecking crew."

She wrapped the towel tighter around her hand. Sam winced. He should've given her a bandage or something when she'd showed up at his door. Too late now. *Way to be a hero, Sam.* "But it was your idea. You said I should refuse to work on any other part of the house until the kitchen was finished. You said I should take my future into my own hands."

"I didn't mean literally," Sam said. "I meant maybe you should talk to your parents about moving the kitchen timetable up a bit."

"Well, then you should've been more specific."

Tinka was the most beautiful girl who'd ever been in his car; that was not even up for debate. She had these deep violet eyes and long, curly blond hair. Even in her still-sweaty running clothes, she was perfect, a Disney princess in human form. And he was Sam. "Are you okay? Like, are you in pain?"

"I'm good." She held up her towel-wrapped hand. "I'm a total chicken—always worried about what might happen—but then when something actually does go wrong, I can usually handle myself."

"You're Walter," Sam said.

"I'm who?"

"Walter, from *The Big Lebowski*. He's a mess about little meaningless stuff, but he's great in a crisis."

"I'm Walter." Tinka nodded in satisfaction. "I like that. How long have you lived here, Sam?"

"Six years? We moved from the Twin Cities."

Her cheeks flushed with a hint of pink as she put pressure on her wound. "I'm from Minneapolis," she said. "Or, well, I was. Do you miss it?"

Sam shrugged. "Not really. I still keep in touch with people I was friends with back then, but we have our own lives now. I was in junior high when we moved. North Pole is home."

She snorted. "This place. Home."

"Do you miss the cities?" He turned right out of the resort.

She groaned, and Sam sensed his question was a loaded one. "No," she said at last. "I don't know. I miss my house and…normal life. I'm off-kilter here, you know? My mom and dad are happy, and I love seeing that, but I'm rootless right now. I don't have a home."

"By the end of the summer you'll be calling North Pole home," Sam said.

"If you say so." She tightened her towel on her hand and glanced out the window, like she was searching for some proof of what he'd just said.

"Seriously. This is a great place, and there's always stuff to do. We live in a beautiful resort. How many people can say that? And in town you've got the arcade and the indoor hockey rink." He paused for drama. "Or if you're in the mood for danger, there's always Jingle Falls."

Her eyes widened. Sam couldn't tell if that was from fear or excitement. Maybe both. "What's that?"

"A ski lodge, north of town. They have these concrete slides they open up in the summer. You take the ski lift up to the top of the mountain, then you ride a plastic sled all the way down. It's horribly unsafe, and it's amazing the place stays open. The owner must be connected as hell." Sam showed her his arm. "See that scar on my elbow? From a wipeout at Jingle Falls. My entire family is covered in these burns. Badges of honor."

Tinka's eyes lingered on his scar a few seconds longer than normal, and Sam thought maybe the pain was finally getting to her. Then she shook her head. "You're suggesting I injure myself for the thrill of it? I've already tried that." She raised her bleeding hand. "Not a fan."

"Well, if that's too edgy for you, there's always the video store," Sam said. "It's my favorite place in town. We show classic movies every Saturday night. Five bucks gets you admission, popcorn, and pop. All the locals our age go. It's kind of the date spot." He blushed, thinking of last Saturday, when he'd told Dottie he already had a girlfriend—a girl he'd never met who was now sitting in his passenger's seat.

Tinka laughed, the lilt of her voice resonating through the car. "Dating, yikes. That is definitely not on my agenda this summer. Had a little too much of that at boarding school this year."

"Yeah?" Sam asked, not sure why he was even slightly deflated. Tinka was well out of his league, and he knew it. What did it matter if she was also out of the game? Especially when he was in the same boat.

"Yeah," she said. "I kind of need some time to myself, to get my head right. You know?"

He nodded. "I get it. I'm leaving for college at the end of the summer."

"Where you going?"

"USC," he said. "I'm leaving in August. I want to enjoy my family and friends and the town for as long as I have them. I just wish my siblings would stop trying to set me up with random people I have no interest in. Why bother starting something that's doomed to end?" He'd thought his brother and sister would give up on teasing him about his lack of a romantic life once they left town, but it had only gotten worse. They'd sensed, correctly, that Sam was upset, and they kept ribbing him and ribbing him. The three of them had a text chain that was supposed to be about the wedding, but it had evolved into a plan to make Sam more attractive to women.

"You, too? My parents are trying to foist their friends' son on me. I start yammering about golf whenever one of them broaches the subject, but that's only a temporary solution." Tinka grinned as she lifted the towel and checked out her wound. "Still bleeding." She wrapped her hand again. "You've got the right idea, I think. No romance, just friends. Friends are my focus right now." She chuffed Sam's arm with her non-bleeding hand and a spark shot up his spine. "Speaking of, thank you so much for driving me."

"Like you told me before, it was basically my fault."

"Still. I owe you." Tinka's eyes lit up. "I know! Maybe I can make a batch of your favorite cookies one day, to thank you for driving me to urgent care and saving me from mortal peril." She frowned. "I'd have to use your kitchen, though."

"Not a problem." This girl could use any room in his house she wanted.

"What are your favorite cookies? I can bake anything."

"*Alfajores*," he said without hesitation. He could almost taste them. Even now, after five years, the smell of caramel took him right to September and the first day of school, with his mom in the kitchen wearing the Wonder Woman apron he'd gotten her for Mother's Day back when he was six.

"Ooh. What are those? I've never even heard of them."

"They're Peruvian. My grandma used to make them for my mom when she was a kid. Shortbread sandwich cookies with *dulce de leche* in the middle. Like, melt-in-your-mouth amazing."

"I'll tell you what. I'm going to make you those cookies, Sam Anderson." She readjusted her towel. "And I will make them so perfectly that no other baker in your life will be able to live up to the impossible standard I have set."

"That sounds almost like a threat."

"Well, I'm incredibly talented."

Sam shivered. She was talking about baking, and that was it. She wanted a friend, nothing more. This wasn't the start of a great romance. It could be the beginning of a beautiful friendship, but that's as far as it would go, which was fine. Friendship was all Sam was in the market for, as well.

It hit him then that he and Tinka had essentially made

plans to hang out again, at least one more time. They were joking easily, enjoying each other's company. She'd come to him when she'd hurt herself. He couldn't keep what he'd told Dottie a secret from her. If she found out from Dottie or someone else, she'd never speak to him again. He had to rip this secret off like the bandage he should've given Tinka back at his house.

"Um...can I tell you something completely embarrassing?"

"Sure." Sam felt Tinka's eyes on him, but he kept his on the road as he tightened his grip on the steering wheel.

"So...I don't know if you remember, but I waved to you the other night when you were on your balcony?"

"That was you?"

"Yeah, so, Saturday night I was at the video store to watch a movie, and this girl, Dottie, well, she kind of likes me and maybe I gave her the wrong impression about how I felt. Okay. I definitely did. I texted her, and it was a whole thing. Anyway. She ended up coming on kind of strong, and I had to come up with a quick excuse to brush her off. I told her I already had a girlfriend."

Sam paused, waiting for Tinka to fill in the gaps for him. She didn't. He was going to have to say the words. The awful, mortifying words.

"So, uh...since I'd just seen you on the balcony, you were the first person who came to mind. I told Dottie that you and I were...together..." He let that trail off.

Tinka was silent.

"I'm sorry." She must think he was such a loser. What kind of guy had to make up a fake girlfriend? "It was a stupid thing to say. I panicked, and I never thought we'd ever meet anyway. It was an innocent little lie. I wanted to tell you, in case word got back to you—"

He glanced over at her. She was staring hard out the

window, turned completely away from him. He'd blown it. He'd completely screwed this up.

"I'm sorry," he repeated. She had no idea how sorry.

"Just drive," she said.

Chapter Four

"Whose cars are those?" There were two unfamiliar vehicles parked beside the new "liquid platinum" SUV in Tinka's parents' driveway. Dread and annoyance dampened the pain radiating from her freshly stitched hand wound. "I bet at least one belongs to Mark and Trish."

"Mark and Trish?" Sam asked.

"My future in-laws." They were probably inside planning the wedding right now, sketching out a monogram entwining Tinka and Dylan's names.

This was why her mom hadn't come running to urgent care. When Tinka had called her from the waiting room and relayed what had happened, her mom had overreacted at first, which was great. It was the reaction Tinka had been banking on. Nervous Mom was normal Mom. But once Tinka had convinced her she was okay, her mom had said they'd meet at home, apparently because their friends were coming over. Mark and Trish trumped Tinka.

"Tinka, again, I'm really sorry." Sam had been saying that ever since he admitted he'd used her as a way to deflect the unwanted advances of some Dottie girl.

At least he'd been honest about it. She had to give him credit for that. "You want to make it up to me?"

"Anything."

Tinka tried to see into the house, to get some preview of what she was about to walk into. The not knowing was the worst part. She was about to head into an ambush unprepared. "Want to come in and act as my buffer? Your presence might keep Mom and Dad from going full-bore with this Dylan thing."

"Dylan?" Sam's hands kneaded the steering wheel, making the muscles in his forearm twitch. Yes, he'd told another girl Tinka was his girlfriend, but those tanned, strong arms almost made up for it. Almost.

"Greene," Tinka said. "You know him?"

Sam frowned. He was trying to see inside the house, too. "Literally the only thing I know about Dylan Greene is that he broke up with his girlfriend a week before senior prom so he could go with someone else."

"Ah, so he's a real winner then," Tinka said.

"A total prince." Sam grinned and there was that dimple again.

Sam and Tinka's entrance made no impact on her parents. Her mom and dad bustled about the living room, carrying paper plates, plastic forks, and napkins. Jane and the Greenes—Dylan included—were perched on the floor around the coffee table, passing containers of garlicky Chinese food. But there was one other person in the room, someone Tinka could never have even imagined would be there. Karen. Tinka's ex-best friend from Minneapolis, the one she'd ghosted after moving to South Carolina.

Karen was sitting cross-legged on the floor next to Jane, who was talking a mile minute. Tinka caught the word "manicure" over the din. Karen looked like Karen, dressed in denim shorts and a plain pink T-shirt with a pen resting on one ear. Her hair had changed, though. She used to wear it in a relaxed bob, but now she'd let it go natural, puffing up around her head. The sunlight coming through the skylight above them filtered through her hair, giving her an ethereal glow that contradicted the scowl on her face. She alone had noticed Tinka.

Tinka raised her hand in a timid wave. Karen sneered and turned away, plastering on an over-the-top expression of amused interest in whatever Jane happened to be saying about nail polish.

"Honey!" Tinka's mom shouted when she finally caught sight of her daughter near the door. "You're home! Look. Karen's here."

"I see that." Tinka waved her bandaged hand to no avail. Her mom hadn't even bothered to ask how she was doing.

Karen folded her arms. "Your mom invited me, and my mom forced me to come. I brought a bag of books and two hundred *New York Times* crossword puzzles. You won't even know I'm here."

Tinka's mom squeezed Karen's shoulder as she passed by with a carton of sesame crispy chicken. "Of course we will, dear. And we're all so happy to have you." She raised her eyebrows at Tinka and nodded pointedly.

"I'm glad you're here, too, Karen," Tinka said. It was true. She'd been trying to figure out a way to apologize ever since she'd found out Karen's parents were splitting up. Tinka had composed and deleted about thirty different text messages— saying she was sorry, asking if Karen was okay, offering her ear if Karen needed to chat. None of the texts looked right. She and Karen needed to deal with each other in person. Here was their chance.

"Bite me," Karen mouthed to Tinka.

No one said it would be easy.

"Karen drove up this afternoon, in her hot new car." Jane scooped a spoonful of fried rice onto her plate. "She's why your mom had us working so hard to finish the guest room. Maybe we should move up there, too. Make it a sleepover."

The look of horror on Karen's face told Tinka exactly how she felt about that idea.

Sam glanced down at Tinka, his forehead furrowed with concern. "You okay?" he mouthed.

She nodded, feeling calmer all of a sudden. She had an ally here. "This is Sam." Tinka gestured toward him.

"We know Sam." Tinka's dad pointed to a spot on the floor. "Come join us. We bought out the Chinese Restaurant, basically."

"Tinka's okay, by the way." Sam nudged her in the arm, and she held up her hand. The room turned to see. "She got five stitches, but they'll come out in a week."

"Oh, honey." Her mom scurried over and gingerly clutched Tinka's hand. Blue paint had hardened on her mom's cuticles. "Did I not ask about your hand? I've been so scatterbrained today, what with Karen coming and all."

"I'm fine, Mom." Tinka's safety and well-being were now lower on her mother's priority list than "guest room bedding" and "feeding Mark and Trish." No big deal.

Her dad shared an exasperated look with Mark Greene. "I guess Tinka won't be golfing with us tomorrow."

Tinka's mom had barely flinched when she'd heard Tinka was hurt, and now her dad was callously talking about how she'd ruined his golf plans. The urge to grab on to something—or some*one*—hit her, but Sam was the only object nearby. She straightened up. Seeking out the closest available warm body was how Tinka would've dealt with sadness and disappointment at school. Those days were done.

"I can ask one of my friends." Dylan scooped some moo shu pork onto a lettuce leaf.

"But this was supposed to be a chance for you and Tinka to get to know each other." Tinka's mom plopped a stack of paper napkins onto the table.

"There will be other opportunities," Dylan said.

Tinka's brain flashed forward to the next few weeks of dinner with Dylan, golfing with Dylan, being tricked into spending alone time with Dylan. She didn't know whether to laugh or cry. Either response seemed appropriate.

Trish refilled her own wine glass. "Maybe you can go out tonight or something?"

Dylan turned to Tinka. He shot her one of his very slick, "I know I'm hot" smirks. If he had come at her with that grin a few weeks ago, she would've been powerless against it. Now it only made her want to run and hide in a dark closet somewhere. "What do you say? It might be fun."

Fun. "Fun" was what Colin had promised the night Tinka betrayed Jane, his ex-girlfriend, and Tinka was done with that. The idea of fun exhausted her, and so did Dylan. It was going to take too much mental energy to keep evading his advances, energy she didn't have to spare because she was too busy golfing and working on the house and trying to figure out what was going on with her parents and dealing with two friends as houseguests—one who hated her, and another who'd have every reason to hate her if she ever found out what Tinka had done.

She glanced up at Sam. Maybe he'd had the right idea. Maybe he'd done all he could do in the heat of the moment. Perhaps he'd realized Dottie wasn't going to leave him alone unless he squashed all her hopes. Tinka's parents were never going to give up on this Dylan thing, either, unless Tinka provided a valid reason why it was never going to happen. Like if they thought she was already dating someone else.

Good thing Sam owed her one.

• • •

Sam had been too busy figuring out the dynamics at play in the Fosters' living room to realize what Tinka was up to. He felt like he was slogging through some three-hour ensemble drama with a huge cast, and it was up to him to remember how everyone was related. He'd barely heard her when she said, "But I'm already seeing somebody."

And he didn't put together that the "somebody" was him until Tinka laced her fingers between his and squeezed. A zing of electricity bounced from Sam's toes to the top of his head. "Um…" was all he could say.

"He was so sweet this afternoon. He held my hand while I got the stitches." That wasn't true. She'd made him stay in the waiting room because she'd still been mad about the Dottie thing. "We got to talking, and one thing led to another…"

Tinka's voice trailed off, and Sam glanced down at her. She was gazing up at him expectantly. He was supposed to finish this story.

He pulled his eyes away from her big blue ones. "And… yes…us," was the genius that trickled from his mouth.

"This is…surprising," Tinka's mom said. She didn't know the half of it.

Tinka's dad and Mr. and Mrs. Greene had nothing to add. They only sat there, shocked. Mrs. Greene's fork had only made it halfway to her mouth.

"Too bad." Dylan winked at Tinka with a cocky grin. Sam checked her reaction. She either hadn't noticed or was pretending she hadn't.

Tinka's friend, Jane, clapped her hands. "This is so romantic." She jumped up from her spot on the floor and hugged both Sam and Tinka. Then she stood between them and linked her arms in theirs, making a Jane sandwich. "We need to celebrate. Let's go out on the town tomorrow, get to know Sam. He can show us around. What do you say, Karen?"

Karen's expression said, "That sounds like torture."

Jane took it as a yes, bounded over to Karen, pulled her up from the floor, and wrapped her in a big hug.

And now Sam was staring into his closet, trying to decide what he should wear today to hang out with his not-girlfriend and her real friends for a not-date. In less than twenty-four hours, he and Tinka had gone from strangers to friends to not friends to pretend boyfriend and girlfriend. If this had been a movie, Sam would've said it was too much, too fast.

Sam threw a *Back to the Future* T-shirt over his blue mesh basketball shorts and ran downstairs, where his sister Maddie's nanny was chatting with the girls in the foyer.

"Hi." He pulled on his favorite high tops, nodding specifically to Tinka. "Hey."

"Hi." She blushed slightly.

Jane squealed, clapping. "You guys are so cute! I can't even take it."

Tinka's other friend, Karen, groaned, turned around, and marched out the front door.

Sam had no idea how he was supposed to behave. They hadn't discussed the particulars of their situation. Tinka was definitely avoiding his eyes right now. Maybe she regretted starting this charade and was about to pull the plug. Sam would let her take the lead, whatever she thought was best. She was the director, and he was her assistant.

He and the girls hopped into his pickup truck, and he drove them into town, pointing out various landmarks on the way. "That's where the Joyces live. They keep their nativity scene and aluminum Christmas tree out all year round." He waved to a woman across the street. "And that's Dolores Page. She named her kids after reindeer."

Sam found a parking spot right in front of Frosty's Dye and Trim.

Tinka stared at the life-sized plastic snowman on the sidewalk outside the barbershop. "It's June."

"This is toned down. Wait a few weeks for Christmas in July. By then it will look like a giant vomited red, green, and gold all over everything." Sam led them across the street to the local cafe. "And here we have Santabucks, where everyone gets their coffee. Anyone need caffeine?"

Tinka raised her hand. "We've been living off Folger's Crystals and stale doughnuts. Give me the good stuff."

Grinning, Sam held the door open for Tinka, Karen, and Jane. Brian Garland, in his Santa hat, was working the counter. His eyes widened when he saw Sam come in with three girls. "Sam," he said.

Sam made his way over to Brian, both sheepish and chuffed to be seen out in public with not one, not two, but three attractive humans of the female persuasion. It wasn't a sight North Pole was used to, unless Sam happened to be walking around with his sister and a couple of her friends.

"Who are they?" Brian whispered.

"My neighbors." The girls had grabbed a table near the back. "Or the blond one is. That's Tinka." He almost added "my girlfriend" to the end of that, just to try it out, but stopped himself.

"What's her story?" Brian's eyes were squarely on Jane.

"What about Abby?"

Brian's gaze was back on Sam. "Abby?"

Sam held his hand up waist-high. "The Canadian gymnast?"

"Oh." Brian shrugged. "Old news."

"Shocker." Sam ordered black coffees for himself and Tinka, an Arnold Palmer for Karen, and an unsweetened matcha iced tea for Jane.

"I'll bring them to you," Brian whispered. "Put in a good word."

Shaking his head, Sam joined the girls at their table,

where they were discussing what to do next.

"We could go shopping," Jane said.

"Or to the bakery." Tinka was sitting alone on one side of the table, her seat as far from Karen's as possible. Sam took the empty chair next to Tinka.

"Of course *you* want to go to the bakery." Karen wrinkled her nose. "Your mom said there's a great bookstore on Main Street."

Brian strolled over with their drinks. He had taken a second to straighten his hat before coming over to the table, where he unceremoniously plopped Tinka's, Karen's, and Sam's drinks in front of them, but handed Jane her tea with a slight bow. "I'm Brian."

"Jane." Her lips puckered around the straw.

Sam rolled his eyes at Tinka, who smiled and rolled hers back. Brian was so obvious.

Brian pointed to Jane's cup. "We care a lot about customer service here at Santabucks, so I took the liberty of writing my phone number on the side there, in case you have any comments or complaints."

"Such dedicated service," Jane said.

Tinka picked up her cup. "I don't see your phone number on my cup. Don't you care about my experience?"

"Or mine?" Sam examined his cup as well. "What if I have a comment or complaint?"

"Karen, too." Jane draped her arm across Karen's shoulders. Karen stiffened for a moment, then relaxed.

With a huff, Brian grabbed each of their cups in turn and gave them his number.

Tinka, Jane, Karen, and Sam laughed as Brian retreated behind the counter.

"He's cute," Jane said. "Maybe I should call him. It's summer. We're in a resort town. We have to have flings. It's, like, the law or something. Right, Sam?"

"I've read the town charter. Mandatory summer flings are not in the bylaws," Sam said.

Jane gestured toward Tinka and Sam. "I want what you two have."

Tinka blushed, and Sam attempted to deflect the conversation. "Tinka mentioned the bakery—"

"We don't have to go to the bakery," Karen said. "Just because *Tinka* wants to—"

"I never said we *had* to go to the bakery," Tinka said. "It was a suggestion. I'm not forcing anyone to do anything."

Jane turned to Sam. "Be careful. I took Tinka to my favorite bakery in Charleston where they make these amazing potato chip cookies. She went back to my grandma's house and elevated the shit out of them. We went to the grocery store and bought twenty different kinds of chips. Then she smothered them in white chocolate and caramel and Nutella and played around with spice and heat—she used, like, garam masala and Sriracha and all these other ingredients from my grandma's kitchen. So delicious. She ruined the bakery for me that day, Sam." She shook her head at Tinka. "Bitch."

"You know you love me." Tinka smiled, but there was pain behind it.

Jane patted Tinka's hand. "I do."

Karen folded her arms. "Gross. And I'm still anti-bakery."

Tinka frowned. "Well, someone pick something."

"I know!" Jane said. "Tinka told me about that Jingle Falls place. It sounds ridiculous. Let's go there."

Tinka hadn't seemed so keen on Jingle Falls a few days ago. "There's so much to see in town," Sam said. "I haven't shown you the arcade—"

"We'll see that later," Jane said. "Let's go do the dangerous slide thing."

"Yeah." Karen pouted. "Let's do *Jane's* thing."

Tinka's face had gone white.

"It is fun," Sam said. "And fairly safe, despite all my scars."

She nodded. "Okay. Let's do Jane's thing."

The four of them left Santabucks, piled again into Sam's pickup truck, and he drove them up north, straight across town from the golf resort. He kept sneaking peeks at Tinka, who sat right next to the passenger's side door, with Jane and Karen between them. She stared out the window and didn't say much, but her mind was obviously working overtime on something. At the entrance to Jingle Falls, Sam paid for their tickets and the four of them picked out their sleds.

Karen and Jane jumped onto the first chairlift and Tinka and Sam boarded the one behind them. Tinka clutched the armrest on her side for dear life.

His legs swinging freely in the warm breeze, Sam studied the grassy mountains and deep valley below them. He watched a family of deer gambol down the side of one hill. This was nothing like the heart of North Pole. There were no Santa hats, no plastic reindeer, no piped in Christmas music.

"It's so peaceful up here," Sam said in a desperate attempt to get Tinka talking.

She only gripped the armrest harder.

When they hopped off the ski lift, Jane met them at the top of the mountain, her sled standing upright next to her. Karen had already gone down the slide.

"Who's next?" Sam asked. He smiled sheepishly at the slide attendant—a guy, Jerry, from school—who pointed to Tinka and then to Sam with a nod and a sly wink.

"You guys go ahead." Tinka gawked at the slide, where a kid of about ten had just disappeared down the first steep drop.

Jane held up her sled. "I'm on it." With full authority and confidence, she stepped over to the slide and handed her sled to Jerry. Seconds later, Jane was gone.

"You want to go?" Sam asked.

Tinka's eyes were so big and sad. And scared. Like an animal in a Disney cartoon who sensed nearby danger. "I don't think I want to do this."

"I kind of got that impression the way you were hanging on to the chairlift."

Tinka frowned. "Jane and Karen are gonna make fun of me."

"So what?" Sam shrugged.

"It's dumb. Karen's looking for any reason to bust my balls, so that can't be helped, but Jane only knows me as a kind of daredevil, and, I don't know, all the riskiness has gone out of me. I'm being Walter again, worrying before there's anything to worry about."

He grinned at the reference to their *Big Lebowski* conversation. She remembered. He snapped his fingers. "I've got it." He handed their sleds to Jerry and said, "We'll take the ski lift back down."

"You don't have to, Sam. You can go ahead."

"It's no big deal," he told her. "I've done Jingle Falls before, remember."

The two of them jumped back on the lift together. Tinka clutched the armrest again. "They're still going to think I'm a wimp."

"No, they won't." Sam pointed to her bandage. "Use your ace in the hole. We'll tell Jane and Karen Jerry wouldn't let you do it because of your hand."

Tinka smiled. "Good thinking."

She could smile at him like that forever, and he'd never tire of it. He pointed to his head. "Not just a hat rack."

Tinka leaned back and stared at the sky. "I'm so embarrassed."

"Why?"

"Because even though the girls won't know I'm a wimp, you always will." She turned to face him.

"I don't think you're a wimp." She was beautiful and nervous and cautiously considered every step before she took it, but she was not a wimp. "Jingle Falls is some scary shit." Sam pointed to a rather large scar on his right knee. "This is from when I was riding down with my sister Harper. She was screaming at me that a sign said 'Slow,' but I didn't listen. I took a sharp turn and we wiped out. I got this, and Harper skinned her shoulder."

"Ouch."

"Yeah," Sam said. "Not recommended."

After a few moments, Tinka said, "So, we haven't talked about...our situation."

"No, we haven't." This was it. This was where she'd tell him they were even, and they could go their separate ways. Sam clutched his own armrest, bracing himself for the rejection. He readied his response. He'd be cool and flippant. He'd make a joke. It wasn't like he'd never been shot down before.

"You're probably wondering why I had a change of heart last night." Tinka stared off to the side as scenery at their eye level flew past them. "My parents are all about me getting together with that Dylan guy, and I don't want to deal with him or romance at all right now." She turned to Sam. All the color had drained from her face. "I did a bad thing."

What could she have done that made her so upset— murder? Treason? His vast movie-watching experience had prepared him for any and all confessions.

"Can I tell you about it? I need to tell someone."

He nodded. Whatever it was, he was going to be so cool about it.

"The last night at school, there was this big party." Tinka held up a hand, letting go of the armrest for a split second. "Let me backtrack. I kind of spent most of last year getting drunk and hooking up, which were things I never did back in Minneapolis, but when I was in South Carolina..."

"All bets were off," Sam said.

"Kind of." Tinka shrugged. "You get it."

Sam didn't, really. Drinking was not something he did. His mom had been killed by a drunk driver, and their whole house had been dry ever since. He wasn't against people drinking or anything—a lot of his friends, even Harper, did—but he wasn't a party guy. He didn't hook up randomly. He, based on recent history with Dottie, was incapable of hooking up randomly. But he certainly didn't judge his friends or Tinka for doing those things.

"Anyway." Tinka shuddered and closed her eyes. Sam wasn't sure if that was because they were on a scary chairlift or if it had to do with what she was about to say. "The party. The last night of school. I'd had a lot to drink and I got to talking with this one guy and we ended up back in his room." Now she opened her eyes and bit her lip for a moment. "But he wasn't any random guy. He was Jane's ex, like, as in they had just broken up."

"Oh." He had been prepared to deal with treason or murder, but not this.

"I stopped it once I realized what I was doing, and all we did was kiss. Literally, that was it. But I felt awful, still do, and of course it's been agonizing carrying this secret around while Jane's here—she has no idea, by the way."

"I won't say anything." He'd be a steel trap, whatever Tinka needed. None of this was his business, after all.

"But it wasn't just *what* I did, but it was the fact I did it at all. How did I go from being this cautious wallflower to getting wasted and hooking up with my roommate's ex-boyfriend in the span of a few months?"

"This is some heady stuff for one ski lift ride." Sam chuckled, trying to lighten the mood.

"I'm sorry. I'm unloading on you."

"It's okay."

"Well, the whole existential thing coupled with how badly I treated Karen over the past year and how my parents seem to be doing better here without me, I realized I needed to reckon with some things, you know?" Tinka turned toward Sam, fully facing him. "It hit me last night—maybe you were on to something. And maybe pretending to date you would get my parents off my back about Dylan at least. It'd take one problem off my plate."

"We're kind of in the same boat," Sam said. "I'm dealing with leaving for college and organizing my brother's wedding, and my siblings have been relentlessly teasing me about not being able to get a date. It's like, they left me with all this work to do and instead of being nice about it, they keep jabbing me where it hurts the most." He paused. "Maybe that's why I caved to their pressure and texted Dottie. I wanted to get them off my back. I wanted some peace. Though it only created more problems. If I hadn't done that—"

"I wouldn't have been able to use you as my excuse to shut down the Dylan thing." Tinka's eyes sparkled. "But A, it was good of you to be upfront with me right away, which leads me to B, I really do think you're a decent guy, Sam." She squeezed his arm. Again, sparks flew right to his brain. "At least you seem to be, based on the twenty-four hours we've known each other. Since our problems aren't going away any time soon, I'm all for keeping up this charade if you are."

Sam hesitated. There was nothing fake about his attraction to her, which would make being her pretend boyfriend both easier and harder in some respects. "I…guess so?"

"That's the spirit!" Tinka grinned. "Sam Anderson, will you be my fake boyfriend until such time as we both decide this is no longer working for us?"

Even though every ounce of Sam's being told him this would send him careening into trouble, he said, "Yes, Tinka. I'd be honored to keep being your fake boyfriend."

Chapter Five

This fake relationship thing had its perks.

When Tinka woke the next morning, she was greeted by the scent of fresh coffee and hot breakfast coming from upstairs. Trying not to disturb Jane, who was still sleeping, Tinka rolled off their air mattress and basically floated up to the kitchen. There she found her mother, father, and Karen perched around the coffee table in the living room, filling up their plates with toast, eggs, bacon, bagels, and fruit. Her dad was even drinking orange juice.

"Food," Tinka said, relishing the sound of her father's knife scraping against his toast. "Finally. Thank you." She sat on the floor next to Karen. "Morning."

Karen scooted to the other side of the table. Well, Tinka, at least, was going to keep trying. If Karen wasn't interested in patching things up, that would be on her.

"Don't thank us." Tinka's mom handed her an envelope. "This is for you."

Bemused, Tinka stared at her mom as she tore the paper and pulled out a note written in scribbly handwriting.

*Tinka, you deserve a real breakfast. You'll notice there are
no stale doughnuts. Sam. P.S. Why don't you, Jane, and Karen
come to my house today to hang out (if your parents can spare
you)?*

She surveyed the spread. Sam hadn't missed a thing. He'd
supplied disposable plates and silverware and butter and jam.
He'd even tossed in a package of napkins and a cloth for the
coffee table, which was normally covered in plastic. Tinka's
mom peered over the lip of her coffee mug.

"Well, that was decent of him." Tinka pretended not to
notice Karen's bitter expression as she grabbed a slice of
cantaloupe and poured herself a cup of coffee. "Sam invited
us girls over this afternoon, if that's okay."

Her parents shared a look across the table. "You went out
with Sam yesterday. Isn't this moving a little fast?" Her mom
widened her eyes at Tinka's dad.

"And don't you have work to do around the house?" her
dad asked.

"Well, I can't do much with this." Tinka held up her
bandaged hand. "And we'll be here for the morning anyway."
She figured her mom for the easier mark and pleaded her
case to her. "Karen and Jane are only here for a few weeks.
They can't spend every waking moment up to their eyeballs
in drywall dust."

"I suppose." Her mom stood, pouring herself one more
cup of coffee. "But not too late, okay?"

Tinka's dad followed his wife into their bedroom, which
was right off the kitchen. He rested his arm across her
shoulders and whispered something in her ear. Tinka caught
the words "Tinka" and "boyfriend."

Grinning, she grabbed a banana. Putting her parents on
edge and escaping hard labor—not bad at all. Thank you,
Sam.

"Sam's a nice guy," Karen said.

Tinka startled. "Are you actually talking to me?"

Karen stared at Tinka with an eyebrow cocked and her lips pursed. Half a bagel sat uneaten on her plate. Sacrilegious.

Tinka peeled her banana. "Fine, Karen. Keep up the silent treatment. You do you."

Karen shrugged and stood up. "Not like you'd take my opinion into account anyway."

"Just say what you want to say."

Karen retreated toward the stairs leading up to the guest room, her fortress of solitude.

"We need to talk, you know." Tinka was not going to give up that easily. "I feel awful about how things went down this year, and I want to apologize."

Karen turned around. "I hope you know that saying you want to apologize isn't the same thing as actually apologizing."

"I understand that."

She squinted at Tinka. "Does Sam know what he's getting into with you?"

Tinka chewed her banana, a sick feeling forming in her stomach.

"You like him now, I'm sure, when it's convenient for you, when it's easy and everything's going your way, but does he know what you're like when things start going south?" Karen paused as if to let Tinka answer. When she didn't, Karen said, "Here's some friendly advice: maybe don't go all Tinka on Sam. Don't treat him like you normally treat the people you allegedly care about."

"What does that mean?" Her words socked Tinka in the gut, but she covered her emotion by grabbing the uneaten bagel off Karen's plate.

"If I even have to tell you." Karen rolled her eyes and disappeared up the stairs.

• • •

A little while later, Tinka, Jane, and Karen had thrown on their bathing suits and cover-ups and were making the trek from Tinka's house to Sam's. Karen's words had been bugging Tinka all morning. She wasn't wrong. Tinka *had* been a bad friend, and she *had* done some regrettable things, like ignoring phone calls and kissing her roommate's ex.

But the operative word there was "had." That was the old Tinka. Yes, she'd behaved that way, but in the past. She was a changed woman. She was ready to prove she could put other people's needs before her own, if only Karen would give her a chance.

"Check out Sam," Jane whispered as the girls approached the Andersons' property. "What do you think of your boyfriend now?"

Tinka stopped in her tracks. She shielded her eyes from the sun to make sure she was seeing what she thought she saw. "That isn't…" She squinted at the stranger standing on the front stoop.

"That *is*." Jane ran up to the door and greeted Sam with a big hug. He looked like an entirely new person. He was wearing a pair of nice jeans and a breezy button down shirt. His face was clean-shaven, and he'd gotten a haircut. He laughed as Jane ran her hand down his smooth cheek. Sam had dressed up.

He'd better not have done that for Tinka's benefit. She and Sam were supposed to be on the same page. This was a mutually beneficial relationship of convenience. Neat and tidy. No one's feelings were going to get hurt, as long as everyone played by the rules and didn't make it weird, like by getting makeovers to impress the other person.

Tinka took her time ascending the steps. "Hi." She fixed the shoulder on the yellow, cotton sundress she was using as a cover-up. Jane and Karen hovered inside the foyer, and Jane was making kissy faces at Tinka. She waved them away, and they scurried down the hall.

Sam leaned down and whispered, "What do you think?" He waved his hand to indicate his new clothes. "Not my idea. I told my sister Harper about us. I hope that's okay."

Ah, so that was why. He'd only dressed up to make it seem like he was trying to impress his girlfriend. Tinka smiled. "Totally fine. Obviously, that's why we're doing this."

"I said you were coming over, and she made me promise to make myself presentable. I even had to send her a picture of me all dressed up as proof."

"I think…" Tinka searched for something witty to say, but she went with, "You look nice." And he did. He cleaned up well. Very, very well. Heat rose up Tinka's neck. He even smelled good, like soap, but with a hint of sweetness underneath.

"Don't get used to it," he said. "As soon as we head outside, it's back to comfy shorts for me."

"Good." Tinka's eyes twinkled. "I like your movie T-shirts. It's sort of a game, trying to guess which one you'll wear next."

"You think about my T-shirts?" Sam's dimple flashed.

Tinka blushed. "No." She shook her head. "I don't know." Ugh, she shouldn't be tongue-tied in front of Sam. He was the same guy he was yesterday and the day before, but in better clothes and with a scent that reminded her of cookies and clean cotton. She expected him to play by the rules and keep things as platonic as possible, but here she was drooling over him.

She brushed past him into the house, and the Anderson mansion opened before her. Tinka had to take a moment to catch her breath. It wasn't simply that the house was beautiful, which it was and she'd always figured it would be, but there was such an aura of home to it. People lived in this house. There was no doubt about it. And after a week of barely surviving in her parents' dump, that was enough.

When she spotted a stately grandfather clock next to the

stairs, Tinka whispered, "I want to live here."

"Play your cards right, and we could take this fake dating thing all the way to a fake marriage."

Tinka's eyes snapped to Sam's. He was blushing, too.

He cleared his throat. "We'd have to fight my sister for the house, though, and she's scrappy as hell."

"We can take her," Tinka said.

The front hallway opened up on both sides to a living room and dining room dressed in sunny yellows and bright blues. The couches were buried in plush pillows. It wasn't too hot today, so a breeze blew through the open windows, ruffling the airy chiffon curtains. In the corner of the living room stood a grand piano, whose top was covered with frames boasting photo after photo of the Anderson family, dating back decades. In fact, pictures were everywhere, all over the house. They lined the walls leading upstairs and the mantel in the dining room. They were on coffee tables and end tables and countertops. Every room of this house seemed to shout, "These are the people who live here."

Tinka's parents' house said, "We're a hot mess. Come get high on paint fumes!"

Sam led Tinka through the first floor and into the great room off the back of the house, where Jane and Karen were waiting for them. This room, stocked with more pictures and a giant television, was attached to the massive, gleaming, state-of-the-art kitchen. Tinka tried hard not to drool as Sam gave them the tour. She basically hadn't seen a real, functioning kitchen in months, but Sam's kitchen was so much more than functioning. It had two sinks and an island and a double oven and, wow, was that a Majestic Pro Industrial Size and Strength Stand Mixer in brushed chrome?

Tinka ran over and caressed the appliance's cool metal. It was beautiful, a work of art. It belonged in a museum. "Your mixer," she said. "I want to lick it."

Sam laughed. "I'm serious. The offer from the other day stands. Anytime you want to bake something."

"You don't have to tell me twice."

Sam led the group down to the beach where they found Sam's little sister, Maddie, and her nanny building sandcastles. A pontoon boat and two canoes were tethered to the dock, and a large cabana sat off to one side.

"This is paradise, Sam," Karen said.

Tinka snuck a peek over at her mom and dad's house. They'd been so busy with the inside of the house, they'd neglected the outside almost entirely. The grass was in desperate need of mowing and the weeds were starting to take over. That was the problem with her parents' place. There was always something to do, something to take care of. It was impossible to relax there.

As the waves lapped the shore of the Andersons' little private beach and Jane and Karen spread a king-size comforter over the sand, Tinka peeled off her cover-up. She blushed when she noticed Sam checking her out in her indigo bikini.

He wasn't so bad, either. Tinka found herself imagining what it'd be like to hug him, to snuggle up on the couch under a blanket with his strong arm around her shoulders. She was willing to bet it'd be pretty nice. He'd make a good real boyfriend for someone someday.

Before they'd come out to the beach, Sam, as promised, had changed out of his fancy gear and into another of his movie shirts. Tinka didn't understand this one. "A hot dog and a house?"

Sam glanced down at his midsection. "From the all-female *Ghostbusters* movie?"

"Haven't seen it," Tinka said.

"It's good. Better than advertised." He grinned. "We should watch it sometime."

They should, and they should snuggle up together on his couch. Tinka blushed. She had to stop thinking like that. This was a fake relationship. Fake. And she had sworn off guys. But if they had to cuddle a little to prove their devotion to each other… "Yeah. Okay."

He grinned and his eyes stayed on her for a moment. Then he turned to the other girls. Jane was lying on her stomach, propped up on her elbows, and Karen had busted out her thick book of *New York Times* crossword puzzles. "What do you ladies want to do?"

"Canoe!" Jane said.

Karen's upper lip curled into a slight snarl. "I'm good."

Here was Tinka's big moment to prove she was able to put someone else's needs before her own. (Even though, honestly, she wasn't too keen on canoeing, which seemed like an accident waiting to happen—she pictured herself getting slapped in the head with a paddle—and, besides, she wasn't supposed to get her stitches wet, but Karen didn't need to know that.) "How about if we take the pontoon boat out instead? That way we can all stick together, and Karen can bring her puzzles along."

Karen's eyes met Tinka's for a quick moment, so fast it barely happened. "Works for me."

They each grabbed a few pops from the cabana and headed onto the boat. Sam undid the rope on the pier, as Jane took a spot along the edge for maximum sunlight. Karen grabbed a seat next to her, and Tinka occupied the swivel chair next to Sam's captain seat.

"You haven't seen much of the resort, have you?" he asked, turning the key in the ignition.

Tinka shook her head.

"This is the best way to do it, anyway. No drunk golfers, no random Christmas decorations. Just nature." He pulled away from the dock. Trees lined the shore on all sides. There were a few private, probably man-made beaches here and there, but there were even more like her mom and dad's place, which had a rocky drop-off to the water.

"It's quiet." Tinka listened to the birds and bugs fighting to be heard. There were a few other pontoons on the lake, plus canoes, paddle boats, and sailboats.

"By design," Sam said. "No speed boats allowed, no skiing, no tubing."

Tinka chuckled. "Fine with me. Those things are out of my comfort zone. I'm always worried I'll fall and get left behind because no one's looking out for me."

"I'd look out for you." Sam pressed the gas and they cruised toward the middle of the lake. Tinka's insides warmed as Sam—hand shielding his eyes—expertly steered their vessel.

"Maybe North Pole doesn't *totally* suck." Tinka's eyes scanned the perfect blue sky and the houses peeking out over the treetops. "At least not all of it." She glanced at Sam again as the warm wind ruffled her hair and caressed her face. Was she having actual fun? And what was this other strange emotion? Contentment? Where was the tension in her shoulders? Where was the pit in her gut?

"It's all in how you see it," Sam said.

"I'd only been seeing it through my parents until now—the stuffy golf course, the decrepit house, the stale doughnuts." Tinka grinned at Sam. "I like your way of life much better."

Back on the beach, they ate sandwiches provided by Sam, then built more sandcastles with Maddie and her nanny. When all was said and done, they'd erected an entire village. When they were sufficiently wiped out, and the nanny had taken Maddie inside for a rest, Jane and Karen resumed their places on the comforter and closed their eyes, letting the late afternoon sun dry their skin.

Tinka glanced back at the house. She had an idea. "Sam?"

The sun was behind him and its rays formed a sort of halo on his head and across his shoulders. "Yeah?"

"You know what I want to do right now?"

Jane made half-hearted kissy noises, but she didn't open her eyes.

Tinka ignored her. "I want to bake something. Is that okay?"

"Of course." Sam hopped over Jane and Karen's legs.

"Sure. 'Bake cookies.'" Jane mumbled. "That's such a euphemism."

Tinka grinned. "Go to sleep, Jane." Then she grabbed Sam by the arm and led him up to the house. "My cookies are better than kissing anyway."

. . .

The house was quiet. Maddie and her nanny were upstairs resting, but Sam and Tinka were alone-ish. He had never been alone in his house with a girl before, at least not that he could remember.

He glanced back at the beach where Jane and Karen were still on the blanket, napping in the sun. Tinka had only jokingly mentioned kissing on the way in, but now it was all Sam could think about.

"It's probably blasphemy to say this in Minnesota where we're supposed to relish every bit of summer we're given, but I want to be inside, in this room, all day long. I still can't believe you have a Majestic Pro Industrial Size and Strength Stand Mixer in brushed chrome." Tinka stroked the top of the appliance and studied all of its angles.

"I can leave you two alone, if you'd like." Sam hopped up on a counter and grabbed an apple.

"That would be kind of you. I think your machine and I need a moment." She flipped the switch on the mixer, and the paddle attachment spun inside the metal bowl.

"'Gets turned on by kitchen appliances.' That's something to add to my list of Tinka." Also on the list? Looks amazing in a bikini. Sam wasn't normally the kind of guy who ogled women, but it was hard not to notice Tinka's street clothes had done her figure no favors. And here he was hiding his belly under an XL novelty T-shirt—with a picture of a hot dog on it.

"This mixer is practically begging for some batter to stir," Tinka said.

Sam shrugged. "So, make something already." And now this gorgeous girl was about to make him baked goods. He'd won the life lottery.

Her hands went to prayer position and she clapped. "Really?"

"Really. I'm desperate to try some of these Tinka Foster confections I've heard so much about." Sam hopped down from the counter, reached under the island, and grabbed a baking sheet from the cabinet. As he passed her the pan, their hands touched. Electricity shot up Sam's arm, and not for the first time that day. He kept having to remind himself that this thing with Tinka was fake, and the feelings he was experiencing were due to the power of suggestion, nothing else. They were not in a real-life rom-com. They weren't going to fall in love. He and this incredibly beautiful girl were only acting like boyfriend and girlfriend, playing the roles they'd assigned themselves, which was confusing the heck out of Sam's head, heart, and, well, the rest of him, too.

Tinka placed the pan on the counter. "You have any cookbooks? Or am I flying solo here?"

He opened a cabinet above the stove. "See anything you like?"

Tinka stood right next to him. She tapped her chin as she perused the books. "*Joy of Cooking*. Classic."

"That was my mom's favorite." He handed her the book. It was heavier than he remembered.

Tinka clutched the book to her chest. "Was?"

Sam winced. Everybody in North Pole already knew about Sam's mom. He rarely had to tell this story. "She died a few years ago."

"Shit. I had no idea." She reached out and squeezed his forearm. Electricity. Again.

He casually removed his arm from her fingers. Self-preservation. "Car accident. The anniversary's coming up, actually. Fifth one." Sam plopped down on one of the stools flanking the island.

"I'm so sorry, Sam." She tilted her head like everyone did for a moment, then, as if remembering herself, she straightened up.

Sam smiled slightly to let her know it was okay. He was always doing that for people—his siblings, his dad. He was Sam, the strong one, and he had to keep up the appearance that everything was fine. "She used to bake all the time. My sister Harper has tried to fill her shoes, but frankly," he glanced around and whispered, trying to lighten the mood, "she sucks." He waved a hand at Tinka. "You do your thing, I'll watch. Unless you want to put me to work. But don't ask me where anything is because I don't have a clue."

Tinka turned her back on him and flipped through the cookbook. "One question: do you have bananas?" she asked.

"Hey, I know that one! They're right there." Sam pointed to the island in front of him.

"I think banana bread it is." She started flipping through cabinets, pulling out ingredients—flour, sugar, baking soda, salt, and baking powder. She gathered butter and eggs from his fridge, as well as a slab of bacon.

"Bacon?" Sam's eyes widened. "You're killing me."

She held the slab aloft. "We can do this Elvis-style—

slather the slices with peanut butter and crumble bacon bits on top."

"I was joking when I mentioned the two of us getting fake married earlier, but I'd gladly make a more serious offer if you keep talking like this." Sam was only half-kidding. Actually, more like one-third kidding.

Grinning, Tinka placed three unpeeled bananas on the baking sheet, put them in the oven, and turned it on. Then, her back to Sam, she started measuring ingredients and dumping them into a bowl. "I'm sorry I said I'm sorry about your mom."

That was a new one. "You're sorry you said you're sorry?"

"Yeah." Tinka shrugged. "I always want to be the one who's ready with the perfect response in this situation, but instead I gave you an 'I'm sorry' and the tilted head-frowny face."

Sam's jaw dropped. "You know about the tilted head-frowny face? I hate the tilted head-frowny face."

"Ugh, me too. It's the worst." She dumped something else into the flour and hunched her shoulders up to her ears. "My brother died."

On instinct, Sam moved to stand, to go to her, offer her a shoulder, but he caught himself, because maybe that wasn't what she wanted. He sat back down, giving her space. "Tinka, I'm sorry."

"I'm fine." She shook her head and turned toward Sam now, her chin out, face hard, like she was trying to prove how fine she was.

"And I'm sorry because I definitely gave you the tilted head-frowny face behind your back," Sam said.

She smiled. "Everyone does."

"We can't escape it." He shrugged. "How old was your brother?"

"Four." Tinka chewed on her lip. This wasn't a story she told often, Sam could tell. Her hunched up shoulders, her jutted chin—she was trying to keep her emotions in check, something Sam knew a lot about. "He was at preschool, first week. He climbed to the top of the monkey bars and fell."

Sam's hand went to his mouth. "How old were you?" Sam knew what it was like to lose someone in an accident. There were always those moments where he found himself thinking about what was going through his mom's head, if she'd suffered, if she'd known.

"I was only a year old when he died, so I don't remember him or the incident at all."

"What's his name?"

"Jake." She said the name like she had to think about it beforehand, like it was an unfamiliar word she had a hard time pronouncing.

"The whole situation is awful, but it really sucks you have no memory of him." Sam's siblings bugged him, but he couldn't imagine life without them. He had an urge to run and hug Maddie or call Harper and Matthew. He settled for running his finger along the edge of the wedding binder, which he kept on the kitchen counter, a constant reminder of how much his family was counting on him.

"Yeah, I don't remember him, and maybe that's why the 'I'm sorries' bug me so much. I got off easy. My parents deserve the sympathy, and the rest of my family, but not me."

"You do, though. He's your brother."

"But he's more like a distant relative. People act like I should cry and mourn him, but I don't, which then makes me feel emotionally inadequate, because maybe I should be doing those things." She turned around and measured something else before dumping that into the bowl, as well.

"There's no right way to handle grief." Sam's family had run the gamut. Harper had leaned on her best friend, Elena. Matthew had Hakeem. Their dad had gotten rid of all the alcohol in the house and cut back his hours at work. Sam had been the rock for whoever needed him, but especially Maddie, who had only been three when the accident happened.

"But it's not grief, is it?" Tinka said. "I'm not sad. If anything, I'm pissed off, which almost certainly makes me a terrible person."

"You're not horrible for feeling the way you feel. I know that for sure."

She shook her head, her back still to Sam, like the only way she could talk about this was if she couldn't see him. "There's a lot of resentment. Everything in my life has happened in the absence of Jake. I'm Tinka because that's what Jake called me when I was born. My parents act the way they do because Jake's not here. I let them drag me around by the leash because they lost their son and I've been trained—by them, by other relatives, by my own instincts—to try to make their lives easier at all costs. And, as a result, my entire life revolves around Jake being gone."

"Your entire life?" Sam thought about his mom every day. He didn't wake up with her consciously on his mind, but inevitably something would remind him of her—whether going into the coffee shop or catching a whiff of her perfume on Harper. But his life didn't revolve around her. He was moving on, moment by moment, little by little. Each day existing got a tiny bit easier.

Tinka started doing calf-raises at the counter, rising up and down on her toes in a steady rhythm. The action was probably supposed to calm her, but one leg was definitely shaking. "I started golfing because of Jake, because he sunk a twenty-foot putt one time when he was three and my dad thought he'd be the next Tiger Woods. After Jake died, my dad pushed all his golf dreams on me, and I've kept up with it because it's the only way my father relates to me. He only pays attention to me on the golf course."

Sam's dad was in real estate. A businessman. He didn't

know much about Sam's movies or Maddie's figure skating or any of the other stuff his kids loved, but he tried to understand. He tried to show an interest. Because that's what fathers did. "I'm sure that's not the only way your dad relates to you."

Tinka turned on the mixer and spoke over its whirring. "I don't know about that. I've always felt like he's kept me at arm's length because he's scared of getting attached to another kid."

"God, Tinka." Sam tried to put himself in her shoes, but he couldn't fathom his dad making any of the Anderson kids feel that way.

"My mom went the opposite route. She scheduled every inch my life and knew where I was at all times. At least she used to. Ever since I went to boarding school, or at least since winter break—it's like they got rid of me and they're much better now. She barely batted an eye when I hurt my hand. I spent seventeen years trying to live up to their standards and make their lives easier, but now that we're here in North Pole, it's like I was the problem. I was the thing holding them back from happiness." Tinka wiped her eyes with the back of her hand. "Shoot."

She walked over to the sink, turned on the water, and threw some of it in her face. Sam stayed on his stool, trying to decide what to do, what the protocol was here.

"If it makes you feel better," he said, "I get feeling resentful. Obviously I knew my mom better than you knew your brother and I miss her as much as anyone, but because I'm Sam the happy one, everyone assumes I'm not as gutted as they are. They take it for granted that I'm doing okay, but... sometimes I'm just not. I wish they'd let me be not okay once in a while."

Tinka turned to face him. She clutched the lip of the counter behind her, like she, too, was trying to decide how they were supposed to act in this situation. "I've never talked to anyone about this stuff before."

"Me neither. It's how I got into my current predicament." Sam stood and picked up the wedding binder. "My brother and sister left me with all of Matthew's wedding details because they knew I could handle it, that I'd make sure everything got done. But sometimes I want to break down. Sometimes it hits me that my mom should be the one here doing these things."

"Can we hug?" Tinka asked. "I think we need to hug."

After putting down the binder, he stepped over to her and she wrapped her arms around his waist. Sam enveloped Tinka in his arms and rested his cheek on top of her head. "Thank you," he said.

"I started this." His T-shirt muffled her voice. "I'm the one who unloaded on you."

"Any time." He squeezed her a hair tighter. "What are fake boyfriends for?"

Chapter Six

Tinka rehearsed her lines on the putting green while waiting for her dad to show up for their tee time on Saturday afternoon. She'd gotten her stitches out that morning, and, though her scar was still a bit tender, Tinka's dad hadn't wasted any time forcing her back out on the links.

"I've been thinking, Dad, and I don't want to play golf this year," Tinka mumbled to no one. She lined up another putt, took a deep breath, and sunk it. "I appreciate you sending me to Florian's. I really like it there." Or she had liked it there, before the whole Colin situation. Tinka shook herself and crouched down to focus on the slope of the green as she whispered the words she'd say to her father. "It's not like I want to give up golf forever. I'll keep playing with you…on occasion. I only want to quit the team. That's it. I no longer want to compete."

She sank a nice thirty-footer and took that as a sign that this afternoon was going to go well. Her dad was always more receptive to her feelings once they were on the golf course. Plus, she'd practiced this conversation with Sam last night when she and the girls were at his house, which was becoming their evening routine—work at Tinka's house all day, hang out with Sam at night.

Sam's house was the only place in North Pole, perhaps the world, where she was at peace. Last night, Jane and Karen had gone down to the basement to play video games with Maddie, and Tinka and Sam had stayed out on the porch, chatting about family issues.

"We need to be honest with them, don't we?" Sam had asked. They were drinking coffee and picking at the remnants of a chocolate-chile cake Tinka had baked earlier that afternoon. It was the most adult she'd ever felt in her life—drinking after-dinner coffee on the veranda with her (pretend) man friend.

Tinka had glanced over at her parents' house, which was dark. Her mom and dad had gone to dinner with Mark and Trish again, of course. That was also most definitely becoming routine.

"There's a first time for everything." Tinka had never, ever given her parents even the slightest inkling that she wasn't happy with her current situation. They'd be shocked to hear it, she was sure.

"I'll do it if you will." Sam drained his mug. "I'll get on the phone with Harper and Matthew and tell them that I can't be in charge of all the wedding details. It's not fair to me. I get that they're dealing with a lot right now, too, but so am I. They tend to forget that. Or, really, I tend to hide how much stuff gets to me. It's time I told them."

Tinka had frowned. "And it's time I tell my dad that I don't want to golf anymore." She could picture his heart breaking in real time.

"You're going to be fine." Sam had punched her lightly on the arm, which made her grin. She almost believed him.

When her dad showed up for their round, Tinka shored

up her shoulders. This was her moment. She had considered waiting until after the front nine or even for when they'd finished and were back in the clubhouse, but no. She'd already waited too long. They needed to have this conversation now. "Hi, Dad." She set her lips in a line.

"Hi, honey." He placed his bag down and pulled out his putter and a ball. He was wearing a pair of khaki pants and a polo with his company's logo on the breast—his uniform.

"Can we talk for a minute first?" she asked.

Her dad dropped his ball on the green, crouched down, and lined up the putt. "Give me a few secs to warm up. We're running late. We can talk on the way to the first tee."

"We" weren't running late. She'd been here for fifteen minutes already. She checked her phone while her dad commenced his warming up.

"No phones, Christina," he warned.

Huffing, she shoved it back in her pocket. Golf, at least with her father, was so arcane, so backward-looking. She couldn't wear jeans or shorts. She had to wear a collared shirt and a visor—no sunglasses. And now, no phones—because in Scotland when this game was invented, no one used phones. They hadn't worn visors, either, Tinka was sure. Or collared shirts with logos on them. And women definitely weren't allowed, but whatever. He was a golf originalist when it suited him.

When he was finally ready to make his way to the first tee, Tinka fell in step with her dad, and tried to broach the subject of quitting the golf team again. "Dad, I've been thinking—"

He sidestepped her, waving vigorously to someone standing outside the clubhouse. "Dylan!" her dad called. "We're over here!"

Dylan? What was he doing here? Well, no matter. She and her dad were still going to have this discussion. As Dylan picked up his clubs and lumbered toward them, a cheesy gameshow host smile on his lips, Tinka said, "Dad, I really need to talk to you."

Now her dad glanced down at her, a frown on his face. "Oh…that's right." He peeked up at Dylan, who was a mere fifteen feet from them now. "I'm sorry, honey, but can it wait? We can talk on the ride home."

"Fine," Tinka muttered.

Still smirking like the Joker, Dylan greeted Tinka's dad with an enthusiastic handshake. "Ready?" He hiked up his bag on his shoulder.

She scowled. "For what?"

"Dylan's joining us." Her dad grabbed his clubs and led them over to the first tee. "Tinka got her stitches out, and I thought I'd drag her out here since she didn't have any plans with her friends this afternoon. But…what are you doing tonight? Something fun, right? You should ask Dylan to come."

A litany of expletives flew through her brain.

The starter sent Tinka's dad over to the tee box, leaving Tinka and Dylan alone a few feet behind him, her dad's proposition hanging over them. Tinka ran her fingers over the dimples on her neon pink ball.

"What are you doing tonight?" Dylan whispered so as not to disturb her dad's concentration.

"Movie night," Tinka mumbled.

"Ah." Dylan grinned. "The great North Pole tradition. You've never been, right?"

Tinka dropped her ball into the ball washer and plunged it up and down. *Whoosh. Whoosh. Whoosh.*

"It's always a fun time." Dylan paused as Tinka's dad launched his first drive of the day. "So, are you having a girls' night out or—"

"Sam's going to be there," Tinka blurted. She couldn't say his name enough in front of Dylan. She grabbed her ball and wiped it dry with her towel. "Sam works at the video store, you know. He said he'd give us the red-carpet treatment, free popcorn and everything."

"The popcorn's always free." Dylan had this idiotic bemused look on his face, like he knew she'd cave to his wiles eventually. She would not.

"I know the popcorn's free. I was making a joke." Tinka nodded toward the men's tee box, which her dad had vacated. Dylan was up.

He grabbed his driver and saluted her with it. "I may see you there."

"It's a free country." Tinka shoved her ball into her pocket.

"So Dylan's going to be hanging out with you ladies tonight?" Her dad wiped the head of his club and dropped it into his bag.

"He said he might be there."

"It's nice to see you two getting along so well. Duke isn't that far from Florian's, really. You two can get together on the weekends—"

"Dad. I'm dating Sam. *Sam*," she added for good measure.

"Right." Her dad followed Dylan's drive with his eyes. "But Sam is going to school in California. You two will be a whole continent away from each other next year."

"And we'll cross that bridge when we come to it." She and Dylan would still be a whole state away from each other. To see him, she'd have to cross state lines as a seventeen-year-old. Why did no one—certainly not her father—see the issue with that?

Tinka grabbed her bag and marched up to the women's tee. She set up her ball and swung the club in nearly one motion, without thinking, completely neglecting to set up the shot. She put it right in the weeds, but Tinka couldn't care less. That was how she'd play the rest of the round—alone and from the rough. She'd leave the fairway to her father and his new buddy, Dylan.

In the clubhouse at the end of the round, after avoiding her dad and Dylan for hours, Tinka grabbed a lemonade at the counter, leaving the guys alone at a table. When she returned to them, her dad was showing Dylan a photograph. Tinka snuck a peek, and her heart immediately started hammering in her chest. It was a picture she knew well—a shot of Jake at age three swinging a golf club.

She'd never seen that photo out in the wild before. It used to be up on the desk in his home office, in the privacy of his workspace. It wasn't a picture people saw when they came to the Fosters' house in Minneapolis. It was private, never mentioned, for Fosters' eyes only.

And here was her dad beaming with pride and showing it to Dylan.

Dylan frowned at Tinka, and she felt his pity, which, ugh, was the last thing she wanted. She'd never even told Jane about Jake. Karen knew the situation, obviously, but she understood that the topic of Tinka's dead brother was verboten. The only person Tinka had ever opened up to about Jake was Sam, and that was merely because he'd been through something similar with his mom.

"Tinka's got the same skills." Her dad smiled up at her. "I swear it was a moment of divine intervention when I saw her pick up a club for the first time and swing it like her brother. It was as if Jake was talking through her."

There it was. The thing that had kept her stagnant her entire life—her dad saw her as an extension of Jake. How could she possibly tell him that she was prepared to cut the tether to her brother, and by extension her father? Without golf, Tinka would be nothing but a disappointment to him. She wasn't even capable of dating the right guy.

Her dad folded the picture and put it back in his wallet, which was apparently where he kept it now. "Tinka needs a little something extra to push her over the edge before her senior year. That's why I was hoping you could work with her, give her lessons. Again, don't judge her by how she did today. Her hand was obviously still bothering her."

"Obviously," Dylan said.

Tinka focused on the rapidly melting ice in her lemonade. Her dad was talking about her like she wasn't there. He was making decisions without consulting her, not that she could do anything about it. To reject this would be to reject him.

"I'm in if Tinka is," Dylan said.

Tinka was not in, but she didn't have the luxury of saying that.

"She played well last season," her dad said, "but there's room for improvement. No doubt about that. This is her last year before college. She has to be great."

"Definitely," Dylan agreed.

"I was thinking, three times a week."

Tinka nearly choked on her drink. "Three times a week? But my hand."

"You hand is fine."

"The house."

"Your mother will get along without you."

"If Tinka's available, so am I," Dylan said.

"Fantastic." Her dad shook Dylan's hand. The deal was done. The men had shaken hands. Tinka was going to spend three days every week with Dylan breathing down her neck—literally—trying to improve her skills at the game she no longer wanted to play. Perfect. She felt an overwhelming urge to run over to Sam's house, curl up in a chair on his deck, and listen to him tell her all kinds of things about movies—like his feelings on horror as a political statement, and how Hollywood needs to make more true rom-coms.

She and her dad said good-bye to Dylan, and Tinka followed her father to his car. Halfway through the parking lot, he turned around. "I forgot, Tinka. What did you want to talk about?"

This was her moment. This was her chance to break her father's heart. She couldn't do it. She could not be that cruel.

It was just one summer, one school year. She would survive, as she had for her entire life. "Nothing," she said. "Never mind."

. . .

"You promised we'd be watching *The Revenant*," said Craig, "as part of Maurice's ongoing Best Actor series."

"I know." Sam handed him his complimentary can of Mellow Yellow. "But we had to change it. Too depressing. And too cold. We can't be watching Leonardo DiCaprio freeze half to death in June."

"Fair points," Craig said, and Sam took note of this. It was a big moment. Craig never relented this easily when he disapproved of Sam's movie night picks. "But why *Popstar* of all things? What does that have to do with Best Actors?"

"I don't know." Sam shrugged. "Maybe Andy Samberg will win an Oscar someday. Consider this a good faith, pre-Best Actor entry in the series."

"I'm not a fool. That's never going to happen." Craig shook his head. "Is nothing sacred in this town?"

"Sorry, Craig." Sam handed him his popcorn, and Craig marched away.

Sam turned his attention to Tinka, who'd been hanging out near the window. She walked over and rested her elbows on the counter. "Why does he even come if the movie choice bugs him so much?"

The door slammed shut behind Craig.

"I'm fairly certain the fact that it bugs him is the point." Sam smiled at Tinka. "Craig takes glee in being able to complain about something."

"Well then, thank you for changing the movie," Tinka said. "For me and for Craig. I don't have to sit through Leo's struggle, and Craig gets to bitch about it."

"Everyone wins," Sam said.

Tinka glanced at the front door as it opened, then spun back to Sam and whispered, "Shit." Her shoulders were practically up to her ears.

In came a quartet of guys, Dylan among them, who'd graduated from North Pole high a year ahead of Sam.

"Hey." Sam waved them over to the counter. "Home for the summer?"

One of them said, "And still doing the same stuff we used to do in high school." The four guys paid, and Sam crouched down to grab their drinks.

Dylan sidled up to Tinka. "Hi."

"Hey." She locked eyes with Sam. *S.O.S.*

Dylan bobbed his head, trying to get her to look at him, but she wouldn't. Sam stood and handed Dylan a can of Diet Coke. "You can go on in now."

Grinning his sly, preppy, Troy from *The Goonies* grin, Dylan took the pop from Sam's hand. "Did Tinka tell you? I'm going to be her golf coach."

Her eyes were stormy.

"Really?" Sam asked.

"Three days a week. I'm gonna get her in shape for next season." Dylan grabbed his bag of popcorn from the counter and raised it as a salute. "See you in there." Dylan followed his friends into the theater.

When the door had closed behind them, Sam turned to Tinka, who was still staring at the counter. "I'm guessing the conversation with your dad didn't go so well, then."

She shook her head. "It never happened. I chickened out, and now I'm going to be subjected to Dylan and his feeble attempts to seduce me three times a week. How about you?"

"About the same," Sam said. "I called Harper and started to tell her I needed some help, but she cut me off and told me how great I've been, taking this stuff on for her and Matthew. Then I ended up agreeing to make the song list for the ceremony on top of everything else."

"We're such chickens," Tinka said.

"At least we're chickens together." Sam glanced up at the door, then said through clenched teeth, "Oh goodie, Dottie's on her way in."

"I finally get to meet the infamous Dottie!"

Dottie in her blue buns and movie ticket dress sauntered through the door with her usual gang of girls. A surly, confident smile on her face, she marched right up to Sam and tossed a five on the counter. "Hi, Sam. Did you save me a seat?" Sam knew she was being sarcastic, but the underlying tone was one of malice, not friendly ribbing.

Sam coughed. "Um…"

Tinka got right up in Dottie's face and narrowed her eyes into a confrontational stare. Sam half expected her to pull out her earrings and slam them on the counter. "Are you Dottie?"

Dottie turned to Tinka and swallowed. "Yeah."

"So, you know Sam is my boyfriend, then?" Tinka put her hands on her hips.

Sam nodded somberly. "Dottie, this is my girlfriend, Tinka."

Dottie sized her up. "How long have you two been together?" She raised a hand, silencing Sam. "From her. I want to hear it from the horse's mouth."

Tinka stepped back, affronted. "Did you just call me a horse? Whatever. Sam and I have been dating for a few weeks now, since I moved here."

Dottie turned to her friends and motioned them over, like she was assembling her backup. "Did you know your boyfriend kissed me last week?"

"Dottie kissed me," Sam said.

"And he texted me to hang out." Now Dottie's angry eyes were trained on him.

"You *did*?" Tinka glared at Sam in mock anger.

Sam backed up, shaking his head. His focus swung from Dottie to Tinka, then back to Dottie again. He was unable to look at Tinka right now. The feigned horror on her face was going to make him laugh and ruin this whole charade. She was really selling the whole "jealous girlfriend" thing. If Sam hadn't known she wanted to be a baker, he'd have wondered if Maurice might be featuring one of her movies in the Best Actress series one day. "Harper did." Sam doubled down on that lie. Harper could handle it. "She was being a jerk."

Dottie shook her head. "Like I'm supposed to believe you weren't in on it." She looked him up and down. "You're no better than your sister or anybody else in this town." She and her friends marched into the back room.

"I'm hoping she'll have cooled off by the time she's working on my brother's cake," Sam said.

"I don't know if she's capable of cooling off." Tinka tapped out a rhythm on the counter.

"I don't want to go in there." Sam shuddered.

"Me neither, honestly." Still drumming her fingers, Tinka stared at the door as Maurice stepped through.

"The movie's started. You two can go on back." Maurice nodded at the room behind him, which was dark except for the screen.

"Idea." Sam mimed a light bulb flashing over his head. "What if we didn't?"

"Huh?"

"What if we skipped movie night? Dottie's probably angling to make a scene, and Dylan will be leering at you like he knows you'll eventually fall in love with him."

"You see it, too?"

"He's laying it on pretty thick." Sam could barely fathom how a person could have that kind of confidence in their ability to seduce anyone. He supposed it probably had something to do with looking like Prince Eric from *The Little Mermaid*. The confidence came as part of a package with the perfect mahogany hair helmet and chiseled physique.

Tinka narrowed her eyes. "What should we do instead?"

Sam nodded to the front window. "Whatever we want. It's a beautiful night."

Eyes twinkling, Tinka grabbed her purse. "Let's do it. Let's go out on the town."

Leaving Maurice to watch the store, Sam and Tinka dashed out onto Main Street, free to do whatever they wanted for the next ninety minutes. "What should we do?" she asked. "I'm up for anything. Short of Jingle Falls."

Sam raised his index finger. "I know exactly the place."

Together, they walked down Main Street—Sam and this girl who should definitely be with someone who looked like Prince Eric and not someone who looked like the Beast's grungy younger brother. They passed Santabucks, where he waved to the owner, Maggie Garland. He sensed a hint of surprise in her eyes. She was no doubt wondering what Tinka was doing with Sam. He nodded to Trip Prince and Tom Chestnut, who were working in Prince's Summer Sports. Tom gave Sam a thumbs-up, like he definitely knew Sam was with a girl who was far out of his league.

Near the end of the street, Sam held the door open for Tinka at Santa's Playhouse. "Here we go. Another one of my favorite places in North Pole."

The arcade was fairly empty, which was how he'd assumed it would be—it was mostly families with young kids and, of course, the servers who were dressed like Santa's elves. Most of the Playhouse's biggest fans were crammed into the back room at Maurice's right now.

Sam bought Tinka a pop and purchased a game card for each of them. She played *Tetris* while he worked on his pinball skills. After a while, they came together and pooled their tickets, winning long strips at Skee-Ball. At the end of the hour, Sam led her up to the counter where they perused their prize options, while Craig's BFF Dinesh, who was working the counter, kept his eyes glued to the Twins game on the TV across the room.

"Two hundred and thirty-five tickets," Sam said. "What do you want? One whole miniature Tootsie Roll? A plastic whistle that probably doesn't work? The world is your oyster, basically."

"I know what I want." Grinning, she crouched down and pointed to a ring in the glass case in front of them. It was silver and heart-shaped with a massive pink gemstone in the middle. "I want that gorgeous plastic ring to commemorate our love." Even though he knew she was kidding, Sam blushed. The smile on his face was becoming permanent.

Sam stood up. "Dinesh, we'll take the ring."

Dinesh made them wait until the current batter had struck out before he reached into the cabinet, grabbed the ring, and chucked it unceremoniously across the counter.

Sam slid the ring onto Tinka's finger. "Now we're officially official."

She clutched her hand to her heart. "I'll never take it off."

"You might want to. It'll probably turn your hand green."

Laughing about embarrassing things that had happened to them as kids, the two of them walked back to the video store to relieve Maurice and wait for Jane and Karen. Sam was lighter around Tinka. He probably should've been more self-conscious around her because she was so pretty, but he wasn't. He was as comfortable with her as he was with Harper. So comfortable, in fact, that when they got back to the video store and Maurice had retreated into his office, Sam handed Tinka a rag and asked her to wipe down the popcorn machine.

"I will make it gleam, boss," she said.

Sam plopped onto the floor to fill the fridge with more pop, while Tinka wiped down the machine. He was in the middle of telling her about the time he got locked in a bathroom stall in fourth grade when she screeched, "Ouch!" behind him.

He jumped up, spinning around. Tinka was clutching her hand—the same hand she'd hurt when she'd tried to remodel the kitchen by herself. "What happened?"

"Burn." Wincing in pain, she nodded toward the popcorn machine.

Sam checked the appliance. "Damn it. We shouldn't have left Maurice alone here. He forgot to turn it off. This place would go up in flames without me." He opened the drawer next to the cash register and pulled out a tube of Alocane. "This works great. Give me your hand."

Tinka held out her hand. Sam rested it in his palm and assessed the situation, holding her hand up to the light. "Not too bad." He squeezed a bit of the gel onto the burn and lightly spread it around with his finger. Tinka's breath caught when he touched her. "Does that hurt?"

"No," she whispered.

Sam's heart beating a tattoo against his rib cage, he backed up, still holding her hand.

Tinka's eyes met his. "Thank you." The air around them had changed, at least to Sam. Electricity bounced between them, and, even though he knew it was impossible, he sensed Tinka could feel it, too. Sam wasn't Prince Eric, not even close; but Tinka, in that moment, was gazing at him like he was.

And Sam, who had never, ever been in this situation before, and therefore had no idea how to handle it, or if he should even let himself believe it, turned away, letting go of her hand. "You need to stop hurting yourself," he joked.

"You're turning into a rom-com cliché." He screwed the top on the tube of Alocane and handed it to her, letting his fingers graze hers again, but for only a second. "Take this. You'll need it."

Chapter Seven

Glancing around the living room to make sure she was alone, Tinka slunk over to the coffee table, opened Karen's crossword puzzle book, and grabbed the pencil she'd been using as a bookmark. Then Tinka crawled over to the wall near the fireplace, behind the drop cloth-covered wingback chair.

In the corner, she drew a dinosaur about the size of her fist. It was a T-Rex, like the sketch that had been on the wall in the Fosters' Minneapolis house.

Tinka leaned back and assessed her handiwork. "Hi, Dorothy," she whispered.

In the old house, Dorothy had been Tinka's touchstone, her confidante. She'd found the picture when she was about three years old, when she'd been hiding from her mom and dad after being scolded about…something. She'd lain under this wingback chair and noticed a dinosaur drawing.

It hadn't occurred to her then that it had been a Jake original. That thought came to her much later, that Dorothy was her own conduit to her brother, like Tinka was for her dad. But on that day when she was three, Dorothy was there to hear Tinka's side of the story. Lying under the chair, talking to a dinosaur drawing was Tinka's version of therapy. She told Dorothy all her secrets—problems with friends, crushes, her fears about going to Florian's. And Dorothy was always there to listen.

Today after finishing the picture, Tinka stared into Dorothy's pencil-drawn eyes and opened her mouth to speak, but she stopped there. What did she want to say? How could she put into words what had been going through her head for the past day and a half?

"I almost kissed Sam," she whispered finally, right at the place where Dorothy's ears would be, if Tinka had bothered to draw them. Then she rested her forehead on the cool plaster wall. That night at the video store there had been a moment. She couldn't deny it.

Tinka reached into her shirt and clutched the ring they'd won at the arcade. It was hot from being next to her skin. She'd been wearing it on a string around her neck for the past two days...for what? As a joke? Was it part of the "we're dating" charade? Sam wasn't here now to see it. No one was here to see it.

She'd been having a ton of fun with Sam. He was a great friend and a terrific listener. She was more comfortable around him than anyone else. But these feelings were probably just her brain's way of processing her frustrations about golf lessons with Dylan and not being able to tell her dad she wanted to quit the team. Hooking up with guys was how she'd dealt with—or, rather, not dealt with—her feelings at school. It was a pattern she had to break. Besides, Sam was a good friend. She wouldn't confuse their situation by escalating it, physically.

A sob from the basement cut through her wallowing. Tinka pulled herself from the floor and dashed downstairs, where she found Jane and Karen on the couch. Karen had her arm around Jane, who was bawling.

"What happened?" A million terrible thoughts flew through her head—Jane's parents were hurt, her grandma was sick, she'd found out that Tinka and Colin had hooked up.

"Colin." Jane sobbed.

The blood drained from Tinka's face.

Karen patted Jane's shoulder. "She texted him. I told her not to."

"Jane, what?" Tinka sat in front of the girls on the coffee table. "You texted Colin?"

"He"—sob—"told me"—sob—"to stop it."

Tinka's eyes met Karen's. Karen had only recently met Jane, but she was the one with her arm around her. Tinka'd had no idea Jane was even considering texting her ex. She'd figured Jane was over him. She should've asked, but that would've meant saying his name, acknowledging Colin's existence.

Jane let out a giant hiccup.

"He broke up with you." *And then he hooked up with your roommate on the last day of school,* Tinka admitted silently.

"I know, but I miss him."

"She needs to get Colin out of her system," Karen said matter-of-factly. "I told her to call the guy from the coffee shop."

"That's not a bad idea. You two can go out with me and Sam." Tinka blushed at his name, which annoyed her to no end. *Stop it, Tinka. Those feelings are fake. They're a distraction. You're confusing comfort for attraction.* "Maybe they have a friend for Karen."

Karen narrowed her eyes. "Not interested, thanks. I don't need your boyfriend to scrounge up a pity date for me."

"I'm only trying to help." She was never going to say the right thing to Karen. Never, ever.

Jane glanced at her phone for a moment, then tossed it to the table next to Tinka. "I don't think that'll work. I don't want to, like, date somebody. I'm here for a few weeks. What am I going to do? Go out with this guy, fall for him, and then get all broken-hearted again when I have to leave? How would that help my situation?" She wiped her eyes and shook her head. When she spoke again, her voice was stronger. "I need to pull a Tinka."

"'Pull a Tinka?' What's that?" Karen asked. "Run away to another state and stop answering people's texts?"

She deserved that. "Jane, I really think you should call Brian. Sam says he's a decent guy, and a good friend of his." There she was, shamelessly working Sam's name into the conversation again.

Jane shook her head. "I want you to teach me your ways. How do I get drunk and make out with people?"

Yikes. A year ago, Tinka would've been the last person anyone would've been asking for hook-up advice. "Well, one pretty much leads to the other." Tinka stopped herself. "But it's not... You don't want that."

"Since when has Tinka been getting drunk and making out with people?" Karen asked. "And also, who are you to tell Jane what she does or doesn't want?"

"Tinka was the queen of drunken hook-ups at school," Jane said. "I'd be off with Colin—being all serious and fighting about him not being around or whatever—and she was having a fun time messing around—guys from class, the golf team, the baseball team. No strings. No heartbreak. No guilt."

Oh, there was guilt.

"I want that." Jane's eyes were big and watery, pleading with Tinka to give her this one thing.

She glanced at Karen, whose mouth had dropped open to the base of her neck. Back in Minneapolis, Tinka hadn't been the girl who hooked up. She'd been the girl who was too busy golfing and being dragged here and there by her mom to hook up with anyone. She'd only kissed one guy before leaving for Florian's. And now, well, she'd done way more than that. Yet another thing she'd kept from Karen. One more barrier between them. And now Karen knew.

"We could throw a party, I guess," Tinka said. Maybe it wasn't the worst idea. She wouldn't have to participate in the shenanigans. Tinka could be there as chaperone, or as the sage old woman who'd been through it all before. She could look out for her friends, put their desires first for once, *Karen*. "My mom and dad are going back to Minneapolis Friday night to pick up some stuff. It'd be the perfect time."

"So that takes care of the venue," Jane said. "But what about the alcohol?"

"I bet your buddy Dylan has a fake I.D. or something," Karen said.

"I bet he does." Tinka glanced toward the sliding glass door leading to the patio. "Or maybe Sam knows someone." She'd rather talk to him about this than Dylan. She'd rather Dylan not know about it at all. Dylan plus drinks equaled disaster, for sure.

Jane clapped her hands. "Maybe he does. Ooh, go ask him. And tell him to bring a bunch of friends for me and Karen."

"Now?" Tinka touched her hair, which was up in a messy bun. Butterflies invaded her body, but she shook them away. She was being ridiculous. She didn't like Sam. She couldn't like Sam.

To be on the safe side, she said, "Why don't you guys go?" She nodded toward the stairs. "I'm gonna stick around here and paint the master bath."

But as she passed through the living room, Tinka snuck a glance at Dorothy, who was watching her with what Tinka read as a knowing, accusatory expression.

"Shut up," she told the dinosaur before grabbing a dry paintbrush and marching into her parents' bathroom.

• • •

"Are you guys okay?" Jane asked Sam. She and Karen were hanging out in his kitchen decorating the picture frames that would be the favors at Matthew and Hakeem's wedding.

"Me and Tinka?" Sam held his handiwork up to the light, making sure he'd applied the exact right amount of glitter, whatever that was. Harper should've been the one doing this, not Sam. He wasn't a glue and glitter kind of guy. "We're fine."

"We haven't seen you together much, is all." Jane pointed to Sam's face, and he wiped away some errant glitter.

Sam glanced out the back door, craning his neck for a glimpse of Tinka's house. She was over there working on stuff with her mom and dad, and the truth was, they hadn't been together much over the past few days, not since Saturday night at the arcade. She'd come over on Monday to bake some butterscotch blondies, but that was about it. Sam had offered to help, but she sent him down to the basement to watch a movie with the other girls. "She's been busy."

Or else the moment that had passed between them at the video store had thrown her off balance. It had certainly done that to him. He shouldn't be feeling this way about Tinka, or anybody, for that matter.

Maybe Tinka had the right of it: if there truly was something happening between them—which Sam was fairly certain there wasn't, at least not on her end—they should stay far away from each other.

"This is just like Tinka." Karen made dots of glue around her frame.

Jane glanced up from what she was doing. "What do you mean?"

Karen looked Sam right in the eye. "Tinka's not good when stuff gets serious. If you keep things light and happy, she's great. Once it starts getting real, she bails." From her seat at the table, Karen mimed a person running away.

That almost-kiss had felt pretty real. "I think she's just busy with her parents."

Karen shrugged. "Like she was 'just busy' with golf at Florian's. It's how she operates."

Sam placed his finished frame on a sheet of newspaper to dry. Karen could be right, but it didn't matter. He and Tinka had an agreement. They were in a mutually beneficial fauxmance. If she wanted to bail, now or a few weeks from now, he couldn't do anything about it. This was always going to end eventually.

"Your thing kind of has an end date anyway, right?" Karen asked, echoing Sam's thoughts. "Not that I'm rooting for you two to break up—I'm mad at Tinka, but I'm not that mean. You're going to be across the country from each other come August."

Sam focused on another frame.

"I remember how Tinka treated me when she moved to South Carolina. She stopped answering my calls and texts. She completely froze me out. I don't want to see that happen to you."

"That won't happen," Jane said. "Tinka feels totally bad about how she treated you, Karen." She squeezed Sam's hand. "And she and Sam are so adorable together."

They were fake adorable. Sam was experiencing his first ever romantic relationship, and it just so happened to be bullshit.

"Let's talk about the party," Jane said. "Brian says he's all set with the beverages, so thanks for setting that up, Sam."

Since Sam's dad was also going to be in Minneapolis this weekend and because Tinka's house was such a disaster, Sam had offered to host. He was throwing a party with alcohol, blatantly breaking his father's cardinal rule. Sam was really leaning into the cliché of the dorky boy who'd abandon all of his principles just to impress the hot girl next door.

"Do you think it'd be okay if people crashed here, if necessary?" Jane asked. "I don't want anyone driving home who doesn't want to."

"Or can't," Sam said. "It's fine if they sleep over." No one who'd had a milliliter of alcohol would be getting behind the wheel, not on Sam's watch.

"It's going to be so fun!" In her excitement, Jane dumped almost a full can of glitter on her frame. She frantically wiped up the mess.

"I'm not big on parties," Karen said, "but even I'm mildly excited. If Tinka figured out how to let her hair down, so can I, I suppose."

"You totally can," Jane said. "Me, too. I kind of want to go old school and play Spin-the-Bottle or something. Maybe Seven Minutes in Heaven. Stuff I haven't done in years. Can we use your cabana, Sam?" Her big eyes blinked at him.

Seven Minutes in Heaven. Spin-the-Bottle. When he was younger and that kind of stuff was going on, he'd usually been in another room playing video games or watching movies. The one time he did play, he ended up in a closet with his sister's best friend for seven minutes. They'd stood near the door, banging on the wall, making silly, lusty animal noises. He'd never played for real. He'd play for real if Tinka wanted to.

"Sam?" Karen snapped her fingers in front of his face.

He shook his head. He had to stop thinking that way. Nothing was ever going to happen with Tinka, which was a good thing. It was the way this was supposed to go. "Yeah?"

"Can we use the cabana?"

"Oh…yeah. Whatever you need." He needed to end

these little fantasies. They weren't helping anything, and they were only making him more confused.

"Are you excited about the party?" Jane was grinning like her life was finally getting good.

"Oh," Sam said. "I don't know."

"It's going to be so fun."

Sam glanced out the door again. Tinka was out on the deck now, checking her phone, frowning at something on the screen. Fun wasn't the word that came to mind. Anxiety-inducing? Sure. There were so many ways this could play out badly. He and Tinka could have another awkward moment like last Saturday night. Or he could have to endure watching her have a Saturday night moment with someone else.

"Yeah." Sam turned back to Jane. "Tons of fun."

Chapter Eight

Because Jane had missed the dark party on the last night of school, she decided that their North Pole party on Sam's beach should also be dark. But the walk to Sam's party on Friday night was decidedly different than the walk to the Florian's Academy dark party. There were no bras or beer bottles littering the way, just flowers and grass and lawn chairs and the occasional tree. The only light came from the moon and stars. Tinka had shut off every bit of light in her parents' house, and Sam had done the same in his. Their entire corner of the resort was sheathed in blackness.

She'd left her phone back at the house, too, both because that was part of dark party tradition and because she'd started getting texts from Colin.

The first one came on Wednesday. "Tell Jane to stop texting me."

Tinka had ignored it.

Then: "I can't stop thinking about you."

She wrote him back in all caps: "YOU HAVE TO."

After that he started writing about how he'd been doing

some thinking and maybe when the two of them were back at Florian's, they could pick up where they'd left off. Tinka deleted every message as it came in. She thought he'd get the point, that she didn't want to hear from him, but apparently not, because the texts kept coming.

Karen grabbed onto Tinka's arm as she tripped over a tree root. "Sorry!"

"It's okay," Tinka said. "Hold on to me if you need to."

"I will, but only because I can't see where I'm going."

The girls clutched each other in the darkness, stumbling over something every ten feet or so. As her eyes adjusted to the lack of light, Tinka found Sam, Jane, Brian from the coffee shop, and three of his friends waiting for her and Karen down by the beach, sitting in a ring of Adirondack chairs around a cooler. Tinka made a silent wish that Jane would have fun tonight and forget all about Colin forever. He wasn't worth it.

A table was set up next to the cooler with whiskey, rum, Jell-O shots, and mixers. The guys and Jane were all drinking from bottles, but Sam had his usual can of root beer. Tinka waved to him nervously. They hadn't seen or spoken to each other since Monday. He gave her a curt nod, which nearly tore her heart in half until Tinka reminded herself that she was feeling rejected by her fake boyfriend, whom she herself had been avoiding, which was the most pathetic thing on the planet.

Over the next half hour or so, the entire teenage population of North Pole showed up to the party in Sam's backyard. There were folks Tinka recognized from walking up and down Main Street. There were others she'd never seen before in her life. And, of course, there was Dylan Greene.

"Who invited you?" Tinka dug her toes into the sand on Sam's beach as Dylan sauntered up to her.

"Jane." He offered Tinka a beer, which she rejected. Dylan opened it for himself instead. "How's your awful, debilitating injury?" He took a swig from the bottle.

She rubbed her shoulder. "Still sore." Tinka had cancelled that morning's golf lesson because her shoulder "hurt."

"You were avoiding me."

Tinka dropped her arm. "Nothing gets by you."

"Your boyfriend's making the rounds." Dylan nodded toward Sam, who was about twenty feet away, talking to two very pretty girls who were not Tinka.

"As he's allowed to do." Tinka stared at Sam, willing him to ditch those other girls—whoever *they* were—and come over to save her.

"Jane told me you're always a lot of fun at these parties. I believe the word she used was 'legendary,'" Dylan said.

"She was being sarcastic."

Sam finally glanced over at Tinka, who tried to subtly wave him over without Dylan noticing. Sam got the message. He left the other girls and trudged over to Tinka.

"Hey." He was making it a point not to look at her, so she did the same to him. She knew when she wasn't wanted. She could take a hint. Her eyes stung, but she blinked the tears away. Tinka would not lose her cool over the end of their fauxmance. She was tougher than that. "I need your help with something," Sam said. "Do you mind?"

Without a word, Sam scooped up an empty cardboard box that had previously held a case of beer. Tinka followed him over to Brian, who was chatting with another guy who looked a lot like him. Tinka guessed they were brothers. "Garlands," Sam said.

"Sam," Brian's brother said. "I can't believe you're finally throwing a party with booze."

"Not my party. Give me your keys." Sam held out the box. The moonlight made shadows on his arms, highlighting the definition of his muscles, not that Tinka noticed or anything, because that would be silly.

"What?" Brian said. "No."

"Yes. No one is leaving this house with a car if they've been drinking. I'm the key master."

Brian and his doppelgänger brother tossed their keys into the box.

"The key master?" Tinka asked, momentarily forgetting that they were giving each other the silent treatment as she followed Sam to the next group.

He turned around, fighting the grin that was playing on his lips, which made Tinka's heart soar. She hadn't realized how much she'd missed that smile the past few days. "Haven't you seen *Say Anything*?"

She shook her head. Sam had spoken actual words to her.

"Shameful."

They were talking again, and all it took was getting him on the topic of movies. She wasn't going to let this moment go. "Maybe you could show it to me sometime."

He peered down at her, right into her eyes. Her heart sped up. "Really?"

"Yeah. You have much to teach me about movies."

He looked both happy and pained, and Tinka knew she was probably wearing a similar expression. Part of her wanted to run away, but the rest of her wanted to grab Sam's hand and drag him up to his house to watch that movie. Actually, that part of her was winning out. Either way, she rooted herself to the ground. They had to stay at the party—to make sure their friends were okay.

"But what's the key master?" Tinka ran to keep up with him, desperate to keep him talking.

"In the movie, John Cusack as Lloyd Dobbler—one of the greatest characters and character names ever—holds on to everybody's keys at this party. He kind of gets forced into it, but he takes the job very seriously. He won't give them back unless they're sober."

"Good guy."

"Very good guy."

Tinka smiled. "You're kind of a Lloyd Dobbler, aren't you Sam?"

"There are worse people to be." He paused, like he was deciding whether or not to keep the conversation going. "And you're kind of a Diane Court, but you don't know what that means yet."

"I hope it's a compliment," Tinka said.

Sam grinned down at her. "It is. Believe me." Heat rose from Tinka's feet to her ears. This was different from the charge between them at the video store. This was real, all-encompassing, "if you ever stop talking to me again I'll dissolve into a puddle of despair" emotion. It was dangerous. Tinka didn't do out-of-control drama. She always kept things even, measured, and safely at arm's length.

Breaking the spell, Tinka grabbed the box from him and shouted at the next group. "Key master here! Put your keys in the box."

After she and Sam had collected all the keys and he had locked them inside a cabinet in the cabana, he and Tinka flopped onto some chairs and opened two cans of pop. She leaned back against the hard, plastic chair. Her shoulders were no longer hunched and her neck wasn't tense, which they had been for days. She'd been so ambivalent about this party before, but maybe it was just what she needed.

Jane had put on some music and was dancing in front of the speaker with two of Dylan's friends. Karen was talking to some guy Tinka had never seen before, but she seemed to be enjoying herself. Little groups gathered here and there, drinking and laughing. They were in the good part, when everyone was loose and happy, before things started getting sloppy.

Sam introduced Tinka to everyone who came by, and she

tried hard to remember their names—Elena and Oliver and Marley and Kevin and Katie and a million other people. Sam referred to her as his girlfriend, and she couldn't help smiling every time.

"Harper told me Sam was dating someone," Elena said. "Treat him well."

"I will." Tinka instinctively pulled the ring pendant out from under her shirt and clutched it.

"You're wearing the ring." Sam wrinkled his forehead.

Tinka gripped it harder. She'd forgotten she was wearing it, probably because she hadn't taken it off in days. It calmed her. She caught herself playing with it whenever she got upset—like at her lessons with Dylan or when a text from Colin popped up on her phone. "It's my good luck charm," she told Sam.

Their eyes locked and Tinka's breath stopped. She'd nearly added, "You're my good luck charm," but she caught herself in time.

Sam's lips parted, drawing Tinka's focus to them. "Good thing you didn't pick a Tootsie Roll, then. Candy is temporary, but plastic jewelry is forever."

Tinka leaned closer to him, under the guise of trying to hear him better. He was a magnet, and she couldn't stop herself. "Sam, I—"

She didn't have an ending for that sentence, but it didn't matter. His eyes were on Jane as she crossed in front of them and bent down to grab a beer from the cooler in the middle of the ring of chairs. When she stood, the bottle slipped out of her hands and into the sand. "Whoops." She picked it up. "It was pointing at you, Brian, guess we have to kiss now."

"Yikes," whispered Tinka. "Here we go. Here comes the sloppiness." She put a hand to her chest, willing her heart to slow. Jane had saved the day. Tinka had never been so relieved to see a drunk person in her life.

Jane sashayed over to Brian and planted a chaste little kiss on his cheek. Then she passed him the bottle. "Your turn."

Brian stared at the label. "Are we really playing Spin-the-Bottle? Are we thirteen?"

Jane traipsed across the circle and took her seat next to Tinka. "Dark party tradition," Jane said.

Tinka shook her head. "That's not accurate." The dark party didn't need little games like these to manufacture debauchery. Tinka knew that too well.

Shrugging, Brian spun the bottle in the middle of the circle. It landed on Marley. "Marley, my dear," he said. "I believe we've done this before."

With a cheesy grin, Marley stood up and kissed Brian on the lips before snatching the bottle from him.

"This is such a colossal mess," Tinka whispered to Sam.

Sam shrugged. "It's just Spin-the-Bottle. In a town this small, most of these people have already kissed each other at some point anyway."

"Have you?" Tinka's face snapped toward him. She'd assumed Sam wasn't the kissing-random-girls type, but what did she know? Queasiness settled in Tinka's stomach.

He didn't answer as Marley spun the bottle and it landed squarely on Sam, who grinned big as this Marley person stepped over and stood in front of him, a flirtatious smile on her lips. "Sammy." She held out her hands and helped Sam up. Tinka bit her cheek hard.

Sam glanced down at Tinka, then turned back to Marley, who was still clutching his hands. "I'm not playing. Spin again."

"Whatever." Marley let go and turned away from him.

The feeling in Tinka's gut was jealousy. She hadn't realized it at first, but that's what it was. She was jealous this other girl wanted to kiss Sam. That emotion was unacceptable. Tinka had no right or reason to feel possessive about her fake boyfriend kissing another person. "Play if you want. I don't care."

"Your girlfriend doesn't care." Marley pivoted toward him again.

Sam gave Tinka one last look, but she refused to meet his eyes. "Okay then." Sam put his arm around Marley's back, dipped her and planted a kiss squarely on her mouth. It was a movie kiss, like from a classic film, all for show. Tinka's jaw tightened, waiting for him to break the connection, but he didn't. She started counting. The kiss lasted one…two…three seconds. Too long. The rest of the party got into it, cheering Sam on. Then he helped Marley stand upright and the two of them high-fived before she stumbled off toward one of the empty chairs.

Sam walked to the middle of the circle and examined the bottle. Tinka's body shivered despite the fact that it was ninety degrees out, and she realized she actually did feel sick to her stomach. Tinka put a hand to her forehead. It was clammy, but cool. Still, maybe she should go lie down. She might be coming down with something. That would explain why she'd been acting out of sorts all night.

Tinka stood as Sam set the bottle on the ground. She'd turned away from the circle before he could spin it.

"Ooh-ooh." Jane clapped. "I finally get to see you two kiss."

Tinka turned back to see where the bottle had landed. It was pointing right at her. There was no mistaking it.

"Go on," Jane sang. "Kiss your boyfriend."

Every eye on the beach was watching them, and the sickness in Tinka's stomach morphed into butterflies. All her concern over potential illness floated away. The bottle had spoken. She was supposed to kiss Sam.

He hadn't moved from his place next to the bottle. He was waiting for Tinka's cue. She touched the ring around her neck and marched toward him. It was just a kiss. One kiss.

She'd kissed plenty of people before. This was no big deal.

And she could for sure kiss better than that Marley girl. Of that, Tinka was certain.

When she reached him, Sam bent down and whispered, "Are you sure?"

Tinka stared him straight in the eye. "Kiss me, Sam."

She didn't have to tell him twice. He wrapped his arms around her waist, and she clasped her hands behind his neck. She drew in a deep breath. This was going to be nothing. The kiss was going to be clinical, on par with a doctor's exam or a handshake. It'd be like the time her Aunt Marie had leaned in for a kiss at Thanksgiving and accidentally hit Tinka's mouth.

But the butterflies multiplied as soon as Sam's lips touched hers. Tingles spread up and down her spine and through her limbs. She had to clutch Sam's neck tighter to stay upright, deepening the kiss, which lasted way, way more than three seconds—take that, Marley.

Soon, however, Tinka's brain kicked in. She'd let jealousy get the best of her. She was acting like a common, emotional fool. Her mind screamed *stop*, but Tinka fought it. This was the first and last time her lips would touch Sam's, and she needed an imprint of this moment. She memorized how the soft bristles of hair at the base of his neck felt against her fingertips and how his strong hands took up so much real estate on the small of her back.

Finally, eventually, Tinka backed away, her eyes lowered, her hands pushing on his shoulders. Party sounds filled her ears. People were chatting, laughing, opening cans and bottles. Time hadn't stopped for anyone but Tinka and Sam.

"So...that happened," he whispered.

"Very convincing." Avoiding Sam's gaze, Tinka dropped her arms and took a step back toward the edge of the circle. "Good show."

• • •

Tinka booked it up to Sam's house after their kiss. She'd mumbled something he didn't quite catch, then high-tailed it across the grass and up to the deck.

Marley sidled up to him. "Where'd she go?"

"Bathroom or something," Sam said. "I don't know."

"I was worried she was mad about our kiss," Marley asked.

Tinka slid the door shut behind her as she disappeared into the house. "She wasn't mad. She'd told me it was fine before it happened."

Marley shrugged. "She looked upset."

"You think?" Sam rubbed the back of his neck, where Tinka's hands had just been.

"Definitely."

Sam's brain hadn't gotten back up to speed yet. He was still living and reliving that kiss with Tinka. It was possible he'd never stop thinking about it. He kept picturing himself sitting in a movie theater, but the projector was showing the same thing on a loop—Tinka and Sam, arms around each other, lips touching. Sam could watch that movie for the rest of his life.

Jane tried to keep the Spin-the-Bottle game going, but people quickly lost interest. Some started heading home. Sam handed car keys back to those who were sober and opened up the cabana for the people who wanted to crash. He put on a movie—*Team America: World Police*—to pacify the crowd, and locked the remaining keys in the cabinet again.

As he left the cabana, he snuck a peek at the house. Tinka was still there, as far as he knew. She was inside Sam's house. She hadn't gone back to her parents' place, which meant she was waiting for him, which meant…Sam had no idea.

Karen was sitting in the abandoned Adirondack circle,

talking to Eric Joyce, who was a sophomore and a decent, if dull person.

"You good?" Sam asked Karen. His palms were sweating. Tinka was waiting for him for one of two reasons: either she wanted to break things off with him entirely or she wanted to upgrade their fake relationship to a real one. Both options were equally terrifying. Door number one led to a broken heart, but door number two led to his bedroom, possibly, maybe, holy crap.

"Yeah." She nodded to her new friend. "Eric was just telling me about his family's Christmas sweater tradition. They wear holiday stuff from the day after Thanksgiving until spring. He owns twenty different ones, all made by his grandmother, mother, and sisters." She widened her eyes.

"Twenty, wow." This wasn't news to him. The Joyces were known for their ugly holiday sweaters. Sam's eyes swung around the party. "Have you seen Jane?"

Karen pointed to the pier. Jane was sitting with Kevin Snow. Not Kevin Snow. Anybody but Kevin Snow. This was going to end in disaster. Since Tinka was M.I.A., he was going to have to take over her job and keep an eye on her friends.

As if reading his mind, Karen nodded toward the house. "I've got Jane. You go find Tinka."

Sam's stomach plummeted. Break up or bedroom. "You sure? I can stick around."

"I'm sure. I haven't had anything to drink, and"—she nodded toward Eric—"I need to know more about these sweaters, obviously."

"Okay. Thanks." Sam's eyes scanned the beach. He recycled some empty bottles, stacked chairs, and blew out the citronella candles.

The kiss still played in Sam's mind, but it was no longer a scene from a fairy tale. Each new version highlighted potential problems—he was too eager, he was too sweaty, she'd been playing a part, she was trying to deflect Dylan, she wasn't really into the kiss at all, Sam had imagined everything. That was the truth, wasn't it? He was the naive nerd, and she was this beautiful, experienced girl who was very good at pretending. So good, she'd managed to convince him.

And now she was going to end this.

As Sam approached the deck, he spotted Tinka in the kitchen, staring into the fridge.

Slowly, he opened the sliding glass door and stepped inside the house. He shut the door behind him, but stayed near the exit. He was about to lose her. He felt it in the air. She was going to run, just like Karen had promised.

Tinka kept her eyes on the fridge. "So, that kiss..."

Sam hovered near the door, waiting for her to tell him how this was going to go.

"I...um...I'm leaving for school in August." She shut the door and turned toward him, leaning against the fridge. She folded her arms across her chest.

"I know. Me, too." A lump formed in his throat. This was it. This was the end.

"I can't..." She pointed to herself and then to him. "I'm a mess. I told you that. You know that."

He was as much a mess as she was. And he knew he'd be even more of a mess if she ran out of here tonight and refused to see him because of one tiny, overzealous kiss.

Sam couldn't let that happen. He couldn't let her start ignoring him again. This week had been torture without her. The wedding stuff was starting to overwhelm him, and she was the only one he could talk to about it. He'd told himself that he didn't want to get attached to anyone right now, but too late. He had a few precious weeks left here in North Pole, and he wanted to spend all of them with Tinka, whatever that meant.

It was his turn to convince her of something. He wanted

her in his arms again, sure, but he was fighting for survival here. Keeping her in his life in any capacity was all that mattered now. He prepared himself for the performance of his lifetime. Sam cocked his head for a moment, staring at her in confusion. Then he shook his head and laughed. "Wait a minute. You don't...?" He ran his fingers through his hair. "Wow. I'm a better kisser than I thought." His theatre teacher better not have been lying when she'd said Sam was one of the best actors she'd ever had in class.

Tinka was staring at Sam like he'd told her the sky was plaid. It was working.

He laughed again, channeling his inner Daniel Day-Lewis. "Tinka. That was, um, a nice kiss and all, but it was basically like me kissing Harper."

Her eyes went wide. "Oh." Then they narrowed, and she scanned the room, putting her hand to her mouth. "Oh."

"I guess I really sold it, huh?" Sam stepped over to the fridge, and Tinka scurried out of the way as he opened the door and grabbed a bottle of water. He unscrewed the cap and took a swig. He had actually thrown her off her game. Not bad.

"Very convincing." Her hands clutched the lip of the counter behind her.

Sam pretended to brush a bit of dirt off his shoulders. "I've always wanted to write or direct movies, but maybe I should think about acting instead. Apparently, I'm quite good at it."

"Yeah, maybe." Tinka straightened her spine and looked him square in the eye. "Wait. Did you think I was going to tell you that *I* felt something during that kiss?" She giggled. "Oh my God."

Sam played with the label on his bottle. "I kind of did, yeah. Isn't that what you were going to say?"

Tinka stepped over, grabbed his water bottle, and took

her own sip like it was nothing, like he was nothing. Or not "nothing." But he was definitely just a friend to her, and nothing more. "See, I only brought it up because I thought maybe you had enjoyed it too much." She screwed the cap on and off a few times.

"No way. Not at all."

"Phew." Tinka, an agonizing six inches away from him, wiped her forehead. "Wow. Good thing we're on the same page." She stepped back, a big smile on her face, and Sam felt the void as the space between them grew.

He'd done what he'd set out to do. He'd calmed the situation and stopped her from leaving him because things had gotten weird. But this wasn't how his mind had storyboarded the scene. She was supposed to call his bluff. She was supposed to tell him, no, the kiss was real, *they* were real.

He gave her a moment to change her mind. When she didn't, he jumped right back into his role, for the sake of self-preservation. "We are the king and queen of fake kissing, bro."

"Yeah, we sure are, bud." She leaned in and lightly punched him on the shoulder. Sam caught her scent of orange and vanilla.

He snatched his water bottle back from her and hopped up on the counter, killing any remaining tension. He'd performed triage and stopped the bleeding, which had to be enough. Tonight had been an anomaly, a blip, and it was time for them to go back to the way things were.

"You mind if I make brownies?" she asked.

"You have to ask?"

Grinning, she turned her back on Sam, squatted down, and started rummaging through a bottom cabinet. He tried hard not to stare at her backside in her tight jeans. If he managed to keep up this charade for the rest of the summer, he really would deserve an Oscar.

Chapter Nine

Jane held up an emerald green, ombré-patterned dress. "I'm telling you, Tinka, that was the hottest kiss I've ever seen. You two." She touched Tinka's shoulder and yanked her hand back quickly. "Scorching." She blew on her burned finger.

"Mmm-hmm." Tinka was rummaging through another rack at Mrs. Claus's Closet, the premier dress emporium in North Pole, Minnesota. Not all of the dresses were Christmas themed, thank goodness, but none of them registered in Tinka's brain either. They were all amorphous blocks of color after color with no shape or style.

Jane put the green dress back. "To have a guy look at me the way Sam looks at you, that's my life goal."

Tinka blushed and focused hard on the dresses in front of her. The kiss had been hot. Sam was hot. It was way more than that, though. When she was with Sam, it was like the first time Tinka'd ever baked a batch of cookies. There was a moment of calm and a feeling of "This. *This* is why I've been put on the planet." At least that's how it had been for Tinka. Sam had been putting on a show, and he'd fooled Tinka—worldly, experienced Tinka.

Karen stepped out of the dressing room, wearing a flowing blue maxi dress with an empire waist. She spun around, her shoulders hunched up to her ears.

"You look amazing." Jane pushed down Karen's shoulders. "Own it."

"Whatever." But Karen tried to shimmy herself into a more relaxed position.

"Tell me about your night," Tinka said. Anything to move the subject away from Sam Anderson and the way he turned her into a blubbering mess. "You've both been suspiciously quiet."

The two girls shared a glance.

"What happened?" This wasn't good.

"Nothing." Karen shrugged and stepped over to the shoe and accessories wall.

Tinka shifted focus to Jane.

"Like Karen said." Jane, too, shrugged and shook her head.

"I'm going to need more information."

"It was fun," Karen said. "We ended up watching movies with people in the cabana."

"Okay." Tinka narrowed her eyes. They weren't telling her the whole story. "I guess what I want to know is whether or not you had the fun you'd been expecting to have."

"Yeah, sure," Karen said.

"So, you two had your flings."

"Yup."

Jane pulled out the green dress again and examined it.

"Who'd you hook up with, Jane?" Tinka asked. "Brian from the cafe?"

Jane shook her head.

"Someone else?"

Jane shoved the dress back on the rack and turned toward

Tinka. Tears flooded her eyes.

Tinka shouldn't have left them down by the cabana. She shouldn't have ditched them to hide out in Sam's house. She'd abandoned her friends and they'd gotten hurt. "Obviously something happened. Tell me." She put her hand on Jane's shoulder and glanced over at Karen, who was about to chew her lower lip off.

Jane snuck a look at Karen, then she turned to Tinka. "Literally nothing happened."

Tinka opened her mouth to protest.

"Jane isn't kidding," Karen said. "Nothing happened."

"I'd been chatting with this guy down by the pier," Jane said.

"And I was talking to this dude who liked Christmas sweaters way too much." Karen shook her head.

"The guy I was with—Kevin—he went to make a move, and I started bawling. Literally, yes. A guy tried to kiss me, and I turned into a sobbing mess."

"Why?" Tinka frowned.

"Because I miss Colin," Jane said.

"I had my eye on Jane the whole time," Karen said. "She left Kevin on the pier and started walking by herself along the beach. She had her phone out."

"I was drunk-texting Colin."

"Oh, Jane." Tinka's shoulders were up by her ears again. Jane needed to stop texting Colin, for her own sake as well as Tinka's. Everyone needed to forget about him. It's what Tinka had been trying to do for weeks. Colin was not worth the brain cells or the data charges.

"I know. Pathetic."

"It happens." Tinka waved her off. "So you didn't experience the glory and shame of a regrettable random romance, but you did partake in one of drinking's other wonderful side effects—embarrassing phone-facilitated communication with an ex. Congratulations!"

Jane grumbled, shaking her head. "Colin never even responded."

Karen put her arm around Jane. "Jane and I sat on the beach for a while, talking through stuff."

"That's good." But Tinka should've been there. She'd turned tail right after the Spin-the-Bottle incident and had hid out in Sam's house for the rest of the night. They'd laughed and joked and watched movies while eating her brownies. Then they'd gone upstairs together and said good night—no hugs, not even a handshake—before she disappeared into his sister's bedroom to crash (the prospect of sleeping alone and on a real bed for one night was too good to pass up). Tinka hadn't meant to abandon her friends in their time of need, but that's what she'd done. "I wish you'd have come to me. I would've listened."

"Tinka, please." Karen crossed her arms.

"We didn't want to disturb you," Jane said. "You were with Sam."

"So? I would've ditched him for you. You're my friends." And so was Sam. Nothing more.

"You wouldn't have left him for us," Karen said. "You don't bother with other people when you have your own stuff going on. It's kind of your thing. Tinka's a decent friend, when it's convenient for her."

Tinka touched her cheek like she'd been slapped. "That's not fair."

"Yes, it is." Karen plucked a pair of earrings from the rack and held them up to her lobe. "You kept me around while you were living in Minnesota, because, I don't know, you didn't have another friend or something. As soon as you got to South Carolina, you cut me out, basically. You stopped replying to my texts."

"Not on purpose," Tinka said. "I had nothing to say. We

were living different lives. I was different."

"You were drinking and hooking up with guys."

"And you would've judged me for it." Tinka would not take all the blame here.

"That is not fair," Karen said.

"You always liked that we were on the same level. Other girls were doing things we weren't, and you…had very strong opinions about that." Tinka truly didn't believe this was something Karen did consciously, but it was what she did. Tinka knew it had more to do with Karen's own insecurities than the other girls' actions, but still. "I didn't want to be on the receiving end of your sanctimony."

Karen's smug expression faltered for a moment before she put the heat back on Tinka. "My parents' marriage was ending and you had no idea. You never once asked me how I was doing." She wrapped a long string of pearls around her neck

"And I'm sorry. I've told you that. I mean it."

"Talk is cheap, Tinka," Karen said. "You're selfish. You only worry about yourself and what makes you feel happy and comfortable. You never go out of your way for someone else."

"I don't think Tinka's selfish." Jane pulled on a pair of tan pumps.

"When has she ever done anything for you?" Karen asked.

Standing up straight, Jane grinned. Tinka's heart swelled. Jane. Jane saw the good in her. Of course, she saw the good in everyone. "She made me cookies all year long."

"That was for her." Karen pointed at Tinka. "She bakes because *she* likes to bake, not because it makes other people happy. She even hurt her hand for a selfish reason—working on the kitchen, even though her parents had told her to wait."

"You know how much pressure my parents put on me,"

Tinka said.

"I do," Karen said. "And I also know that you treat other people the way your mom and dad treat you. You expect everyone to forgive you no matter what, no matter how shitty you behave, because why? Because your parents are overbearing? Because your brother died and you don't even remember him?"

Jane was now giving Tinka the frowny-face head tilt. She'd managed to keep her brother a secret in South Carolina and escape the thing that had weighed her down back in Minneapolis.

"You think no one else's problems compare to yours," Karen said.

"I don't think that." Though, maybe she did. Tinka'd never really thought about it before. Maybe she did act like she deserved a pass because of Jake and her overbearing parents.

Karen turned toward Jane. "Tell me. What did she do to make you feel better after your boyfriend dumped you?"

Jane glanced at Tinka. "She baked me cookies." Jane's face fell as she now understood the meaning behind the cookies.

"Anything else?" Karen asked. "Did she stay up late with you, commiserating? Did she put her life on hold to take care of you?"

Jane clamped her mouth shut.

Karen had sunk the putt. She and Tinka knew each other too well. It was like they were in a bad marriage, only able to see the other's faults—Karen was insecure and judgmental, and Tinka was selfish and closed off. They used to have such fun together. They'd been each other's cheerleaders. Karen would trade her pudding for Tinka's carrots at lunch every single day. Tinka used to read through every one of Karen's newspaper articles before she'd hand it in to her editor. They used to be a team.

Tinka's eyes watered. "I honestly didn't realize. No one's

ever said what you just said to me, Karen. That doesn't excuse my behavior, but I hope it explains it."

Jane stepped over and enveloped Tinka in a big hug. "Let's all lighten up!" She pulled Karen over and draped her arms around both girls' shoulders. Tinka relaxed against Jane's side. "We're on vacation. You both hurt each other, but that stops now. We're spending the rest of the day together, having fun and acting like friends. Let's start by getting food, because I'm starved."

On the way out, Tinka's phone buzzed. Jane and Karen held the door open as Tinka checked the text. It was from Colin, at this moment, of all people. "Tinka, get Jane to stop texting me, or I'm going to tell her everything."

Tinka's whole body stiffened. Yeah, Jane was on her side now, but that could all change in the time it took Colin to press "send."

· · ·

Harper leaned on the counter next to Sam. "Why's Dottie so pissy at you?" She nodded toward the back room, where Dottie was currently grabbing a form for the pies Sam and Harper were ordering for the rehearsal dinner.

"You," Sam hissed. "You're why she's pissy. Because you made her think I was interested, when I was not."

"Sure, you weren't interested." Harper had come back into town for her last dress fitting, which had been a surprise to Sam. He'd been in the process of removing the alcohol evidence from their house when she'd shown up. Harper, however, didn't chastise him or threaten to tell their dad. She'd jumped in and started scanning the house and yard for any hidden bottles or cans. Sometimes Sam's sister had the capacity to be awesome. It was easy to forget that when she spent so much time poking fun at him. "I guess it's moot, anyway." Harper glanced toward the front door. "When am I going to meet this girlfriend, Sammy? Elena tells me she's gorgeous."

"She's…yeah, she is." Sam blushed. He'd barely slept last night knowing that Tinka was on the other side of his wall. He'd longed to go next door and tell her that he'd been lying, the kiss had meant everything to him, but he kept picturing her running away in terror, so he'd stayed put.

Dottie emerged from the back room and slammed the order form down on the counter. "What do you need?" Dottie glared at both Andersons.

Sam cleared his throat. "We need to order some pies for Matthew and Hakeem's rehearsal dinner. They want one citrus pie, a chocolate one, and some kind of berry…"

"Strawberry?" Dottie scowled at Sam.

"Strawberry is fine," Harper said. "Strawberry would be fabulous."

Dottie scribble notes on the paper, muttering under her breath, "Strawberry would be *fabulous*."

"You got all that?" he asked.

She nodded.

"And the date? The Fourth of July?" Sam tried to catch a glimpse of the order form, but Dottie blocked it with her arm like she was shielding a test from cheating eyes.

"I've got it, Sam." She shoved the form under the counter and the pen into one of her blue buns.

Something about this conversation didn't sit right. Maybe he should ask to see the order form. But no. Sam couldn't let on that he didn't trust her. She thrived on conflict. He'd have to keep his fear hidden. "You sure?" he asked.

Dottie huffed. "I am capable of taking an order."

"Thanks, Dottie." Harper waved as Sam dragged her, stumbling, out of the bakery. "What the hell, Sam?" she asked, brushing herself off.

"She's more than pissy, right?" He eyed the bakery window, hunting for a clue, some evidence that Dottie was going to ruin everything. "She's going to mess up the cake. I can feel it."

Harper glanced back at the bakery. "What? No. I was exaggerating her pissy attitude. She seemed fine."

"Did she?" Sam asked. "Did she really?"

"Well, she was a little flat and unfriendly, so totally normal for Dottie."

"You didn't get the sense that she wanted to murder us?" Again he peered into the store. Dottie had vacated the counter.

"Not any more than usual."

Maybe he was being paranoid. That was probably the case. He had been so worried about staying on Dottie's good side, making sure that the wedding went off without a hitch, he was seeing things that weren't there. "Maybe I'm stressed about the wedding stuff, getting it all done."

"It's gonna be great." Harper patted his arm.

"It'd be greater if you or Matthew or, hell, Dad were here to help me."

"Eh." Harper grinned. "We'd only get in your way."

Sam opened his mouth to tell her, no, her help would actually be quite appreciated, but he was cut off by his own name.

"Sam!"

He and Harper spun around to see who was calling him from all the way down Main Street. Jane was running toward him, shopping bags slapping against her legs, while Tinka and Karen followed behind. From about a half block away, Sam's eyes met Tinka's. She gave him a subtle, shy wave, and he returned it, his cheeks warming.

"That's Tinka," Sam whispered. "The blonde."

"Ooh, she *is* hot, Sam. Nicely done." His sister squinted

her eyes at him, like she was seeing him in a new light. "I'm impressed, brother. Look at you." She nudged him in the side.

Jane skidded to a stop in front of them and pulled both Andersons into one of her customary hugs.

As Jane released her from her clutches, Harper eyed Tinka. "So, you and my brother."

Blushing, Sam glanced at Tinka, who was the same amount of flushed. Sam suppressed the grin that threatened his cool demeanor. He was still playing a part. He was still trying to convince her—and himself—that the kiss last night had meant nothing.

"Yeah. He's a really great guy." She shot him a sheepish look, and he nodded nonchalantly, barely acknowledging her existence, though his insides were bursting with glee. Fake or whatever, this relationship was the best thing that had ever happened to him, and he almost didn't care how foolish that sounded.

"What are you girls up to?" Harper asked.

Jane held up a shopping bag from Mrs. Claus's Closet. "Dress hunting. For your brother's wedding. Sam invited us."

"Fabulous," Harper said. "I'm headed there in a bit for my fitting, but we were about to get lunch." She elbowed Sam in the ribs. "You girls want to come?"

"Sure," Jane said. "We'd love—"

Sam jumped in. "They're probably too busy." Dining with Tinka would be too much to handle right now. He needed a minute away from this playacting.

"We really are." Tinka was quick on the trigger. "We're having a girls' day out. You two go ahead." Sure, Sam had been the first to put the kibosh on lunch, but he still wished Tinka had looked more bummed about the situation.

Harper waved to the girls. "You ladies have fun. I'll be in town soon for the wedding. We should all hang out."

"Okay." Tinka and her friends took off down the street.

"We should invite them over to play games or something," said Harper.

"Maybe," Sam said.

Harper peered at him, squinting. "Everything okay?"

Was everything okay? That was a loaded question. He'd broken down crying yesterday because he'd gone to check on the flower order for the wedding, and Matthew had picked hydrangeas, because of course he had. They were Mom's favorite. But the smell took Sam back to when he was a kid and his mom used to help him hold the shears while they cut the stems on the hydrangea bushes together, which then made him think about how he was able to hold the shears just fine on his own now, which naturally spiraled into a whole thing about the passage of time and Matthew getting married and how the two of them used to get into these heated one-on-one basketball games when Sam was a kid, but they hadn't done that in years, and maybe they'd never do it again. Oh, and he was falling for his fake girlfriend, on top of all that. But Sam plastered on a grin and shook his head. "Everything's fine. Couldn't be better."

Chapter Ten

A few days after the party, Tinka was back on the putting green for a golf lesson with Dylan.

"May I?" Dylan asked.

Tinka rolled her eyes. "Fine."

Dylan stepped behind her, pressed his chest against her back, wrapped his arms around her torso, and placed his hands on top of hers.

"I really don't think you need to be that close." She squirmed away.

He backed off slightly, placed the putter in her hand, and wrapped her fingers around the handle in the correct position. "This grip will change your life."

"Oh, I'm sure."

She glanced back at the pro shop. Her dad was inside working on his laptop, missing Dylan's whole display, not that he'd be bothered by it. He was rooting for Tinka and Dylan to pair up, after all.

"I've seen you help my dad." Tinka lined up her putt all by herself. "Somehow you manage to keep a six-inch-plus buffer zone between your groin and his ass."

Dylan laughed. "That obvious?"

"Very, very obvious." Tinka gave him the stink eye. "So, stop. Thanks."

He held up his hands and backed even farther away, giving Tinka plenty of space.

With a deep breath, Tinka swung the putter like a pendulum and sank the putt from twenty feet away.

"Nice." Dylan nodded like he was surveying his own work of art.

"I was using my old grip there, by the way." Tinka tucked the putter under her arm and adjusted the glove on her left hand.

He grinned. "I know. I only taught you the new grip so you'd have more confidence in your old one." He glanced back at the pro shop. "Your dad doesn't realize how much you hate this, does he?" He waved his hand to indicate the golf course.

She glowered at him.

"Don't worry," he said. "I know the whole story. I was talking to your friend Jane at your little party the other night. 'Tinka hates golf. She wants to quit, but doesn't know how to tell her dad. She wants to be a baker.'" Dylan raised an eyebrow. "A baker?"

"And?" she asked.

"I thought you might want someone to talk to, because I understand what you're going through."

"Oh, you understand me, do you, Duke boy?" Talking to him was exhausting. He was like a persistent gnat she couldn't swat away.

"More than you know." He grinned. "You think you had me pegged since the second we met, but you and I are in the same boat. I want to keep doing the golf thing full-time, maybe move down south after graduation. But my mom and dad expect me to go to law school and take over the family firm here when they retire. I don't want that, and I'm having trouble telling them the truth, like you with your dad. You and I, we're not that different."

Tinka bit the inside of her cheek. Maybe he had a point, but she wouldn't let him know that. "I really don't think that's true. We are not even remotely in the same situation."

"I beg to differ," Dylan said. "Our parents expect certain things from us. There's an obligation. My parents' firm is their legacy. And you're expected to fill your brother's shoes."

Screw this guy. He barely knew her, and he was bringing her dead brother into the conversation. If he thought that was the way to get her on his side, he was very, very wrong. "You know absolutely nothing about anything."

He rubbed the head of his putter with a towel. "I know you see me as a sleazy jerk, but I'm seriously offering myself up as a friend. That's it. I'm someone who gets what you're going through. You and I have never had it easy. Not like your boyfriend."

Okay, really. Who the hell did this guy think he was? Tinka touched her cheeks, which had warmed at the mention of Sam. Their kiss had been running through her mind for days. Back at Florian's, she never thought about a hook-up after the fact (okay, except Colin, but that was a completely different situation). Come morning, that stuff was all in the past. But the thing that happened between her and Sam Friday night? She couldn't shake it. "What does Sam have to do with this? Sam doesn't have it easy." Yes, she made sure to say his name twice. She liked the way it felt in her mouth. *Sam*.

"Sure he does," Dylan said. "He's got the big house and the gobs of money. He can do whatever he wants with his life. He's going to film school in L.A. I mean, come on, Mr. Silver Spoon. Must be nice."

"You don't know him at all. He's not like that."

"But he doesn't get you, does he?" Dylan said. "He probably sees you as this perfect girl—the pretty baker who's tons of fun. He's all happiness and joy. You need someone more experienced, more realistic. I'm saying, if you ever get tired of him, come find me."

"I won't get tired of him," Tinka said. "And Sam's not the bubbly doormat you seem to think he is. He knows I'm not perfect, and he doesn't judge me for it. He's loyal. He's wonderful. He's one of the nicest, most caring—" She stopped, when she heard an "a-hem" from behind her.

She spun around, and there was Sam, drinking a lemonade.

Tinka's jaw dropped and she blushed to the roots of her hair, but Sam grinned. "Do go on." His brow was cocked as if he was challenging her, but his face had gone pink, too.

She couldn't help laughing, mostly from nerves. The situation was so absurd. It shouldn't have mattered that Sam had heard her saying those things. So what? Her fake boyfriend had caught her in the act of defending him. Though, no matter what she'd told him in the kitchen after the kiss, there was nothing fake about her feelings for him. She couldn't deny it, not with the way her skin tingled when she saw him standing there in a *Kill Bill* T-shirt and his omnipresent basketball shorts. She'd barely seen him since Friday night—he'd been busy with wedding stuff, and she'd been trying to keep herself busy tearing up the shag carpeting in her parents' basement—and it had been like a piece of her was missing. But for some reason she couldn't tell him all that. Why not? What was she more scared of—rejection or acceptance?

She ripped off her glove and shoved it into her golf bag, which she swung over her shoulder. "I think I've had enough for one day." She stepped over to Sam, hooked her arm in his, and dragged him toward the clubhouse.

"What are you even doing here?" she asked once they were far enough away from Dylan.

"Rehearsal dinner stuff. We're having it here at the club."

"Well, thank you for rescuing me," she whispered, resting her head on his shoulder, as if it fully belonged there. Waves of heat pulsed through her body. He smelled like summer and sunscreen and she wanted to eat him, which was definitely not part of their deal.

Tinka lifted her head and dropped his arm. She'd taken things too far. "Your timing is impeccable, fake boyfriend." She jabbed him in the arm. "Dylan was all over me back there."

"Just doing my job." Sam sped up, leaving Tinka in his wake. He shouted over his shoulder. "Dylan can't see us anymore. We're safe, dude."

Tinka stayed a few steps behind him as tears stung her eyes.

Yeah, she'd started it. She was the one who'd called him her "fake boyfriend," but she almost started bawling right there in the parking lot, telling him everything—that she'd meant what she'd said to Dylan, that she'd never get tired of him. Sam had called her "dude," and it had broken her heart.

But she kept her mouth shut. It was for the best. He was doing his job, sticking to the party line, the one they'd agreed to Friday night. This was what they both wanted. No strings, no mess. She'd keep up her end of the bargain. "Thanks, pal." She tossed her clubs into the back of his truck.

• • •

"Finally!" Craig slammed a five-dollar bill down on the counter at Maurice's video store. "After weeks and weeks of you showing terrible movie after terrible movie—"

"Your opinion," Sam muttered, grabbing Craig's complimentary can of Mellow Yellow from the fridge under the counter.

"—you're finally showing something decent." Craig gestured toward the poster on the wall outside the screening room.

"You're a big fan of *Girls Just Want to Have Fun*?"

"I am, Samuel," Craig said. "This film marries absurdity with real emotion. Helen Hunt is a revelation. She wears gigantic dinosaur barrettes. A dude somersaults through a window into a party. This film has something for everyone."

"Well, good," Sam said. "We aim to please."

"No, you don't."

"That's true. We don't." Sam handed Craig his popcorn.

As Craig headed into the screening room, Sam kept an eye on the door. Tinka had promised last night, when she and the girls had come over to make cookies, that she'd be here tonight. She was the reason Maurice was showing *Girls Just Want to Have Fun*, actually, because Sam had suggested the film. It had been Tinka and Karen's favorite movie growing up. They used to watch it at least once a month.

Maybe he'd done too good a job convincing Tinka that their kiss last Friday night had meant nothing. He'd fretted for days about pushing her away, that he'd been too persuasive about his feelings for her being only platonic.

But when he'd shown up outside the pro shop on Tuesday and heard her saying those really nice things about him, he'd hoped maybe they were about to admit their feelings to each other. Then she'd made it a point to drop his arm and call him her "fake boyfriend," which told him for sure where he stood. He was a tool to keep Dylan at bay, nothing more. It was the part he'd agreed to play, and he'd continue doing it, no matter how much it hurt.

Maybe he was a fool, but the agony was worth it, if it meant keeping Tinka in his life.

The door to Maurice's opened and a herd of girls pushed in—Dottie and her friends. She was once again in her movie ticket dress and the expression on her face suggested vengeance. "Where's your girlfriend?" she asked as Sam gathered the group's popcorn and beverages.

"She'll be here," Sam said.

"Whatever." Dottie pressed her lips closed as her friends marched to the back of the store. Then she said, "You're like all the rest of them—picking style over substance."

He hadn't picked style over substance, though. Tinka had both of those things. Dottie, on the other hand, well, if she thought Sam had rejected her based on her looks, that wasn't the truth at all. He'd rejected her based on her personality. Totally justified.

"Your girlfriend likes style, too, you know. I saw her flirting with Dylan Greene at the golf course the other day. I was delivering cookies for an event, and there he was, fondling her." Dottie mimed squeezing a set of boobs. "And she liked it."

Sam's stomach plummeted, but he shook his head. "He wasn't fondling her. He's her golf coach."

"Potato, po-tah-to." Dottie snatched up her popcorn and headed into the screening room.

Minutes before movie time, Tinka rushed in with Jane and Karen. Tinka beamed at him, but he couldn't return the gesture. Fabricated Dottie story or not, he couldn't stop picturing Dylan Greene with his hands all over Tinka. What game were they playing? He wasn't sure anymore.

Obviously, Tinka had been trying to thwart Dylan's advances earlier in the week, but maybe she'd changed her mind about him. Maybe she'd decided she was okay with Dylan—Prince Eric in the flesh—running his hands all over her. Sam couldn't be mad about it. He and Tinka weren't actually together. She could do whatever she wanted with whomever she pleased. But, in that case, she should let Sam off the hook and allow him to get on with his life.

Tinka rested her elbow on the counter. "Sorry we're late. My parents took us out for dinner and it ran long." She glared at the front door, through which Dylan was now entering. "And my dad's BFF followed us here."

"I told you guys to wait for me." Panting, Dylan sidled up to Tinka, who shifted away, but not too far. Dylan feigned surprise at seeing Sam. "Hey, man."

"Hey." Sam busied himself with the popcorn machine. His brain kept insisting all of this was totally normal, but his heart burned with jealousy, anger, sadness, and several other emotions that science had yet to identify.

Dylan grabbed his stuff and headed into the back room with Karen and Jane, but Tinka hung back, waiting for Sam, who was still avoiding her eyes.

"You know, you can sit with him if you want," Sam said. Thank God he hadn't told her his real feelings at the party. He'd be at least ten times more embarrassed now if he had.

"I don't want," Tinka said. "Ignore Dylan. He was just being an ass."

"I mean, you're under no obligation to sit with me." He glanced around the empty room. "It's not like we're really together," he whispered.

She furrowed her brow. "Are you trying to get out of sitting with me?"

"No. We're supposed to sit together, right? To keep up the ruse." Also, there was nothing he wanted more in life than to share one of Maurice's make-out couches with Tinka. It may have been a recurring dream since he'd met her, no big deal. "But I want to let you off the hook, if you feel like doing something else."

She reached across the counter like she was about to grab his arm, but instead she grabbed the salt shaker and traced its pattern of raised squares with her finger. "I have no desire whatsoever to sit with Dylan, or anyone else for that matter. I want to sit with you." Her wide eyes locked on his.

He tapped his molars against each other in a quick rhythm. He had to keep his cool and remember his motivation. Tinka would run away fast if she knew how he really felt. Sam shrugged. "Fine. We can sit together, if you want."

The movie was starting when they entered the back room. There was an empty couch on the right side, near Jane and Karen, who were sitting with Eric Joyce and his brother, Ken. Sam plopped down on the empty love seat, right next to one armrest, and Tinka hugged the other one. Their containers of popcorn sat between them as a barrier. But a few minutes into the movie, when Sam reached for some kernels, his hand brushed Tinka's and his breath caught in his chest. She tickled his fingers.

He should've pulled away, but he didn't. He let her fingers dance across his. He was prepared to let them dance for as long as they wanted.

She leaned over and whispered, "I feel like we're being watched."

Sam glanced around the room. At least two sets of eyes were squarely fixed on them—Dottie's and Dylan's.

"You're right." Ah, so that's what this was. She was putting on a show. Well, so could he.

Tinka lifted up the popcorn between them and moved the containers to the floor. "May I?"

Sam nodded and she scooted toward him, leaning hard against his side. His heart sped up as he wrapped his arm around her and she rested her head against his chest. Suddenly the room emptied. He no longer saw Dylan or Dottie or Jane or Karen. No one else existed except Sam and Tinka, the weight of her head on his chest, her hair teasing his cheek, her scent of vanilla and orange shampoo. He pulled her in tighter and she nuzzled into him.

"We could kiss again." She was looking up at him with big

eyes that were gray in the darkness. "I mean, because it's what people expect. That's what happens here on Saturday nights."

"Too true." The cool, indifferent Sam who'd told Tinka their first kiss had meant nothing to him could totally handle another one. The real Sam, the one who was having trouble forming words with his mouth because his entire consciousness was full of Tinka, would not walk away from this unscathed.

She rested her hand on his chest, and any possibility of Sam staying rational tonight fled the room. "I'm only saying this," she said, "because, obviously, when the two of us kiss, it's no sexier than a handshake."

This conversation was sexier than a handshake. Sam took a deep breath and squeezed her arm. He would be cool, indifferent Sam, because cool, indifferent Sam got to kiss Tinka. "Obviously. I believe I compared kissing you to kissing my sister. It'd be transactional, like using an ATM." An ATM that dispensed rainbows and hearts and heat and completely took his breath away.

"So?" Her lips parted, inviting him to her. He could stop this. Maybe he should stop it. Or maybe he should stop thinking and see where it went, even if his head knew this had the potential to end in disaster.

Well, screw you, brain. Disaster or not, the rest of Sam really wanted this.

He leaned down and touched his lips to Tinka's. She straightened up, improving the angle of their kiss, and wrapped her arms around his neck. Sam was fully prepared for her to pull away after a few seconds, after they'd proven their point, and he was ready to let her, but she didn't. She deepened the kiss, her tongue searching his mouth, and his searching hers. Sam's heart slowed down, but his breath sped up.

He shuddered with pleasure as she left a trail of kisses from his mouth to his ear, where she whispered, "We are really good at this fake kissing thing."

"So, so stinking good at it." And then his mouth was on hers again and his hands were in her hair and the two of them stayed like that for the rest of the movie—tasting each other and nibbling earlobes and touching necks and arms and hands—until the credits rolled and the lights came up.

Tinka pulled away, panting. Her eyes met his. "Wow," she said. "Well."

"I hope that convinced them," Sam said.

She hesitated a second, then leaned in and whispered, "I think it may have convinced me."

Chapter Eleven

"I am not the Pinterest-y girl you're looking for," Tinka said, as she and Sam climbed the front steps to her house.

They'd been out all day doing wedding stuff, boyfriend/girlfriend-type stuff. The line between real and fake was so blurry at this point, Tinka was considering LASIK. She'd actually helped Sam buy candles and mason jars for centerpieces and a decorative birdcage to hold gift envelopes. She'd offered her expert opinion on ribbon colors. She didn't do those kinds of things with just anybody. But she was happy doing them with Sam. She'd do anything with him.

"But you're a baker," he said.

"Yeah. And that's where my craftiness ends." On the front porch, Sam stood next to her, towering over her. All day there'd been this electricity between them, though neither of them had done anything about it. That was one way the two of them were currently not acting like a couple—there was no touching. They didn't hold hands, hug, kiss. They didn't do any of the things they'd done back when "fake" dating was a joke, back before they spent ninety minutes making out in the back of Maurice's video store.

It was a conscious effort on Tinka's part. She'd let things go too far during *Girls Just Want to Have Fun*. They needed to dial it back—revert to the safety of friendship.

She nodded toward the house. "Jane is who you want to talk to about tying ribbons and whatnot."

"Jane, huh?" His eyes flashed and a smile played on his soft lips, and she caught herself before brushing an errant curl off his forehead. He had her off-balance. He had her thinking about dragging him downstairs to her 1970s bachelor pad, and never letting him go. But that's not what he wanted, and it wasn't part of their deal.

Tinka shook the sense back into her head. "Definitely Jane. She's the queen of craftiness."

All business, she pulled open the door. But in the living room, they found Tinka's mom plopped on the floor, resting her head on the coffee table. Her dad was perched on the drop cloth-covered couch, rubbing her mom's back. Both of them had obviously been crying. They were surrounded by boxes and other assorted items— kid's stuff, Jake's stuff. His favorite toy dinosaur, the real, 3-D Dorothy, was standing in the middle of the coffee table.

Tinka expected to see shock on Sam's face, or maybe embarrassment over witnessing this private moment between her parents, but there was none of that. His eyes were sad and watery. He got it. He understood.

Her mom and dad had been so happy since moving to North Pole, and Tinka's heart broke for them now. One toy dinosaur still had the power to crush them. "You found Jake's stuff."

Wiping her eyes, Tinka's mom lifted her head and plastered on a smile. "We were trying to find the Christmas decorations. When in Rome."

Tinka's dad kept staring at the opposite wall, not turning

around. He was shielding his teary face from her and Sam. Tinka went to her mom and wrapped an arm around her shoulders.

Her mom nuzzled a cheek against Tinka's arm. "We opened the wrong boxes."

Tinka rubbed her mother's back. She'd once found her mom, who had coincidentally been looking for Christmas decorations back then, too, cradling that same dinosaur in their garage in Minneapolis. She'd wiped her eyes, and said it was nothing. Then she and Tinka's dad had disappeared for three days, leaving Tinka with her Aunt Marie, who'd spent the weekend telling Tinka that it was her duty to keep her parents happy.

Tinka wouldn't let them skip out on her this time. Maybe they'd talk to her, finally.

"You guys had been doing so well." And they had been. They'd been like completely different people.

"We still are." Her mom straightened up. "We're having a moment of grief, that's all. Carol says—" She clapped a hand over her mouth.

"Who's Carol?" Tinka asked.

Her dad hesitated. "New friend. Lives in town."

"Whatever." She was trying to help, but they still refused to tell her anything. They'd built a wall between themselves and Tinka, and they were determined to make sure it stayed standing. Tinka got up and started tossing the toys back into the boxes. She'd hide them somewhere her parents wouldn't find them, because that's how they'd always done things. *Suppress emotions, deny the past, act like everything's fine.* The Fosters should have that stitched on a pillow.

But Sam picked up Dorothy before Tinka could shove the dinosaur back in its box. "I had one of these. Or one similar. Jake liked dinosaurs?"

Tinka's dad coughed and turned his face away from Sam.

"He did. Very much."

Sam sat in the covered armchair across the room from Tinka's dad and folded his hands in his lap. "I find stuff of my mom's around the house all the time. It always shocks me. I'll find one of her lipsticks under the bathroom sink or a grocery list in the kitchen drawer. Every once in a while I'll smell her in the house, and then I realize it's my sister, who wears the same perfume."

"It reopens the wounds," Tinka's dad said.

"Yeah," Sam agreed. "But it also makes me feel like she's still there, somewhere, keeping an eye on me and my brother and sisters, like every little reminder is her way of saying, 'I'm here.'"

"That's lovely, Sam." Tinka's mom frowned. "That was the hardest part about leaving Minneapolis, leaving those memories."

Tinka snickered and almost said, "You think?" but stopped herself. This wasn't the moment to be snide. If they were ever going to open up to her, maybe she'd have to be the one to start. She plucked Dorothy from Sam's hands and ran her palm along its rubbery skin. "Jake drew a picture of this dinosaur on the wall in our old living room."

Her parents turned to face her, stunned. It wasn't like her to discuss Jake. She usually avoided the topic at all costs.

She pointed to where Sam was sitting. "You two put that chair in front of the drawing, but I knew it was there. When I was mad at you, I'd lie underneath it and talk to Jake through Dorothy."

"Oh my goodness!" Her mom wasn't upset; she was beaming.

Tinka smiled. "I'd tell her how mean you were being."

"Him." Her mom laughed for real now, which made her dad chuckle. "Dorothy's a boy."

Tinka grinned harder. She'd made her parents laugh. She

couldn't remember the last time that had happened. They only laughed for Mark and Trish, as far as she knew.

"I had no idea," her mom said. "When did you stop doing that?"

"I never did. When I found out you guys had sold the house, losing the drawing was maybe the hardest thing to take." She went over to the fireplace, knelt down, and pointed to where she'd drawn her own Dorothy. "I made a new one."

"Honey." Her mom reached for her from across the room.

Tinka shook her head. "I'm fine. Really."

Her mom wiped her nose with the back of her hand. "And so are we, so don't worry about us. Your dad and I were long overdue for a meltdown. We've been able to start fresh here, for the most part, but sometimes things hit you when you least expect them. We deal with it head-on now, instead of tamping it down."

"It's like Sam said." Tinka smiled at him. "It's good to remember Jake."

"It is." Her dad stood and pulled a photo from his pocket. "This is him." He handed the picture to Sam, the one of Jake swinging the golf club. Her dad was showing it to everyone these days, apparently.

Sam glanced at it, and then handed it back to Tinka's dad. "Good form."

"Did you know Tinka golfs because of Jake?" Her dad folded the photo and put it back in his pocket.

Frowning at Tinka, Sam pursed his lips and shook his head.

"She was three, I think. About the same age Jake was in the photo." Her dad was chipper all of a sudden. "She saw this in my office and said, 'I want to do that.' I took her out to the driving range immediately, and she's golfed ever since." He mimed putting. This was almost an exact replica of the conversation he'd had with Dylan a few weeks ago.

Apparently he was reciting his little monologue to everyone. "It's like she channels her brother through the game, and it's one way we keep his memory alive."

Tinka felt Sam's eyes on her, but she couldn't look at him. This was why she could never have the "I don't want to golf" conversation with her dad, and Sam was seeing it firsthand. There was too much mixed up in it. She couldn't break his heart. This, her tie to Jake's legacy, was the thing keeping her dad going.

Rescuing her, Sam stood and hugged Mr. and Mrs. Foster. "If you ever need anything, someone to talk to, golf with, whatever, I'm your guy."

"Thank you, Sam," her dad said.

"Is Jane around?" Tinka asked, though the thought of working on wedding centerpieces right now sickened her.

Her mom frowned. "I think she and Karen went into town. They'll be back later."

"I'm going to steal Tinka, if that's all right." Sam stepped toward the door, and Tinka followed him.

When they were safely outside, he clasped his hands behind his back. "Are you okay?"

She nodded, noting the absence of his arms around her. "Who the hell is Carol?" She blinked back tears.

"Carol?"

She nodded toward the house. "Their new friend in town?" Again, here were her parents with this secret life Tinka knew nothing about—moving to new places, making new friends, talking like they've been reading self-help books.

Sam hesitated. "I don't think there's...I kind of got the impression that maybe Carol is a counselor or something, you know? A therapist."

She wiped her eyes with the heels of her palms. "Crap, you're right. They've been seeing somebody. That's what all this is about." She waved her hand to indicate the mess of a house her parents had bought. "Why not tell me? Why not be honest about it?"

Sam wrinkled his nose. "Like you've been honest with them?"

Smiling, she moved to punch him lightly on the arm, but she stopped herself and wrapped her own arms behind her back. "Shut your face." She retreated a bit, widening the gap between them.

"Do you really talk to a dinosaur drawing?" Sam smirked.

"Yeah? So?" But it hit Tinka then that she hadn't been using Dorothy the same way she had back in Minneapolis. In their old house, Dorothy got all the news, all the drama. But here, the only thing Tinka talked to Dorothy about was Sam, because Tinka talked to him about everything else. He was more to her than just a cute guy she liked to kiss. He was her only confidante.

She glanced back at the closed front door. "I can't go back in there. Not right now. You want to go somewhere else?" It hadn't been what she'd meant, but her mind jumped to the couch at Maurice's. That had been a colossal mistake, and it was all on her. She was the one who'd initiated it. Sam had balked, and she'd talked him into it because she was a selfish person who drew people into her vortex and held them there until she spit them out. She reached up and touched the plastic ring, which was still around her neck, hidden under her shirt. She would not spit out Sam.

Sam's eyes went to her hand. "Good luck charm."

"Exactly." Tinka swallowed. The lump in her throat overwhelmed her. "Sam."

His eyes went to hers, and she nearly told him everything. He was the neo-Dorothy, after all. She opened her mouth, but the words got stuck.

"You need a distraction," he said.

She nodded.

Sam gestured toward the steps. "Then I know just the place."

• • •

Sam led Tinka over to his house. He could think of no better distraction than the Anderson clan. "Hello, family," he said.

The entire crew, who were setting up to play *Trivial Pursuit* at the kitchen table, glanced up as Sam and Tinka crossed the threshold. "I hope this is okay?" Sam whispered.

"Not where I thought you'd take me," Tinka said, "but yeah. Board games might be exactly what the doctor ordered."

Sam coughed nervously. "Hi, everybody. This is Tinka. Tinka, this is everybody."

He waved his arm to indicate his entire family plus Hakeem, who would finally, officially become family for real this weekend, and Harper's friend, Elena, whom the Andersons had always treated like family, anyway.

Harper whispered, "The girlfriend," to Matthew and Hakeem, whose eyes swung right over to Tinka. Sam's face went hot. He had never, ever brought someone home before. Now he was bringing home the girl who was pretending to be his girlfriend, who he wanted to be his actual girlfriend.

If Matthew and Harper ever found out he and Tinka had been fake dating, Sam would literally never hear the end of it.

Sam's dad stood and shook Tinka's hand. "It's a pleasure to finally meet you. Sam has told us all about the cookies you've made for him."

Harper passed out game pieces. "He had to tell us about them, because it's not like he saved any to share."

"Maybe I would've saved you some, if you hadn't abandoned me for summer camp," Sam said.

"I can make some more," Tinka said. "Any excuse to use your kitchen."

"Join us." Hakeem pulled out the chair next to him. "I need another non-Anderson over here, someone who doesn't have the entire box of questions memorized."

"He needs you to help him feel better about his own lack of trivia knowledge." Matthew nudged Hakeem in the side.

Hakeem feigned outrage, then rested his head on his fiancé's shoulder. Sam grinned. His summer had been fine so far—better than anticipated, with Tinka around—but having his entire family back together lit him up from the inside.

Tinka took the seat next to Hakeem, shaking his hand and Matthew's.

"Do you like dissecting things?" Matthew asked.

Tinka shook her head.

Sam shot him a "cut it" look, swiping his hand across his neck.

"Let's do teams." Harper pointed to herself. "Me and Elena, Matthew and Hakeem, Dad and Maddie, and Sam and Tinka."

"Sounds good." Sam pulled up a chair next to Tinka. "So, what are your strengths? Obviously, I've got entertainment covered. Harper's also pretty good at that one, so watch out. Elena knows sports—"

"Let her figure this stuff out on her own," Elena said.

"She needs to know, in case one of you fools ends up in the center. We're not giving you a freaking hockey question," Sam said.

"Fair enough." Elena's family owned a sporting goods store, and she'd managed to absorb a lot of knowledge from working there.

"Matthew's the history buff. Hakeem is an English grad student, so no arts and literature questions for him ever." Sam widened his eyes at his father. "And Dad." He grinned.

His father smiled knowingly back at him. "Yes, Sam? What are my strengths?"

Sam winced. "Dad doesn't have any."

Mr. Anderson tossed a piece of green pie at his son.

Sam ducked and whispered to Tinka. "It's true, though."

"I think I'm with you, Mr. Anderson." Tinka had folded her hands in her lap. "Assuming there's no food-specific category, I'm probably a jack of all trades, master of none."

"I'm in good company, then." Sam's dad rolled the die, a six. Maddie moved their pink game piece to a blue space. "I'm not sure Sam told you, but my good friend, Marge, owns a very successful bakery near where you go to school."

"I didn't know that." Tinka eyed Sam accusingly.

His insides flipped like they did whenever he knew her eyes were on him. "Sorry. I forgot."

Hakeem read the first question. "The largest fresh water lake in the world, Lake Baikal, is located in which country?"

"Marge is coming to the wedding on Saturday. I can introduce you."

"You're avoiding the question, Dad," said Matthew.

"I am not. I'm having a conversation. Maddie can answer it. Would you like that, Tinka?" Sam's dad asked.

"Maddie," Harper said, "name a country. Any country."

Maddie tapped her lips, thinking.

"She doesn't know any countries," Sam said. This was always his dad's M.O. When he didn't know the answer to something, he'd punt to Maddie, under the guise of getting her involved in the game.

"Yes, I do." Maddie pouted. "I'm going into third grade. I'm not a baby."

"Then name one," Harper said.

"That would be great. Thank you, Mr. Anderson," Tinka said. "I'd love to talk to your friend."

"Egypt?" Maddie scrunched up her nose.

"Ennnnhhh!" Matthew, Hakeem, Harper, and Elena made a buzzing sound.

Tinka startled next to Sam.

"Wrong!" Matthew said.

"It was Russia." Hakeem stuffed the card into the back of the box and handed the die to Sam, who shook it.

Sam's dad was still talking to Tinka. "Maybe she can set you up with an internship or something, or whatever it is you bakers call it—apprenticeship?"

Sam's arm stopped mid-roll.

"Oh." Tinka ran her finger along the edges of a piece of orange pie. "Maybe. I don't know how much time I'll have for that sort of thing. There's school. And the golf team."

"She has a lot going on, Dad," Sam said.

"Just roll, Sammy," Harper whined. Then she whispered to Elena, "This game is going to take *forever*."

"Your dad mentioned you're quite a golfer," Sam's dad said. "We'll have to hit the links sometime, you and your dad with Sam and me."

"Yeah," Tinka said. "I'd like that."

Sensing that this conversation was not helping her forget the scene at her house, Sam rolled the die and moved to grab Tinka's hand, but he stopped himself. It would've been too real, too much of a boyfriend move. They'd stopped casually touching each other since the other night at Maurice's. Sam had been avoiding contact because he was scared flagrant touching would push Tinka to end their fauxmance and, thus, their friendship. He couldn't have that.

He shifted his chair away from her a few inches, just to be safe.

After the game ended, Sam walked Tinka back to her house to the soundtrack of Matthew and Hakeem belting out the song "We Are the Champions" from the deck.

In the distance, Harper squealed, "Shut up, you losers!"

"We're not losers," Matthew said. "We're winners." Then he and Hakeem started another chorus of their victory song.

On her doorstep, Tinka said, "Your dad was so nice to mention his friend and her bakery. Working there would be amazing."

"It would be great for you."

"In another life." She stared at the sky. "It's too complicated. You heard my dad."

"You could do both." Sam was heading off to L.A. in the fall to study film. There had never been any doubt about that. But Tinka, who wanted something so simple and so tangible, couldn't face her parents with the truth.

"Not in the fall. No time," she said. "There are practices or matches every single day."

"In the spring, then." Sam was determined to make this happen for her.

She shook her head, staring him right in the eye. "You heard my dad. My golfing keeps Jake alive for him. What I want doesn't matter. Not right now." She drew in a long breath, held it for a moment, then exhaled. "Why do I feel like I'm constantly waiting for my turn? It's like I've put everything on hold. Unless I come clean with him, what? Am I going to keep pursuing this golf thing forever?"

Sam's hand flinched. He was about to reach out to her, to hug her, and he stopped himself. They weren't doing that anymore. But this was different. This wouldn't be a romantic embrace. Tinka needed a friend, and Sam was her friend. He would've hugged Harper in this moment. Or Jane even. It would almost be worse not to hug her. He'd just made up his mind to offer Tinka his arm, when her phone buzzed.

Groaning, she checked it. "Shit." Her shoulders dropped as she glanced up at Sam. "Thank you. Really. I had so much fun tonight."

"You're welcome." His arms were back down at his sides. The moment for a friendly hug had passed. Probably. Maybe.

Tinka hesitated a second, then stepped toward Sam. He

braced himself. He'd give her the friendly double pat on the back and send her on her way. He leaned in, but Tinka cut him off, using her phone as a barrier between them. "I have to deal with this." She waved the phone and ducked inside, leaving Sam to follow the sounds of Matthew and Hakeem butchering Queen back to his house.

Chapter Twelve

The next morning, while Tinka was eating a sad breakfast of instant coffee and stale doughnuts on the living room floor, using old newspapers as a makeshift picnic blanket, someone banged hard on the front door. Groaning, she hoisted herself up and pulled open the door. There was Sam in red basketball shorts and a T-shirt designed to resemble an ugly Christmas sweater. His sister, brother, and Hakeem stood behind him, all dressed in red and green.

"Merry Christmas." Sam's eyes stayed on Tinka's feet as he handed her a candy cane. Then he stepped back, pushing Harper to the front.

"Uh…" Tinka said.

"I'm as confused as you are," Hakeem said.

"It's July First," Harper explained. "Today is the Christmas in July festival." She had a mistletoe barrette in her hair.

Sam kept playing with the drawstring on his shorts, looking anywhere but at Tinka. He'd gone in for a hug last night, and she'd cut him off. He was obviously upset about it.

Harper handed Tinka a green T-shirt, which said "On

the Naughty List." "After six months of slightly subdued Christmas cheer, North Pole goes whole hog on the first of July with a town-wide re-Christmas-ing party. There's eggnog and sleigh rides."

"And Santa comes. You can sit on his lap," Matthew explained.

"*You* can," Hakeem muttered.

"Maurice marathons Christmas movies all day." Matthew checked his watch. "He's showing *Scrooged* right now."

"But you're under no pressure to come," Sam said.

He did not want to be here. The way he kept fidgeting with his clothes and glancing back at the driveway, he was about to take off running. That was fine. Tinka'd let him off the hook. "I don't know. The other girls —"

Harper grabbed a shopping bag from Hakeem and handed it to Tinka. "We have shirts for Jane and Karen, too."

Now Sam was looking at her, a blank expression on his face. Tinka couldn't tell if he wanted her to say yes or no. So, she went with what she wanted, instead, which was any excuse to get out of the house for the day. "Okay. I'll rally the troops." She and Sam had had a nice time together the day before; and they'd survive today, too, as long as the two of them kept their distance.

Their group took two cars into town, and Harper assigned the vehicles. Tinka rode with Jane and Sam in his truck, while everyone else took Harper's car.

So the whole "keep their distance" thing was already an abject failure.

"Everything okay?" It was the first thing Sam had said to Tinka since she'd agreed to go into town. Right now he appeared to be making an effort to stay as close to the driver's side door as possible.

Tinka was making a similar effort to keep her own body near Jane's on the passenger's side. "Yeah. Why?"

"Last night you got a text and seemed kind of upset about it." Sam shrugged, eyes straight ahead.

"Oh." Tinka snuck a peek at Jane, who was gazing out the window at Main Street. Stores had set up sale racks crammed with Christmas paraphernalia along the sidewalks. There were deals on skis and jewelry and shotguns. An actual sleigh pulled by two shiny black horses adorned with jingling bells clomped down the road. Tinka felt like she'd been transported to another world. "Yeah. Everything's fine. Golf stuff."

That was a lie. The text had been from Colin, again, wanting her to get Jane off his back. She'd nearly marched down to the basement to tell Jane to cool it, but she didn't. She'd texted Colin back instead, telling him he was being a jerk and if it meant so much to him, he should block Jane's number. Tinka hadn't heard back from him. Maybe he'd finally gotten the hint that she wasn't going to be bullied by him.

As Sam hunted for a parking spot, they drove past the town square, where restaurants had set up booths for the Taste of North Pole. A very authentic-looking Santa and his elves—all of them wearing shorts, tank tops, and sunglasses—held court in the middle of the commotion. In the park, a band played old-timey Christmas songs from the gazebo.

"The bands get better as the day goes on," Sam said as he parked his truck on a side street near the playground. "Eight Maids A-Milking closes out the night."

"Eight Maids A-Milking?" Jane adjusted her silver skirt that looked like tinsel, which she'd borrowed from Harper.

"The best rock band in North Pole. All girls, but there are only six of them. I guess the name's supposed to be ironic." Sam flashed his dimple at Jane, and jealousy coursed through Tinka's veins, even though Jane hadn't done anything wrong. That dimple belonged to Tinka, and Sam had been hiding it from her all morning.

The Andersons, Hakeem, Tinka, Jane, and Karen stayed together while perusing the food offerings in the town square. Sam kept a casual, but not unfriendly distance. He interacted with Tinka the same way he interacted with Harper. That put things in context. They were doing the brother/sister thing. Even though she didn't have much experience in that realm, Tinka knew she could roll with it, especially because they had so many people around them as a buffer.

But after everyone had had their fill of figgy pudding, savory gingerbread crackers with goat cheese and cranberry chutney, and iced peppermint lattes, the group splintered. Matthew and Hakeem met up with some of Matthew's old high school friends. Harper and Jane ran off with Harper's buddies. Karen wandered off with Eric Joyce, who was wearing a plain white T-shirt under a moth-ridden homemade Christmas vest. Soon Sam and Tinka were alone.

"And then there were two," Sam said.

Tinka scanned the crowd. They'd lost their safeguard.

Sam appeared to be searching for a chaperone as well. "We can meet up with some of my friends. I'm sure Brian is around, or we can hunt for Harper and Jane, see what they're up to."

None of that sounded good to Tinka. She didn't want other people. She wanted Sam, her good *friend* Sam. Emphasis on the "friend." There was no reason the two of them shouldn't be able to spend the day alone together. They'd done it before. Besides, who better to show her around town today than him? He was basically the mayor of North Pole. "Maybe we can hook up with them later."

"Really?" Sam's eyes darkened. "You sure?"

"I'm sure." Tinka straightened her posture. They were doing this. Brother and sister all day long. "I'm a shapeless mound for you to mold into a Christmas in July expert. Where do we start?"

"You're putting me in charge of your Christmas festival destiny." Now Sam flashed his elusive dimple at her. The day, her life, the world could've ended right at that moment and it would've been fine with Tinka.

"Do your worst," she said.

"Such awesome responsibility." He put his hand to his mouth and surveyed the scene. Townsfolk in red and green frolicked along Main Street and through the square. Tinka was actually starting to recognize people. She saw Maurice from the video store, and Craig the guy who complained a lot, and the other Garland boy from the coffee shop. "We have to see Santa," Sam said finally.

"Lead the way." Beaming, she followed him to the square.

The two of them got in line behind a bunch of young kids and their parents, and Sam immediately stepped out of the queue. "I'll be right back."

"You're abandoning me?" Tinka playfully wagged a fist at Sam.

Walking backward away from her, he said, "It's for a good cause."

As Sam spun around and traipsed away, Tinka realized she was grinning like a lovesick fool. She bit her lip to put an end to that, as he stopped to chat, hug, or shake hands with almost everyone he ran into. Her heart warmed involuntarily. He was so the mayor.

When Sam returned, he handed her a bag of warm pecans covered in cinnamon sugar. Tinka popped a few into her mouth and let the spicy-sweet coating dissolve on her tongue. "Yum."

"See, I told you I was abandoning you for a good reason."

"The best reason." She grabbed another handful of nuts. "You can abandon me anytime if this is what you return with."

When it was their turn to see Santa, Tinka sat on his lap, and Sam snapped her picture. They got a few happy ones and one of her pretending to bawl like a two-year-old. Then they had a third grader in line snap a few pics of her and Sam together with Santa—Tinka on Santa's knee, Sam all the way on the other side of Santa's chair.

Outside Mrs. Claus's Closet, Tinka shivered as she assessed the sky, which was bright blue and cloudless. "Does it feel colder? The sun is shining, and it's, like, eighty-five degrees, but I feel like I should be wearing a scarf."

"They have those." Sam pointed to an entire rack of wool scarves on display.

"Of course they do." Tinka bent over the accessories table and held up a pair of earrings. They were dangly irregular quadrangles with a pearly rainbow design. "These are cool," she said. "They'd go with my dress for your brother's wedding, actually." She flushed at the mention of the wedding. There'd be dancing there, and moonlight, and everyone would automatically be in a romantic mood...

"So get them."

"Maybe later." Tinka patted her shorts. "I didn't bring any money with me."

"And those nuts cleaned me out." He pulled out the pockets of his gym shorts to show her that he was all out of cash.

Tinka frowned. "Well, now how are you going to take me on a carriage ride? Isn't that one of the main events of North Pole's Christmas in July?" She'd always thought romantic carriage rides were cheesy, but she would make an exception for Sam. There were a lot of things she could imagine doing with Sam that she'd never do with anyone else.

Sam grinned mischievously. "It is. But we don't pay for carriage rides."

"We don't?"

He shook his head. "Trust me."

Her heart pounded in her ears. She wasn't sure of those

words: *trust me*. Nothing easy and safe came after "trust me."

They dashed down Main Street, dodging a group of carolers in Christmas-themed swim attire—bikinis and swim trunks with masks and snorkels.

The carriage was up ahead, starting to pull away from the curb. "Do what I do," Sam said.

Checking for cars, Sam led Tinka into the street until they were right behind the carriage, which hadn't yet reached full speed. He jumped onto one of the rails and held on tight to the wrought iron curl that snaked up from the bottom. He looked like he was wind-surfing through Main Street on the back of a horse-drawn sleigh. Shutting out the part of her brain that was screaming, "No! Danger! This is how you die!" Tinka followed his lead and jumped onto the other rail.

"Holy shit." Her hands clutched the rail in front of her. "That had to be more dangerous than the Jingle Falls slide."

"Oh, it totally was," Sam said. "You did great."

She was street surfing on the back of a sled, yet she was still alive and unharmed. Amazing.

The people who'd actually paid for their sleigh ride turned around to see who'd jumped aboard.

"Tinka, you've met Craig before," Sam said. "And Dinesh."

"From the arcade." If Tinka hadn't been gripping the carriage for her very survival, she would've touched the ring around her neck right now.

"Where are you guys off to?" Sam asked.

"You're stealing our ride." Craig narrowed his eyes.

"We are," Sam agreed.

"We're going to the park." Dinesh elbowed Craig in the side. "Hang on tight."

Sam saluted him. "Thanks."

The sleigh took them all the way down Main Street, past the elementary school, and toward the park. Tinka closed her eyes as the wind whipped at her face. She was hanging on to a sleigh for dear life, but somehow she'd never felt calmer. When she opened her eyes, she was looking right at Sam. He was flashing that dimple again, making her melt—he, her good friend, Sam, whom she thought of as a brother, and absolutely nothing more.

Sam and Tinka hopped off near the playground and ran toward the gazebo, where six girls were setting up to play.

"That's Marley, right?" Tinka recognized the girl who'd kissed Sam at the dark party. She was tuning her guitar.

"That's her." Sam waved to Marley. "The other girls go to North Pole High as well. Allison, the drummer, was my prom date."

A pang of jealousy hit Tinka hard. This band contained a girl Sam had kissed and a girl he went to the most important dance of his life with. She had to remind herself that A) Sam was still only her fake boyfriend, and B) it wasn't like she didn't have her own past. "Did you two have fun?" She tried to make it sound jokey, like how his sister would've asked.

"Sure." Sam turned toward Tinka. "But we only went as friends."

"Oh. So, like, *friend* friends. Nothing…more?"

Sam grinned, watching her curiously. It reminded Tinka of the day they met in his backyard, when he'd looked at her like he was trying to figure her out. "Did you go to prom?" he asked.

Tinka winced, taking her gaze off his dimple. "Almost. We only have senior prom at Florian's, but some guy asked me to go with him. We were not friends." She shook her head for emphasis.

"And you only 'almost' went with him?"

"Yeah, he was really sweet leading up to it." The band started playing their first song, a blues-rock version of "Away in a Manger," and Tinka tapped her toe in time. "But he was friends with some guy I had…hung out with a few weeks earlier, and I found out he had certain 'expectations' about prom night."

"Asshole," Sam said.

"The dumb thing is that if he'd been upfront with me from the beginning, I might have gone along with it. He was cute and fun. If we'd hooked up at a party, it would've been no big deal. But the fact that he bothered with, like, romancing me beforehand was insulting for some reason. Does that make sense?"

"Don't pretend to want more if all you want is sex…or you know, whatever." Sam's face went slightly pink.

Tinka's cheeks could've heated her parents' house right now, but she shrugged off the embarrassment. "The suckiest thing was that I'd been excited about the dance itself, but I ended up not even going. I'd never been to a dance before."

"Never ever?"

She shook her head.

The two of them turned to face the gazebo. Tinka focused hard on the bassist, because Sam had neither kissed nor gone out with her, as far as Tinka knew.

"So…" Sam said.

Tinka didn't look, but she could sense him fidgeting next to her.

"Maybe *we* should dance, then. Or whatever."

Tinka's mind swirled as she focused on the bassist plucking her strings. "Maybe." She turned to Sam, and his expression convinced her to chuck all propriety out the window. She'd seen that look before, on other guys. Sam wanted her. The difference was, this time, she wanted him back.

She took Sam's hand. It was the first time they'd touched skin-to-skin in days, and the sensation almost brought her to tears. She wrapped an arm around his neck, pulling his cheek closer to hers. He held her tight around the waist, and they swayed together as Marley Ho serenaded them with "I Saw Mommy Kissing Santa Claus."

Tinka leaned back and stared him straight in the eye. "Can I be honest with you right now?"

She felt his breath catch. "Okay."

She focused on his mouth. "I want to touch your dimple." She wanted to touch more than that, but she'd start there.

He laughed and the dimple appeared. "What?"

"I've wanted to touch it since the day we met. May I?"

He shrugged. "Not what I was expecting, but sure."

Tinka licked her lips and leaned in. She pressed her index finger to the little divot on his cheek. Then she let go. "That was very satisfying," she said.

"Any time you need it, my dimple is here for you."

She wrapped both arms around his neck and pulled him in close, resting her head on his chest. He rubbed her back and held her tight as they swayed in time to the music. All her troubles faded away—her parents, Colin's texts, Dylan, Karen. Sam, the guy who lit every nerve in her body on fire, was her key to inner peace.

When the town clock struck seven, Sam pulled away, breaking the spell.

"What?" Tinka asked, the space between them suddenly agonizing. "Are you about to turn into a pumpkin?"

"Better," he said. "It's time to watch the greatest Christmas movie of all time."

He grabbed her hand, and Tinka laced her fingers between his. They'd broken their unspoken no-touching rule, and, apparently, they were going to blatantly keep violating it. The two of them dashed through the streets to Maurice's. "What movie is it?" asked Tinka.

"You'll see." Sam opened the door to the video store.

"I saved you a spot." Maurice tossed a small bag to Sam as he and Tinka ran toward the back.

The screening room was packed mostly with strangers, but there was an empty beanbag chair right in front, with a hand-written sign that said "Reserved." Sam flopped down, and Tinka joined him. The two of them sank into each other, side by side. Nervous, Tinka hugged her own chest. Seeing a movie while sitting close like this wasn't a very brother/sister thing to do. Seeing a movie was when they'd spent almost two hours kissing each other after they'd agreed to keep things platonic. So far tonight they'd only danced, but here in the dark…

Sam nudged her with his elbow. "Get ready."

A few moments later, the opening shot of *Die Hard* appeared on screen. Tinka settled in with Sam next to her. The beanbag chair was so comfortable, and she was so tired from running around all day. She closed her eyes for what she thought was just a minute, but the next thing she knew, the credits were rolling, and she woke up with her head on Sam's chest.

He had his arm around her and his head had fallen limp against the top of hers. He was sleeping, too.

Tinka lifted her head and sat up. The room had cleared out. A few people were up front, talking to Maurice.

Sam stirred and sat up as well. He ran his fingers through his curls and glanced around. "Ghost town," he said.

"Yeah."

"We fell asleep. During *Die Hard*. I'm so disappointed in us."

Tinka reached up and touched his dimple again, which made him smile more. Breathing hard, she pulled his face toward her and kissed him—a sleepy, fervent, messy kiss. He kissed her back just as hungrily. And it struck her, they were all alone. They weren't putting on a show for anyone right now. It was just the two of them. She put her hands on his cheeks and ducked away from his lips. He grinned, and she pulled him in for another long, slow kiss.

That ended a moment later when someone behind them coughed. "A-hem."

Tinka and Sam straightened up and turned around. Karen and Jane. The look on Karen's face could freeze lava, and Jane's eyes were puffy and red from crying.

"Colin called," Karen said.

Shit. Tinka jumped up from the beanbag chair. "Jane."

"How could you?" Jane sobbed, backing toward the exit. "You spent the past month lying to my face. Karen was right about you this whole time. You only care about yourself." She spun on her heel and dashed out of the video store. Karen followed behind.

Tinka should've seen this coming. Colin had told her this would happen. She'd tried to do the Tinka thing and ignore the problem until it went away, something that had never, ever really worked.

She and Sam were doing that now, floating along, kissing each other occasionally, not dealing with the fact that the summer was going to end, they'd go their separate ways, and Tinka would push him away until he ended up hating her.

"You should probably take me home." She stepped toward the door, putting a very necessary chasm of space between them.

"As you wish," he said.

Tinka knew what that meant, and it broke her heart. With one movie quote, he'd managed to shatter this illusion of friendship they'd worked so hard to maintain. "*Princess Bride*," she said.

Sam grinned, but Tinka couldn't return the smile. He'd known from the start that she consistently railroaded the people in her life. Yet, here he was, standing by her, using Wesley's famous words to tell her he cared about her. There was only one thing to do. It'd kill her, but she had to end this now.

· · ·

Sam ran after Tinka as she jog-texted her way down Main Street, sending people scurrying to jump out of her way. When he finally caught up with her, she shoved the phone into her pocket. "What's the point, right? Just another friendship I've ruined. Might as well do my normal thing and let it go, pretend like it doesn't bother me." She rested her hands on her knees, and a sob escaped her lips.

Sam put a hand on her back, but she shrugged him off, stood, and took off running to his truck. He followed behind, but not too closely. She wanted to be alone. He got the hint.

The two of them sat in silence in the car. Sam waited for her to speak, but she didn't. Tinka stared out the window, seeming content to stay in her head. Sam wouldn't push the issue. She'd talk when she wanted to talk. He drove them silently through the streets, passing houses that were newly decorated for Christmas in July. There were blowup snowmen and trolls from the movie and even a terrifyingly realistic Santa mannequin reclining on a Barcalounger. Sam commented on each of them in his mind, but kept his thoughts to himself.

He pulled into her driveway, and she immediately gripped the door handle.

Sam spoke quickly before she had a chance to escape. "I had an amazing time today." Though things had taken a turn when Karen and Jane showed up, everything before that had been perfect, the whole, entire day. Their kiss on the beanbag was the icing on the cake. He wouldn't allow that to get lost in the drama.

"Me, too." She was still staring out the passenger's side window.

"Tinka, I know it's easy for me to say, but what if you talk to Jane, explain to her what happened—"

She turned to him, tears welling in her eyes. "You don't get it, do you? This is who I am. This is the real me. I'm selfish. I don't think about other people. Over and over again, same story."

"You know that's not true, at least not anymore."

She gestured toward the door. "You've seen firsthand what I'm capable of. I cut my best friend out of my life without a word of warning. I got drunk and kissed my roommate's ex-boyfriend. Who does that? What kind of monster does that?"

"*Did*," Sam said. "*Did* is the operative word. All that stuff's in the past. It's what you told me from the beginning."

"Yeah." Her eyes turned hard, erasing the tears that had threatened to spill. "And what kind of person lets someone like that into his life?"

"Excuse me?"

She took a second, as if really thinking this through, then said, "It's been bugging me the whole ride home. Why would you—why would *anyone*—trust me after all the things I've done? I'm honestly asking."

"Tinka." He was walking a tightrope right now. This conversation could end a few different ways—with her fleeing or with her agreeing to stick it out and talk through the problem. She was right on the edge of bolting. "I *know* you. Right from the start, you've been honest with me. I've never thought you were perfect. You've shown me all your flaws, and I accept them. I always have."

She frowned, the moonlight hitting her face at harsh angles. "Why?"

Tinka was about to exit his life forever. Sam felt it in his bones. "Be—because I've seen how you want to make up for those things. I know you regret what happened between you and Karen and Jane, and you don't want to make those mistakes again." He reached into the pocket of his shorts and pulled out the bag Maurice had tossed him earlier at the video store. Desperate times. "I…I care about you, Tinka. I think, more than I can even say."

She held the bag, but didn't open it. "You care about some idea of me you've concocted. You see me as you want to see me."

"I see you as you are."

She shook her head and handed the bag back to him, her jaw tense. "I'm a pretty girl who started talking to you, and you're willing to give me the benefit of the doubt because of it. You don't like *me*, Sam. You like the idea of me. You like the fact that I like you. Let's be honest."

Her words filled the space between them as if they had mass. They were almost corporeal. Sam crumpled the bag slowly, then shoved it back into his pocket. "Is that really how little you think of me?" he whispered.

"You had a choice between me and no one, basically. You chose me because what other options did you have?"

His mouth fell open.

"I'm trying to do you a favor here, Sam. I'm thinking of someone else for once. You should stay away from me. It's for your own good." She turned and clutched the door handle again.

"Maybe you have done me a favor," he said. "There was something between us, a real connection. At least I thought there was. I was willing to see past the stuff you told me about, not because of how you looked, but because of who I thought you were." He paused. "But I'm starting to think I was wrong about you, about all of it. Since apparently you only see me as this ugly sad sack who has to take what he can get."

"I didn't mean that." She turned toward him again, her lip trembling. "That's not what I—Sam, that's not what I think."

"Well, it's what you said, so what am I supposed to believe? Seems to me you think I'd have to date someone who'd treat me like shit because no one else would have me. You're no better than Harper and Matthew or any of them."

"That's not true." She reached toward him, and he backed away.

"You know what?" He faced forward, and put his hands on the steering wheel. "This is actually great. We started fake dating because neither of us wanted to get attached. It didn't work, though, because I was starting to fall for you, but now…"

"Sam, I didn't mean it."

"Sure you did. It's fine. It's better than fine. We'll go our separate ways and be able to leave for our respective schools in August. No tears, no drama."

He aimed his face forward, though he could feel her eyes on him. After a few moments of silence, Tinka threw open the door, slammed it, and ran up to her house. She'd left the truck, but her words stayed behind with Sam.

Chapter Thirteen

Tinka slammed the front door and glared out the window as Sam's truck backed down the driveway and out onto the street. How dare he! How. Dare. He…

How dare he…what? Dump her? Tell her to go to hell? It was what she'd been practically begging him to do.

She never thought he'd do it. Not her Sam. He wasn't supposed to give up on her—on them—that easily. She was the flighty one. She was the one who'd bail. He was supposed to keep pushing back against her until he convinced her to see things his way. But she'd pushed him too far.

Shit. She literally did ruin everything.

"Tinka?"

She spun around, startled. She wasn't the only one home. As far as she knew, Karen and Jane were still in town doing Christmas things. She'd assumed her parents would be, too.

But no, they were in the living room with Dylan's parents, and Dylan himself, sitting on the couches, whose drop cloths had been removed for the occasion. The adults were all drinking beers or hard ciders. Dylan had a can of pop in his hand, and he was staring at her, mouth wide open.

"Join us!" Tinka's mom said, completely missing the fact that her teenage daughter was in a messy, crying tailspin. She swung her hand around the room to indicate that they were all having a lovely, festive time in their Christmas paraphernalia. Also, Tinka could tell by the unfocused glassiness of her mom's eyes that she was drunk.

Oh hell no. No thank you.

Tinka gave them a courtesy wave and marched through the living room, into the kitchen, and out the sliding glass doors leading to the back yard. She trekked across the deck—not even once peeking at Sam's house, for which she was very proud of herself—through the grass, and down to the lake, where she perched on the decrepit pier.

She stared out at the water, which shone black and shimmering under the moon and stars. Her brain kept begging her to look back at Sam's house, but she wouldn't. She would not.

Her entire existence was a disaster. She checked her phone. Still no replies from either Jane or Karen.

A strong desire to run hit Tinka. What if she...escaped, started over somewhere new. North Pole was a bust, like Minneapolis had been before she left for Florian's. And down in South Carolina, she'd been able to create a new life for herself, and a fun, new identity. That had worked out well, hadn't it?

Until she'd blown it by hooking up with Jane's ex.

"Want some company?" came Dylan's voice from behind her.

"I'm good." Still focused on the water, she willed him to get lost.

"Okay, well. I'm going to sit over here on this structurally unsound bench with this bottle of cider I stole from your parents' cooler, if you change your mind." Tinka heard his feet swishing through the grass.

Eyes to the moon, Tinka gave him the news. Everyone was going to find out eventually. "Sam and I broke up."

"Sorry."

"Please. You're glad. You never thought we were right for each other anyway, and you've been hitting on me all summer." Her lip trembled.

"Well, yeah, but still. You seem bummed about it, so that sucks."

"It does suck."

A flash of loneliness hit her, of true despair. She hadn't felt this way since her parents dragged her to North Pole a few weeks ago, since they'd told her they'd sold the house in Minneapolis. Sam had been the one to bring her out of that funk, and now he never wanted to see her again. She couldn't blame him. She'd basically called him a loser. There was no coming back from that.

She and Sam were never going to talk again. She was never going to hear his thoughts on this new movie or that old one. He wasn't going to sit on the counter and make her laugh while she baked cookies. She'd lost yet another best friend.

"I love him," she told the lake. "I love Sam."

"Wow," Dylan said, startling Tinka. She'd forgotten he was there. "I had no idea it was that serious."

"Yup." Her breath was suddenly shaky and uneven. "Me neither."

"What happened?"

"Well, I fucked it up, as I do. And now I'm out here with you, so."

"Glad to be of service."

She hoisted herself up from the pier and walked toward the bench where Dylan was sitting. "You're the only person left in North Pole who'll talk to me." She and Dylan Greene were of the same ilk. She was no better than him or Colin or the other countless preppy douchebags from her past. Maybe preppy douchebags were her destiny.

Tinka sat next to him and plucked the bottle of cider from his hands. He pulled out his keys and popped off the top.

She took a swig. "What are you doing here, anyway?"

"I'm the designated driver. I've been driving our drunk parents all over town tonight. You're welcome."

"Okay, maybe your night hasn't been much better than mine." She glanced around the yard. She hadn't spent much time down here since moving to North Pole. The Fosters didn't have a sandy beach like Sam did, but there was an unkempt magic to it in the darkness. It felt wild out here, primitive, dangerous. The buzzing cicadas filled her ears, creating a sort of white noise machine that tamped down her thoughts, thoughts like "Danger! You should not be sitting this close to Dylan" or "If you do this, you'll definitely kill any chance of getting back together with Sam."

Eh, that chance was already dead. Sam saw her for who she was now, for sure, and he was better off. He and Karen and Jane could start a little club for people who'd been crushed by Tinka Foster.

She held out the bottle to Dylan. "Want some?"

He shook his head. "Like I said, designated driver."

"Good boy." Her eyes wandered over to Sam's beach next door, which was a mistake. That's where they'd kissed for the first time while playing Spin-the-Bottle. The thought that she might never have the chance to kiss him again or wrap her arms around him or feel his breath against her skin as he whispered in her ear yanked at her heart.

Sam was kind of right, wasn't he? She had done them both a kindness by squashing his feelings, and he'd done them a favor by verbalizing the end of their relationship. Things were only ever going to end badly between her and Sam. If they'd started dating for real, she'd have cocked it up once she got back to school, because that's what she did. She used people, got what she needed out of them, and let them go. She was selfish. Always had been, always would be. Karen was right. Jane was right.

Why deny her destiny? Why leave any possible thread to Sam uncut?

She took a swig of cider. "Maybe you were right, Dylan. I should be with a guy like you."

He hesitated. Tinka prepared herself for him to make a move, but he didn't. "You know, Tinka, I thought I had you figured out, but maybe I'm not as smart as I like to think I am. You don't want me."

Her sinuses, eyes, and throat were about to burst with tears. "No, I don't."

"And besides, you and I should keep things platonic. Our relationship goes way deeper than romance."

"Ew. What are you saying?"

"We have a big job. We have to be grownups and protect our midlife crisis-ing parents from themselves." Dylan put his arm around her, like a friend or a big brother. He squeezed her shoulder while she cried.

* * *

Sam was a pathetic loser. It was official. He'd suspected it all his life, and now he had the proof. Knowledge was power, though, and he was never, ever going to put himself into another position like the one he'd been in tonight. He was done dreaming. No more Disney princesses.

He parked his truck outside his front door and ran into the house, where he found Hakeem sitting alone in the living room, reading.

Shooting him a wave, Sam turned his head and wiped his eyes with his other hand. He'd come in here ready for a good post-breakup cry. He hadn't anticipated company. "Where is everybody?"

"Your dad and Maddie are sleeping. Harper and Matthew are in town at some party. I took the opportunity for some peace and quiet." Hakeem shut his book and placed it on the end table next to his chair.

"Sorry I interrupted you." Sam's instinct was to dash upstairs, but he stood rooted to the floor. Maybe company wasn't a bad idea.

Hakeem gestured toward the couch across the coffee table from him. "You okay?"

Taking a seat, and feeling like he was walking into a shrink's office, Sam shook his head. "I'm fine." He folded his hands in his lap.

"No, you're not," Hakeem said.

Sam glanced over at the piano, which held dozens of pictures of his family. There was one big one in the middle of his mom and dad on their wedding day. They looked so happy, so sure of themselves and each other. "Tinka and I broke up." His eyes swung back to Hakeem.

"No." Hakeem stood and came over to Sam. He took a seat on the couch next to him and sat the same way, hands in his lap. "I'm sorry, man. I liked her."

"Yeah, well…" Sam's knee bounced up and down like a piston. "We were only pretending to date, really. Our relationship was a mutually beneficial way to get our families off our backs for the summer. It was always going to end. Just happened a few weeks earlier than anticipated." He shrugged.

"You're telling me that the girl who played *Trivial Pursuit* with your whole family, who ran around town with you all day today in Christmas garb, who I definitely saw looking at you like you were her favorite member of One Direction—"

"Oh, Hakeem, get new references." Sam couldn't help smiling a tiny bit.

"A girl who looked at you like you were the hottest member of 98 Degrees—"

Now Sam actually did burst out laughing.

"Sam." His future brother-in-law put a hand on Sam's knee, putting an end to the bouncing. "She liked you. Believe me. I don't know what happened between you two tonight, but her feelings were real. I have a sixth sense about these things. I'm a professional."

"You teach English literature. No, not even. You're a teaching *assistant*."

"Exactly. Reading things is literally my job." Hakeem folded his hands again.

"We…the two of us talked about everything, like my mom and stuff. And it wasn't one-sided, either. She told me things she'd never talked about with anybody. And beyond that…" Sam blushed. "I don't know, I don't have a *ton* of experience, but I actually managed to kiss two whole other girls this summer—"

"Good for you."

Sam sighed. "And kissing them was nothing like kissing Tinka. And maybe it's cheesy as hell—I mean, I've seen enough movies to be skeptical. I'm not a guy who believes in soul mates or anything. But with Tinka I honestly felt like maybe there was something deeper happening there. You know, until tonight."

Hakeem sat quietly for a few seconds before speaking. Sam loved that about Hakeem. He never rushed to judgment, not like Harper or Matthew. He always took his time to analyze every situation. "Okay. Let's walk this back. What exactly happened tonight and what did she say?"

"Well, she and her friends got into a fight. It was something that had been brewing for a while, but tonight it all came to a head. She feels guilty for what she did, like hurting people is in her DNA. She told me she was doing me a favor by letting me go, that I'm better off without her." Sam paused. "Maybe she's right."

"Dude." Hakeem squeezed his knee. "I pulled this same shit with your brother."

"Please," Sam said sarcastically.

"Really. You've only seen us all happy and in love and stuff, but it was a rough road getting here. I definitely gave Matthew the 'It's not you; it's me. Go find someone who can love you for real' malarkey."

"You did not."

"I sure did." He shook his head. "When your brother and I first met, I was still in the closet and trying to stay there, honestly. I had a lot of concerns about my family and their reaction, and I thought denial, denial, denial. I'd dated other guys who tried to drag me out, but I dug my heels in, man. But Matthew and I, we started dating senior year; and when we got closer to graduation and the real world outside our college bubble, I panicked. I was like, this has been great, but I'm only going to hurt you, and I can't give you what you want." He waved. "'Boy, bye.' How's that for a current reference, smart-ass?"

Sam grinned. "So what happened?"

"We broke up, and it was terrible. I was completely miserable; but, having a bunch of time to myself all of a sudden, I realized that I hadn't been giving him, my family, or myself credit that we'd be able to deal with this. I had set up this wall of avoiding 'real' relationships because I hadn't wanted to upset the compartments I'd created. But I realized that having your brother in my life was more important than keeping this bizarre peace I'd made for myself. Especially because this peace wasn't really peace at all, since it meant I couldn't be with Matthew the way I wanted to be, and I couldn't be honest with my family about who I was."

"I always thought your family was totally cool with

everything," Sam said. "Wow, I just realized I'd only assumed that, and, like, I never bothered to ask. I'm sorry."

Hakeem shook his head. "Probably because your brother was lucky. Your parents had always been super supportive, so why wouldn't other people's families be the same way? But, you know what? Mine were cool, too...eventually. It took them getting to know Matthew and seeing how happy we were compared to how stressed and closed off I'd been before opening up to them." He waggled his eyebrows. "Also, everyone loves Matthew. It's the law."

Sam smiled at their playful banter. "True, but everyone loves you, too, Hakeem. If I were forced to choose between you two—"

Hakeem nudged him in the side. "I know, I know, but let's not tell your brother. We wouldn't want to bruise his fragile ego." He nodded toward the Fosters' house. "But back to your thing. I'd be willing to bet that Tinka's over there right now, regretting her life. You could wait for her to come to you—wasting the precious few weeks you two have left—or you could go over there and let her off the hook."

Sam took a deep breath and stood. Maybe it'd make him extra pathetic if he went over there and she rejected him again, but he had to try. "I'm going to do the Sam thing and be the good guy."

Hakeem went back to his chair and picked up his book. "And I'm going to do the Hakeem thing and read as much as I can before your brother and sister get home and start bugging me about shit."

Sam ran right over to Tinka's house. He rang the front doorbell, hopping from one foot to the other, rehearsing his lines in his head. *You're wrong, Tinka. You're only trying to push me away because you're scared. I'm not going to let you do that, because I'm in love with you.*

Yikes. Where did that come from? He wasn't in love

with her. Talk about pathetic. He liked her. A lot. He couldn't imagine living life without her, and he spent most of his waking hours thinking about her. But he wasn't *in love* with her. He was about to leave for California. Love was meant for grown adults in romantic comedies, not teenagers about to leave for college in a matter of weeks.

Tinka's front door opened, and Sam's heart skipped a beat, but it was her dad at the door, not her. He threw an arm around Sam's shoulders and pulled him into the house.

"Uh..." Sam checked out the scene in the living room. Tinka's parents were playing cards on the coffee table in the living room with Dylan's mom and dad. Shot glasses and tumblers littered the area. They were having a fine time. "Is Tinka around?"

"She's in the back yard."

Sam's heart slammed against his ribs as his steps crunched over the plastic sheeting that covered most of their first floor. He skirted the tools and rags and buckets in the dusty kitchen and went out the sliding glass door. Tinka was sitting on a bench down by the lake. Someone else was with her, but Sam couldn't tell who. Was it Karen? Jane? Maybe they'd made up.

As he got closer, dread filled his stomach. It wasn't Karen or Jane. It was a guy. Yes, it was definitely a guy. He had his arm around her. She was leaning on his shoulder.

Sam yelped as he tripped over something in the yard, and Tinka and the guy spun toward him. "Sam?" She jumped up. The guy stood, too, and Sam could make out his features in the moonlight. Dylan Greene. Prince Eric, in the flesh.

Sam backed away. "I...I..." He tried to come up with a reason for why he was there, something that wouldn't totally mortify him.

Tinka panted as she ran up the hill from the lake. "Sam." She was grinning at him like everything was wonderful.

Sam's eyes were fixed on Dylan. "I pulled out of your

driveway, what, twenty minutes ago?" He glanced at the time on his phone.

Dylan, who'd reached them by now, said, "Dude, nothing happened."

A cloud of confusion passed over Tinka's face. She glanced back at the bench. "What do you think was going on?"

"It's fine." Sam's jaw tightened. "It's great. It's exactly how you told me it'd go down. You told me you'd hurt me and, hey, you were right. I should've believed you." Maybe he should've believed Dottie, too, when she'd said she'd seen Tinka and Dylan flirting on the golf course. Maybe Sam had been wearing blinders this whole time.

Tinka reached for him, but Sam ducked away. She let her arm hang there for a second, then dropped it to her side. "We were just talking. About you, if you must know."

"Okay, so, you left me, regretted it, and instead of coming to my house to talk things over, you ran right to *him*." Sam pointed at Dylan. "After all we've been through together, you went to Dylan before me. I thought we could talk about anything."

"Not when you were the one I was upset about."

"*Especially* because I was the one you were upset about. You're treating me like the other people in your life, like I'm a problem to be avoided."

"You're here now. Let's talk now."

Sam hesitated. The girl who'd called him a loser not a half hour ago, whom he'd just caught cuddling with Dylan Greene in the moonlight, wanted to talk. Hakeem had told Sam to cut Tinka some slack, but he didn't have to actually hand her the rope to hang him.

He spun on his heel and shouted over his shoulder, "I think I've heard enough from you tonight."

Chapter Fourteen

After her parents had gone to bed, Tinka grabbed a blanket and went out on the front porch with her phone. She curled up in an old lawn chair and tried texting both Jane and Karen again—notes of "I'm sorry" that went unrecognized. She didn't even bother trying to contact Sam.

Well, whatever. She'd wait. They'd have to come home sometime, and she'd be ready.

Around one in the morning, lights illuminated their little street. The car turned into Tinka's driveway and her heart caught in her throat. She sat up straighter as Jane and Karen jumped out of Harper's little red sports car.

The girls tried to push past Tinka without a word, but she blocked the door. "We need to talk. Please."

Karen refused meet Tinka's eyes as she nudged Jane toward the back of the house.

"One minute," Tinka said. "And then you can go back to hating me."

Karen put her hands on Jane's shoulders and tried to steer her away from Tinka, but Jane planted her feet. "One minute," Jane said. "One."

Tinka's face crumpled. Of course Jane would listen. That's what Jane did. She saw the good in people, even someone as worthless as Tinka.

Jane gave Tinka the kind of scowl she usually expected from Karen. "I want to hear whatever bullshit excuse you've come up with to rationalize hooking up with my ex."

"I don't have one," Tinka said.

Jane turned her back on Tinka and went to Karen, who'd stopped at the corner of the deck at the point where it made a right turn toward the back of the house.

"I could tell you how I was sad and confused and Colin happened to be there," Tinka said. "I could explain it away by telling you I was drunk and wasn't thinking. But the truth is, I kind of did know what I was doing. All I cared about was making myself feel better."

"Tell us something we don't know." Karen hugged Jane's shoulders.

"I push people away. I don't know why. I did it to you two, and I did it to Sam tonight." Tinka's throat tightened, but she coughed away the lump. "I want to start over. I think it's what I've been trying to do since I got here, but in kind of a half-assed way. I should've been honest with you right from the start, Jane. I should've listened to Karen when she was telling me how selfish I'd been. I should've been straight with both my parents and Sam."

"Harper talked to him," Jane said. "Sounds like you broke his heart, too."

Tinka blinked back tears, but a few escaped and rolled down her cheeks. "I'm so sorry. For everything."

"Talk is cheap, Tinka," Karen said.

"I know it is." Tinka stepped aside to let the girls in the front door. "But it's all I have at the moment."

As Karen and Jane disappeared into the house, Tinka

checked out Sam's driveway, where Harper's car was now parked. His truck wasn't there. She looked at her phone. It was after one, and he still wasn't back yet. He could be anywhere, or with anyone. And she had no right to begrudge him that. He'd tried to open up to her, and she'd pushed him away.

She curled up in the chair again, eyes fixed on Sam's driveway. He'd been right. Tinka sought comfort in other people, instead of dealing with her issues head-on. It's what she'd been doing all year at Florian's. It was why she'd gone and kissed Colin—to distract herself from her problems with her parents.

Well, no more. She'd said when she moved here, she was going to start over. She hadn't really done that. But from now on Tinka would be honest with herself and other people. She'd stay up all night waiting for Sam if she had to. She'd apologize and expect nothing in return. Maybe she'd burned that particular bridge, but it was going to be her last one.

Tinka stayed awake for as long as she could, but she gradually nodded off into a restless sleep. Sometime later a woodpecker tapping on a nearby tree woke her for good, and her eyes adjusted to her surroundings and the sunlight. She glanced over at Sam's house. His pickup wasn't there. Sam still hadn't come home.

The sounds of birds chirping and people chatting floated on the air. The voices were coming from Sam's house, where the back door was open. Tinka heard a "holy shit" from Harper, and then an incomprehensible bellow of frustration from a man.

Sam. Tinka's heart started thumping. She pushed the blanket to the ground and ran over to his house, jumping over the hedge between their properties and bounding up the back steps to the deck. Matthew, Hakeem, and Harper were in the kitchen. Matthew was on the phone. Harper was pacing and grabbing her hair. Hakeem, in running clothes, stood stoically near the refrigerator. Tinka knocked lightly on the open door, and Harper, a hint of a sneer on her face, said, "What?"

"I heard someone yell." Sam wasn't here. He'd been in an accident. He was in jail. Dottie had decided to do a science experiment on him involving knives and/or acid.

Matthew, pacing with the phone, said, "Nancy, this is Matthew Anderson. Please call me back as soon as you get this. It's an emergency."

"Nancy?" Tinka asked.

"Gold," Harper said. "The baker."

"The baker? What happened? Where's Sam?"

"Well, we have no idea where he is, and, frankly, why should you care?" Harper sized up Tinka.

Hakeem, who looked slightly—but only slightly—less pissed off at Tinka than the others stepped over. "I went running this morning, and I found this." He showed her a picture of the bakery door on his phone, which bore a sign that said, "*Gone fishin'. Closed until July 6.*"

Tinka stared at it for a moment, then shook her head. "What does that mean?"

"That's what we're trying to find out."

Matthew's phone buzzed and he answered it. "Nancy." He put the phone on speaker and set it on the kitchen table. Everyone huddled around, even Tinka.

"Hi, Matthew," came a woman's voice from the other end. "What's the emergency? I think we're still on track for next weekend, right?"

Matthew's jaw dropped and he looked from his fiancé to his sister. "Not next weekend. This weekend. The fourth."

Nancy hesitated. "No…no…the eleventh. It's been on my calendar for months. There's no way I would've scheduled a wedding for this weekend. I've had my vacation planned since last September. I blocked off the dates in the bakery calendar."

"Sam and I have been talking to Dottie about this all along, since March," Harper said. "She's known the whole time that the wedding's been on the fourth. Like, she's literally said the words 'Fourth of July wedding' to me, I swear it."

"I…" Nancy stammered. "I…No. I remember the day she told me about the wedding. I was so excited, and happy that I'd be able to make the cake for Matthew. I adore Matthew. When Dottie told me the wedding was in July, I said, 'Oh no! Tell me it's not on the fourth.' Dottie said, 'Nope, the eleventh.'"

Harper glanced around at everyone, including Tinka, like she was part of the group now. Dottie was their shared enemy. "Shit."

"I'm terribly sorry about this mix-up," Nancy said. "I'll make it up to you—"

"Well," Matthew said, "what are we supposed to do?"

"Do you have cakes in your store we can use?" Tinka asked.

Hakeem mouthed, "Good question."

"Maybe," Nancy said. "But no. You can't get in there. There's no key. I had new locks put on to keep Dottie out during off hours. I really need a better assistant."

"Yes," Harper said, "because your current one is a vindictive weirdo who lives to cause trouble."

"I can put you in touch with a friend—"

"That's okay. We'll figure something out," Matthew said.

The answer was obvious. They needed cakes. Tinka knew cakes.

"Matthew, I'm so sorry," Nancy said.

"I know. Have a good trip, Nancy." He ended the call. "Well, what are we gonna do?"

"What about the French restaurant?" Hakeem asked. "Maybe we can do a pastry table or something."

Tinka coughed, but no one heard her.

"That's asking a lot of them on Christmas in July weekend. They're probably strapped." Matthew put a hand to his chin.

"God, I wish Sam were here right now." Harper sent a frantic text. "Where the hell is he?"

Tinka raised her hand. "I can do it. I'll make the cake and the stuff for the rehearsal dinner, and whatever else you need."

Harper raised an eyebrow. "You? You know how to make a wedding cake?"

"No, but any cake can be a wedding cake, if that's what you call it."

Hakeem handed Tinka his phone again. "This is the cake we want."

Tinka tried to keep her expression as neutral as possible, but it was difficult. "This cake?" This cake was hideous.

"It's the same cake my parents had back in the day."

Tinka stared at the photograph and disco music played in her mind. It was 1979 in cake form—three tiers resting on columns with a working fountain underneath. A plastic bridal party lined the miniature staircase connecting the top tier to a lone cake at the base of the display. The whole thing was topped off by a bride and groom surrounded by a tulle heart. The piping on the cake was fairly simple—white on white— but the structure would be an issue. "Where are we going to get a cake fountain in the twenty-first century?"

"Well, there's one in Nancy's bakery," Matthew said.

"Plus she has all the people, the columns, the stairs, even a groom and groom for the top," Harper added.

Tinka stared at the photo for a moment. "Okay. We can do this." She glanced at the clock on the stove. It was six thirty on Thursday morning. "We have two days to make this cake."

"And all the pies for the rehearsal dinner."

Holy crap. What had she just agreed to? No matter. Tinka was going to make the heck out of this cake for Matthew and

Hakeem. She reached into the drawer next to the stove and pulled out a pad of paper and a pen. "Matthew, write down what each of the tiers is supposed to be and what kinds of pies I'm supposed to make."

"I'm on it," Matthew said.

"Hakeem, if you could start pulling out cake-related ingredients and supplies. We need to take inventory. I'm going to run over to my parents' house and see what they have squirrelled away in terms of cake pans and whatnot."

"And what do you need me to do?" Harper asked.

"Figure out a way to rescue the fountain and other cake decorations from that bakery."

• • •

A sound jolted Sam awake on Thursday morning at...he couldn't tell what time. He was in utter darkness except for the video screen on the wall in front of him, which was playing the DVD menu of *Star Wars: The Force Awakens* on a loop.

After he'd left Tinka last night, he'd driven into town and texted his sister. Harper had been at a party with Jane, Karen, Matthew, and a bunch of other people. She'd invited Sam to join them, but he'd said no.

A party had sounded terrible. Sam had not been in a party mood. So he'd let himself into Maurice's store instead and holed up in the back room with an armful of *Star Wars* DVDs.

Now thunder shook the walls. Ah, so that was the noise that had startled him awake. There were no windows in the screening room, and Sam hadn't even realized it was raining.

He hoisted himself up from the beanbag—the same beanbag he'd shared with Tinka during *Die Hard* last night. That felt like a hundred years ago.

Thunder rolled again, but it wasn't the only sound.

Someone was pounding on the front door of the video store. Sam held his breath. Someone, some girl, was calling his name.

Sam shut off the TV and cleaned up his mess, taking his time. It was probably Tinka, and he didn't know what he wanted to say to her. He'd run through their last conversation in his mind all night long. She hadn't sought Dylan out, not really. He'd happened to be at her house, apparently, and he'd been the only one there to talk to. It had been a conversation of convenience. Maybe Sam had been too hard on her.

But still. She'd basically told him he was a loser for standing by her. It'd make Sam even more of a loser if he were to go back to her at this point.

He pulled open the door between the screening room and the main part of the video store. Rain poured from the awnings in front of Maurice's place. The sky was a dark, heavy gray, and Sam's sister was standing at the front door. Harper was soaked through, like she'd been swimming in all her clothes.

"Open the door, damn it!" She hit the glass with her palm.

Sam sprung into action. He rushed over and pulled the door open for Harper, who dashed in and shook her head like a dog.

"Took you long enough." She paced the floor. Her feet made squelching sounds in her sandals.

"I was sleeping."

Harper stopped walking and put her hands on her hips. "Why the heck weren't you answering my calls?"

"Dead." He held his phone up to prove it.

"Well, everything has gone to shit." She started pacing again. "Dottie screwed us."

Sam's stomach lurched. This was his fault. One stupid text message had ruined everything.

Harper pointed to the door as if Dottie were right outside. "She'd been planning this all along. She wrote down the wrong date on the calendar from the get-go. She told her aunt it was next weekend, even though she kept telling us she knew it was on the fourth."

"Okay…but my whole Dottie text mishap only happened a few weeks ago. Why had she been trying to ruin the wedding all the way back in March?"

Harper's face flushed. "It's possible that I neglected to mention something."

Sam narrowed his eyes.

"I may have hidden her clothes after gym class one time."

"Harper." Sam was going to kill her.

She raised her index finger. "In my defense, she had it coming. She accused Katie Murphy of cheating on her biology test, which was total bullshit. Katie's, like, an angel. Everyone knows that. But Dottie full-on framed her, and Katie got two weeks of detention."

"This would've been valuable information weeks ago." It might've saved him a lot of agony. He could've been more proactive, made Dottie show him the calendar and their order form. He could've dealt with Nancy directly.

"I know. I'm sorry."

"I've been stressing for weeks about staying on Dottie's good side, but the whole thing was a mess from the start, Harper, thanks to you."

Harper slapped on a massive, pleading smile. "On the bright side, there's something we can do to fix it. We can rescue the fountain and other cake decorations from the bakery."

"Are there cakes in there we can use?" There had to be some pies or cakes or, heck, bagels Nancy had left behind.

Harper shook her head. "Nancy didn't seem to think so. I guess she probably cleaned out the shop before she left on vacation. But…it's okay." Harper grinned. "We're making our own wedding cake."

"We. You're making a wedding cake." Harper had once

tried to make their dad a birthday cake and it came out like a concrete slab.

"Uh…" Harper grimaced. "Not just me."

Sam hesitated. "Tinka." Of course.

"She heard us fretting about our cake issues this morning and offered to help right away." Harper nodded toward the door. "She's out there right now hunting down ingredients. In the pouring rain."

Sam knew what Harper was trying to say, that Tinka was doing this for him. "She's doing this to help Matthew and Hakeem. She would've done this for anybody. She loves to bake."

"Regardless," Harper said, "I think you should call her, let her know you're alive. She was worried sick about you this morning. I don't think she slept all night."

"Yeah, well, she can join the club."

The two of them grabbed newspapers from behind Maurice's desk and used them to shield themselves from the downpour as they ran to Dottie's house.

"Why didn't you bring an umbrella?" Wind and rain whipped Sam's face.

"This rolled in out of nowhere. Besides, would it have made a difference?"

"Probably not." Sam chucked the paper into the nearest garbage can and ran faster toward Dottie's while the rain soaked through his hoodie.

He and Harper banged on the front door of the Golds' little bungalow. Dottie's mom answered and let Sam and Harper stand in the foyer while she retrieved her daughter. When she arrived, Dottie's electric blue hair was hidden by a bandana, and she was wearing pajamas with little sheep on them.

"We need to get into the bakery," Harper said right away. No time for chitchat. Besides, Dottie didn't deserve pleasantries at this point.

Dottie smirked. "Can't help you. Aunt Nancy changed the locks."

"Yeah, but you have a special way of getting inside." Sam stared her down. She was letting them in that store. She owed them that much.

Dottie shrugged. "I don't know what you're talking about."

"Yes, you do. You told me your aunt took your keys, but that wasn't going to stop you."

Dottie stared him down with another smug smile. She wasn't going to cave easily.

Harper put a hand on Sam's shoulder. "We'll find another way. Maybe Sheriff Parsons can let us in—"

Sam brushed her off. "No. Dottie is going to do it. She screwed this up. She's going to fix it."

"I screwed nothing up." Dottie nodded toward Harper. "She did. She and her mean little girlfriends."

"You accused Katie of cheating," Harper said.

Dottie raised her brows. "Because she disinvited me to her birthday party."

"Because you ruined Star's cake." Harper stepped closer to Dottie. They were almost nose-to-nose.

Sam shoehorned himself between them. "I don't care who did what to whom when. At some point, Dottie, you have to accept your role in all this. I tried to be nice to you, but for what? You are a mean, vindictive, paranoid person who thinks everyone is out to get her. And you know why people are out to get you? Because you're an asshole. Because you ruin their birthdays and treat people like garbage and the only way you can get them to be nice to you is by threatening to ruin things." He pointed to the door. "Here's your chance to be the bigger person for once. Go get my brother's cake fountain."

Frowning, Dottie hesitated for a minute. "For you, Sam. *Not* for her." Sneering at Harper, she pulled on her rain boots and raincoat, and the three of them ran to the bakery where Dottie slithered in through a basement window with a broken lock and fetched them the decorations plus a few frozen French silk pies.

Armed with the cake paraphernalia, Sam and Harper ducked under awning after awning as they made their way through the rain to their cars. They stopped under the window outside Prince's Summer Sports. Harper's car was parked right in front. "I should text Tinka," Harper said. "See if she needs anything."

She handed her bags to Sam and pulled her phone out of her purse. "Damn it."

"What?" Sam was juggling all the pies and supplies at this point.

"I never felt this buzz." She glanced up at Sam, worry coloring her face. "Their car. The girls slid off the road. They're in a ditch."

"Crap." Sam's chest tightened. "Are they okay?"

"Doesn't say." Harper frowned. "Can you take this stuff back to the house? I'll go pick them up." She pulled the keys out of her purse.

Sam glanced at his sister's tiny car. It was so low to the ground, and there were bound to be puddles on the road that could swallow it whole. At least their house in the resort was close by. "Not in that car, you're not." Sam handed the bags to his sister. "You get home as fast as you can. I'll get the girls."

Chapter Fifteen

Karen banged her head on the steering wheel. "We're never getting out of here."

"Yes, we are." Shaking, Tinka pulled out her phone again and held it up as high as she could in Karen's car, which she, Karen, and Jane had taken to shop for ingredients. After working out a game plan with Sam's siblings, Tinka had gone to her mom and dad's to hunt for baking supplies. There she'd found her mom and dad sitting in the living room, half-dead. Their eyes were bloodshot and her dad had been massaging his temples. They looked like how Tinka felt when she got off the plane in Minneapolis at the beginning of the summer.

Ignoring her hung-over parents, Tinka had rummaged through every box she could find, looking for pans, bowls, or measuring cups. Down in the basement, she'd run into Karen and Jane, who were watching a movie on Jane's iPad.

"What's going on?" Jane asked.

Tinka had pulled a big cardboard box out of a closet. "The bakery screwed up Matthew and Hakeem's cake. I'm going to bake them a new one."

"Oh," Karen had said.

Tinka had kept digging through the box, finding—yay—one set of measuring spoons. When she'd looked up, she found Karen and Jane standing over her. "Do you need help?" Jane had asked.

"You don't have to," Tinka had said.

"Sure we do." Karen had nodded. "For Matthew and Hakeem."

Suppressing a smile, Tinka had said, "I'm sure Matthew and Hakeem would appreciate the help." Karen and Jane weren't doing this for Tinka, but they were talking to her again. It was a start.

When the girls had left that morning to scour various grocery stores in the greater North Pole area, the sky had been bright blue; but it turned gray, windy, and stormy almost immediately after the girls had exited the golf resort.

And on their way home, when they were just past the Wal-Mart, still a few miles out of town, Karen had swerved too fast around a corner, and her car had careened into this ditch.

The girls were fine, but they were stuck. There was no service where they were. Tinka had tried sending Harper a text right after they crashed, but Tinka had no way to tell if it had gone through. They couldn't call the police or AAA or anything. They were so far down from the road that no one driving by would be able to see them.

"What are we gonna do?" Jane asked.

Tinka shoved her phone into her pocket and pulled open the car door. "There's no use sitting here. I'm going see what's what."

"By yourself?" Jane said.

Thinking of Sam, Tinka channeled her inner Walter and took charge of the situation. She was the queen of crises. She could handle this. "I'll be fine."

In her sandals, Tinka climbed to the top of the ravine, slipping in the mud every few feet. When she got to the road, she checked her phone again, shielding it with her hand as best she could. Still no service, and she was surrounded by nothing but trees. Who knew when or if a car would pass by. Who knew if she'd even want to flag down the kind of person who'd drive a car down a deserted country road during a horrible rainstorm. Horror movies were built on that very premise. She brushed her hair from her face. The rain wasn't letting up.

She glared up at the sky and flipped it two very emphatic birds. She was supposed to be back at the Andersons' house baking cakes right now. They had precious little time as it was.

But there was no point blubbering like a baby or getting pissed off. That wasn't helping anyone. She stood up straight, smoothed down her soaking wet shirt, and surveyed the situation. Right now, with water streaming down her arms and nose and little bits of hail hitting her in the face, Tinka was as wet as she was going to get. Her clothes and hair were fully saturated. More rain wasn't going to make a lick of difference at this point, so why not walk to safety? She hadn't seen lightning in a while. She glanced down the road, in both directions. How far were they from that Wal-Mart they passed? Were they closer to the store or to North Pole?

Taking a guess, she took off in the direction of the Wal-Mart, but after about fifty feet or so, she heard a car coming from the opposite direction, from North Pole. She turned around and saw headlights coming toward her. Doing a fabricated math equation in her head, she tried to determine the likelihood that this was a person who wanted to murder her versus a person who might drive her somewhere for help. She bet on kindness and waved her hands, the raindrops and the bright headlights obscuring her vision. The car pulled over.

"We need help!" she shouted, praying this dude was friendly.

The guy jumped out of his truck and slid to a stop a few feet shy of her.

"Sam?" Tinka brushed hair and rain from her eyes.

"Are you okay?" His hands were in the front pocket of his hoodie.

Tinka's whole body rushed with so much relief that she almost started crying. "I'm okay! Karen and Jane are down there. They're fine, too." Tears started streaming down her cheeks, mixing with rain. "I can't believe you're here."

"Someone needed to help you." He faced the ditch, making a big show of assessing the condition of Karen's vehicle down below.

"Yeah, but you…the pontoon boat." She remembered that first day at his house, when they'd gone out on the lake. "I said I was worried about no one looking out for me, and you said you'd do it. And here you are now." She paused. "I'm so sorry."

He shook his head. "Not now. It's raining."

"We can't possibly get any wetter." She pushed the dripping hair off her face.

"Seriously. Let's just go." He took off toward Karen's car.

Tinka grabbed the sleeve of his wet hoodie. He still wouldn't look at her. "I stayed up all night waiting to say this, and I'm going to say it. The Dylan thing. It was dumb, but seriously nothing. He was a sober person in my vicinity with two working ears. That's it. I was so *sad*, Sam. I'd lost you just when I was starting to realize I luh—" She dropped his sleeve and clamped her hand over her mouth.

His eyes snapped to hers. It was the first time he'd looked at her since he got out of his truck.

Tinka's hand still covered her mouth. She could spin this. She could figure out a way to cover for what she'd almost just said. She was starting to realize she…"loved professional wrestling." No. It was time to be honest. As she dropped her hand, she widened her eyes, willing him to see that she was finally hiding nothing. "I was starting to realize that I… love…you." She winced, waiting for him to laugh or run away screaming.

"That's a big word," he said.

She nodded. "It's stupid, I know. We've known each other for a minute."

His dimple flashed for one bright, glorious second. Then he shrugged. "Maybe, but I kinda think it's the right word."

"You do?" She could've sworn her heart was banging out the Hallelujah chorus against her ribs.

He crossed the space between them and pulled her toward him. She never had a second to think as he put his lips to hers. Tiny bits of hail cracked Tinka on the head, but none of it mattered because Sam was kissing her again. Sam was holding her in his arms and it was like all her problems—past, present, and future—had been solved.

She pulled away from him slightly and aimed her mouth at his ear. "I was worried we'd never get to do that again."

"Can we keep doing it?" His lips tickled her earlobe, and she shivered.

"Yes, please," she whispered. "But not right this second. I have cakes to make." She rested her head on his chest. Her tears dribbled onto his "Goonies Never Say Die" hoodie. "I spent all last night on my parents' front porch waiting for you to come home, and when you didn't it almost killed me."

He pulled away, holding her at arm's length, a glint in his eye. "You slept on the porch all night?"

"In a horribly uncomfortable lawn chair."

"For me?"

"For you."

His lips parted, and Sam started to lean down to kiss her

again, but he stopped himself. "Matthew," he said, almost like he was in pain. "Cake."

Tinka nodded with a sigh. "And we should probably rescue Karen and Jane, too. They were *just* starting to maybe like me again. I don't want to blow it." She grabbed Sam's hand, squeezing it hard to convince herself this was real, and the two of them half slid, half ran down the hill to Karen's car together.

. . .

"It's a privilege to watch you work," Sam said as Tinka spread frosting on the bottom layer of Matthew and Hakeem's wedding cake late Friday afternoon.

She smirked at him, and Sam had to bite his cheek to keep himself from grinning even bigger and more like a goofball. Tinka was smiling at him. For real. She liked him, and not in a friendly fake-boyfriend way. For the past twenty-four hours, she'd been in his house baking cakes and pies, and the two of them had used every small opportunity to touch each other — hands grazing at the sink, rubbing shoulders near the oven, "accidental" kisses behind the pantry door. Karen had said they were disgusting, but she'd said it with a smile.

Tinka stood back from the layer of cake she'd finished frosting. "I think this is good for now. I'll come over early tomorrow, put it together, and decorate it. That will give it less time to collapse."

"It won't collapse." Sam hopped off the counter, hoisted up the cake, and carried it toward the fridge. "Door."

She pulled it open; then Sam crouched down to place the cake on the bottom shelf of the refrigerator, where every available square inch was crammed with pies, cookies, and the other three frosted layers of cake. The Andersons had had to move all their actual food down to the basement. "Everything looks delicious," Sam said. "I can't wait to try it."

Tinka crouched down next to him and rested her head on his shoulder. She turned her head and kissed his arm. They stayed like that for a moment, leaning against each other, until his dad's voice behind them boomed, "We have air conditioning, you know."

Blushing, Sam stood and helped Tinka from her crouch. His dad was standing in the kitchen with a middle-aged lady Sam didn't recognize.

His dad gestured toward the woman. "I wanted to bring my friend Marge over to see what you've done today. She's the one who owns the bakery in South Carolina. Marge, this is Tinka. Tinka, Marge."

"It's so nice to meet you," Tinka said, shaking her hand. When Marge turned toward the fridge, Tinka shot Sam a scared face. He gave her a thumbs-up.

As Marge perused the baked goods Tinka had made over the past two days, Sam walked her through each item. "There's a sour orange pie, chocolate chess pie, grasshopper pie, strawberry-radish pie—"

Marge turned around. "Radish?"

Tinka flushed. "For something different."

"Can I try a slice?"

Tinka pulled one of the strawberry radish pies off the top shelf and cut a piece for Marge. "We have a couple of these, so…" Shrugging, she backed away. Sam wrapped an arm around her waist for support.

Marge took a tiny bite of the filling, savoring it. Then she broke off a piece of the crust. "Nice flaky crust," she said. "And I really enjoyed the spice of the radish. You have a good hand with flavoring, not too sweet."

"Thank you."

Marge ate a second, larger forkful. "John says that you go to Florian's Academy."

"I do."

"My bakery is near there. If you're interested in working during the school year, I'm always looking for help."

"That would be amazing."

Marge handed her a business card. "Call me when you're back at school."

"Thanks." Tinka stared down at the card. After his dad and Marge had left the room, she turned to Sam. "Wow. This is for real."

"Sure is."

"I mean, I'm really going back to school," she said.

"And I'm going to L.A., but not for, like, six weeks." He tried to put a positive spin on things.

"That's practically a lifetime."

"We'll probably hate each other by that point, and I'll never want to see your face again," Sam said.

Tinka stepped closer to him and put a hand on his cheek. "I won't hate you. Guaranteed. Not six *weeks* from now, at least. Six *months*, on the other hand…" Joking, she wiggled her eyebrows.

Sam wrapped his arms around her and pulled her in close. "We're setting ourselves up for a lot of heartache."

"Maybe. But it makes me want to enjoy every minute we have together here. I can't imagine going to the movies on Saturday night or the arcade or anything without you. North Pole is Sam." She hugged him tighter. "And I want Sam."

"You have Sam."

She squeezed him one more time and then backed away. "But you don't have Tinka, at least not tonight."

He made a sad face.

"Don't look at me like that. You've got your brother's rehearsal dinner over at the golf club, and I have to sleep for, like, the next fifteen hours." She opened her eyes wide to show him how puffy and glassy they were.

"But you don't have to go yet, do you? It's still early." Sam checked his phone. He still had an hour or two before he had to start getting ready.

She leaned in close and kissed his cheek. "It's not early when you've been up for almost thirty-six hours straight."

"You have a point." But they had so little time together, he wanted to spend every moment with her for the next six weeks, taking mental snapshots in full color. "Hey, were you aware that it's customary for the wedding cake maker to save a dance for the best man, you know, if she wants?"

"She wants." Tinka grabbed a plate of cookies for Karen and Jane and headed toward the back door. "Oh." She spun around. "By the way, I left you something on your pillow to remember me by." She winked and headed out the sliding glass door.

Not hesitating for a second, Sam ran upstairs and found a plate of cookies on his pillow, the kind his mom used to make, the ones Tinka had said she'd make him as a thank you for driving her to get her stitches the first day they met. "*Alfajores*," the note said, "*as promised.*"

Sam took a bite of one and the flavor exploded inside his mouth—silky caramel and flaky, buttery shortbread. They were even better than he remembered.

He glanced at the suit hanging over his closet door. He wasn't about to put that on until the last minute, so he grabbed the plate of cookies and went to Harper's room.

She was doing her makeup and turned toward him. With only one eye done so far, she looked a little like Alex from *A Clockwork Orange*.

Sam held out the plate. "Here."

Eyeing him warily, Harper stood and grabbed a cookie. "These look like Mom's."

"Try it."

Harper took a bite. "Oh my *God*." She held a hand to her

forehead and dramatically swooned against the doorjamb.

"Right?"

Harper snatched the plate from him and dashed into the hallway. She banged on Matthew's door.

"Harper, your face," Matthew said when he saw her. He'd just gotten out of the shower and was wearing only a towel.

"Shut up," Harper said. "Try this."

Matthew took a tiny bite. A slow smile spread across his face. "Mom's cookies. I forgot about these. Ugh!" He dabbed the corner of his eye with a bent knuckle. "I'm going to look like a blubbering mess at the rehearsal."

"And no one will care." Tears stung Sam's eyes, probably because his brother was crying. Older brothers weren't supposed to cry, even on days like these. Sam blew out a shaky breath. "We're allowed to be sad. Everyone will understand."

"Sam!" Harper hugged his arm. "You're crying."

"No, I'm not." He wiped a rogue tear from his cheek.

She squeezed his bicep. "You're going to make me ruin my makeup."

Matthew sniffed and wiped his nose with the back of his hand. "Which would be for the best."

Harper playfully kicked his shin.

"I'm really glad you're both here," Sam said. "I kind of hated you for leaving me with all the wedding minutiae, but it was a good distraction. I miss Mom. I missed you guys. I'm going to miss this place."

"We're going to be so spread out," Harper said. "Matthew and Hakeem will be in New York. Sam, you'll be in California. Everyone's abandoning me. I'm gonna be stuck here in North Pole with Maddie and Dad."

"And all your friends." Sam's voice broke. This weekend was bringing a lot of feelings to the forefront. The whole college thing seemed so unnatural to him at the moment, so cruel. He was having the best time of his life right where he was; but then one day the calendar would flip, and he'd be whisked away to a whole other state where he'd know no one. "I can't believe I have to leave."

"Everyone does at some point," Matthew said. "And you can always come back. This is your home."

"But I don't want to go," Sam said, even though he knew that wasn't totally true. He wanted to go to college and he wanted to study film, just not right this minute. He was going to miss too much and too many people. "I'm sad."

Harper threw an arm around him. "Sam's the emotional wreck for once. I love it."

Matthew ushered them into his room, cookies and all. "We've got some time before the rehearsal. Unload on us, Sam. It's our turn to make you feel better."

Chapter Sixteen

Tinka trudged home from Sam's house, armed with a plate of cookies for Jane and Karen. They'd been such a huge help over the past two days, they deserved to admire (and taste) their handiwork. And Tinka was pretty sure she deserved to collapse in a heap on her blowup bed for the next twelve hours or so.

But sleep, however, had to wait. When she opened the front door of her parents' house, she was greeted by her mom and dad, who were lounging on one of the drop cloth-covered couches in the living room.

"The mechanic called," her dad said. "Karen should be able to drive the car home early next week. The damage wasn't too bad."

"That's good," Tinka said.

"You've been gone a while." Her mom closed her book and set it on the coffee table. "Jane said you were working on Sam's brother's wedding cake?"

"The bakery screwed up, so we decided to make our own."

Her dad filled in an answer on his crossword puzzle. "It

was nice of you to help."

She was ready to let this go, to disappear downstairs and hit the bed, but here was her chance to finally have this conversation. "I wasn't just helping, though. I was kind of in charge of the whole thing."

Her parents stared at her as if they didn't understand her words.

Tinka stepped into the living room, put the plate of cookies on the coffee table, and sat across from her parents. "I'm pretty good at it, actually. Baking."

"Since when?" her mom asked. "I've never known you to eat a cake, let alone make one."

"I've been baking for a long time. I used to do it at Karen's, though, because you were pretty strict about me using the stove, and you didn't like me eating sugary stuff."

Both parents stared at Tinka for a moment. She got the picture that maybe they were questioning whether or not they were still drunk from the other night.

"Baking?" her mom asked.

"Baking," Tinka said.

Again, they peered at her for a few beats.

"I know I shouldn't be shocked by this. I mean, you're talking about baking, not cliff diving or something, but it feels so out of nowhere," her mom said.

Like you guys moving to North Pole, Tinka added silently. "Actually." Tinka cleared her throat. "I've been wanting to talk to you guys about this for a while. I spent most of last year thinking about it, and this is what I want to do with my life. I want to bake. I'd like to go to culinary school."

Again, they gawked at her like she was an alien being. "Culinary school?" her dad said. "Really?"

"Yes."

"But Duke."

"Was your idea," Tinka said quietly. "Not mine."

"You've been working toward a golf scholarship."

Tinka sighed. "I don't want that anymore. I never really did, if I'm being honest."

"But the team, all the lessons, Florian's—"

"I did those things for you."

Her dad's mouth was pursed, a vein throbbing in his forehead. Her mom was the one who spoke. "So you want to quit the team. Is that what you're saying?"

Tinka nodded. "I do. Yes." Her eyes swung to her dad. "It's not like I never want to play again. I do. With you. I...I just don't want to be so serious about it. I found something else I love to do." She pushed the plate of cookies toward them, but neither her mom nor dad grabbed one.

Her dad massaged his temples. "Why weren't you honest with us? When I think about all the time we wasted—and money. Do you know how much tuition at Florian's is?"

"It wasn't wasted, though, Dad. I had a great experience at Florian's. I made friends and got to have some independence for once. I figured out for sure that baking was what I wanted to do. I'm so grateful you sent me there." She paused. Her father wasn't convinced. "And, Dad, that time on the golf course with you was never wasted. Without it"—she had to take a second to compose herself—"we never would've spent any time together."

Both her parents fell silent.

Tinka's throat tightened into a ball that was threatening to dissolve into tears at any moment. She glanced at the door, willing Sam to come in and save the day, to rescue her from this conversation. But no. She was on her own this time. She had to do this herself. "My golfing has always been how you've kept Jake alive in your mind. I had no idea how to admit to you that it wasn't what I wanted anymore. How would you look at me if I told you that? If I were the one who basically cut that last tether to him?" She blinked back the tears.

Her parents' faces were stone white. "That's not our last tether to him," her mom said. "There's no last tether to Jake. He's always going to be with us, no matter what."

"I get that…I mean, logically." Tinka let out a long shaky breath. If she managed to get through this conversation without bawling, it'd be a miracle. Her complete exhaustion was not helping matters. "But you have to understand that I've been living in his shadow my entire life. I've been told— for as long as I can remember—that my job was to keep you two happy."

"Who told you that?" her mom asked. "I never told you that."

Tinka shook her head. "Aunt Marie. Grandma and Grandpa. It was something I felt for myself. I'd see you get sad, and I'd think, 'It's my job to not let that happen.'"

Both her parents put their hands to their mouths.

"And then…" Oh, now the tears were coming. There was no stopping them. "I flew home in June and you'd totally uprooted our family and moved here. And you've completely changed." She waved a hand to indicate her parents. "Completely. You're happy and lovey-dovey and you're making friends and doing shots and I don't even know. You seem like you're fixed all of a sudden, and what was the catalyst? It was me going away—the girl who always felt it was her job to keep you happy." She dropped her head into her hands.

Her parents ran over and sat on either side of her, rubbing her back and smoothing her hair. Her mom kissed her head, then pulled Tinka upright. "That is *not* what happened." She put her hands on Tinka's shoulders and turned her so they were face-to-face. Tinka's mother stared her straight in the eye. "We are not better because you were gone. We're better because we've been working hard on ourselves and our relationship."

Her dad leaned closer to her and spoke softly. "When we found out that Karen's"—he glanced toward the basement stairs to make sure she wasn't there—"parents were having trouble, your mom and I saw ourselves in them."

"We didn't want to get to that point," Tinka's mom said. "So we started seeing a marriage counselor."

"Carol," Tinka said. "You mentioned the name before."

"Carol," her dad said. "She helped us see how our lives were on hold and we were putting our grief and anxieties above everything."

"It's why I was always such a helicopter parent," her mom said.

"And it's why I...wasn't." Her dad wrapped an arm around Tinka's shoulders. "Maybe you weren't wrong when you said golf was the only way I related to you."

"I always got the sense that you kept me at arms' length because you didn't want to get too close to another kid you might lose."

Her mom hugged her harder.

Tinka's dad shared a look with his wife. "I'm so sorry I ever made you feel that way. The fact is, I love you more than you could ever know. And we should've included you in our counseling."

"Or at least let you in on our plans to move. I think we were embarrassed. I know I was." Her mom closed her eyes for a second. "And you've always gone along with things without complaint. We definitely took advantage of that this year, which was not fair to you. Not at all."

"I think we were so excited that we were doing better and about the prospect of moving to North Pole, we assumed you'd feel the same way about it as we did."

Tinka had been right all along. They hadn't considered her feelings at all.

"We thought it'd be a fun surprise."

"I mean, I am starting to like it here. I really am," Tinka said. "But that has nothing at all to do with you guys. I like it here in spite of you. You sent me away to boarding school without giving me a choice, then you sold our house and dragged me out to the middle of nowhere and this ridiculous Christmas village without giving me a say. You forced me into golf lessons I didn't want and tried to set me up with a guy I didn't like. You made me spend the entire summer working on this terrible house you bought. I'm…I'm mad at you."

"You have every right to be," her mom said.

"Damn right I do." Tinka stood up. Her eyes scanned the room. "It's like you don't know me. You've never known me. And now you're going to be shipping me back to Florian's in six weeks, so what are we even doing here?"

"You should come with us to see Carol—or another counselor, or you can see someone on your own, if you want. We can work this out. At least we're talking now," her dad said. "We're finally being honest with one another."

"And maybe you shouldn't go back to Florian's," her mom said quietly.

Tinka's eyes swung to her. "What are you saying? You're going to pull me out of another school? I'm going to be subjected to another of your whims? I've been offered a job in South Carolina, you know. At a bakery." She pulled Marge's card out of her pocket and waved it at her parents.

Her mom shook her head. "No. It's your choice. I'm giving you the option. Go back to Florian's, if you want. You have our blessing. Or stay here in North Pole so we can work things out."

"We'll work things out either way," her dad said. "I want to be clear. If you decide to go to Florian's, we won't be mad. We won't hide things from you. We'll still do the work to be better parents and a stronger family. We'll just have to do it remotely."

Tinka glared at them. So now after years of telling her what to do, they were giving her exactly two options—go back to school where everyone probably hated her or stay here in North Pole where she didn't know anybody. Great choices, Mom and Dad.

Tinka grabbed the plate of cookies. She had been about to take them downstairs to Karen and Jane, but instead she tossed them onto the couch, to the spot between her parents that she'd just vacated. "Here," she said. "Get to know your daughter."

She marched down to the basement and flopped onto the couch between Karen and Jane, who were in the middle of painting their fingernails.

"Uh…" Jane said. "Are you okay?"

"We heard the whole thing," Karen said.

Of course they had. Tinka wiped her eyes. "I don't know what they expect me to do," she whispered. "Like, if I choose to go to Florian's, am I abandoning them? Is that me opting out of a better relationship with them? But if I stay here, I go to a school where I basically don't know anyone, and I miss out on working with Sam's dad's friend."

Jane patted her knee. "I think you need to work things out with your mom and dad."

Tinka grinned at her mirthlessly. "Is this your way of getting rid of me at Florian's?"

Careful not to nick her fresh polish, Jane tossed a pillow at Tinka. "Maybe I'm a glutton for punishment, and maybe that's obvious because I did keep texting my ex-boyfriend for weeks after I knew he no longer wanted to be with me, but I'd miss you at Florian's. I loved having you as a roommate."

"I loved having you as a roommate," Tinka said. "I was so worried about being the new girl, but you welcomed me with open arms. You made me feel—after having been abandoned by my parents, basically—like a worthy human being. And I will never forgive myself for what I did to you." She turned to Karen. "Or to you."

Karen pursed her lips. "You had a lot going on."

"So did you. I was a terrible friend. I will never treat anyone like that again. I will never treat *you* like that again, if you'll let me be a part of your life." She frowned. "We go way back, Karen. Way, way back. And, regardless of where our lives take us, I want you to know that you can always count on me. From this moment on. I am starting fresh."

"And I'm sorry I made you feel like I'd judge you if you were honest with me." Karen nudged her in the side. "But the second you don't text me back…"

"Not even an issue. You are on my immediate 'text back' list. I'll text back so fast your head will spin."

"I look forward to putting that to the test." A reluctant smile played on Karen's lips.

Tinka turned to Jane. "Now you…"

"I still think you should stay here with your parents." Jane blew on her fingers. "Not because I don't want you at school, but because I don't think you want to be there."

Tinka frowned.

"I've seen you at Florian's, and I've seen you here. I used to think you were having fun there, that you were super carefree and loving it. But now that I've seen you here with Sam, and *actually* relaxed, I know that wasn't the real you in South Carolina. What are you going to do when you go back and people expect fun, reckless Tinka?"

"I'll show them this Tinka instead. Besides, I've got a job there. I'm going to be learning about running a bakery."

"There are other bakeries in the world, is all I'm saying." Jane patted her knee again. "You only have one set of parents."

. . .

Under the arch of flowers on the Andersons' beach, Sam tried to focus on the minister as she married Matthew and Hakeem, but he kept having to stop himself from glancing back at Tinka in the folding chairs on the groom's side.

Best man duties had kept him from her all day, and it was driving him to distraction. He'd seen her for a millisecond that morning when she'd come over with Jane, Karen, and—whoa—her parents to put the cake together and finish the decorations. He'd run over to her, but barely had time to plant a kiss on her cheek, before Matthew was dragging him into town to pick up flowers and their tuxes.

Now she was sitting in the crowd, and he could feel her presence behind him. She was wearing this amazing strapless indigo gown that set off her eyes, and she had her hair done up in a braid-bun thing. She actually looked like Cinderella.

And Sam felt confident that, even if he didn't look like Prince Eric, he was Prince Charming to Tinka.

After the ceremony, he walked with Hakeem's sister down the aisle, and they were immediately dragged off to the house for pictures with the wedding party and both families. They posed in the living room, in the garden in front of the house, and on the deck.

By the time pictures were done, dinner was starting. As they took their seats at the head table, he managed a quick wave to Tinka, who returned it with a big grin that sent his heart racing.

Finally, after the salad course, Sam stood to find her, but his dad caught him and dragged him around to meet all his college friends and people he worked with. By the time Sam had been introduced to nearly the entire wedding reception, the main course—fillet and lobster tail—was already on the table.

Then Matthew and Hakeem did their first dance ("At My Most Beautiful" by REM), the parents danced with their sons (to the Ugly Kid Joe version of "Cat's in the Cradle," because Matthew and Hakeem, as always, thought they were hilarious), and the wedding party was called up to bust a move *en masse* to "Let's Dance" by David Bowie. Sam, wiped out and in desperate need of some water, left the dance floor to finally find Tinka.

She was over near the pastry table talking to Elena Chestnut and her boyfriend, Oliver Prince. As he approached, Sam overheard Elena saying, "I hope you do stick around."

"Stick around?" Sam said, grabbing a bottle of water from a passing waiter.

Tinka ran over and put her arms around him. "You've missed a lot over the past twenty-four hours."

"Apparently."

"When do I get to dance with the best man?"

"After he catches his breath." Sam opened the bottle and downed half of it. Wiping the corner of his mouth with the back of his hand, he said, "What?"

Tinka was grinning at him. "I was thinking about the time we first met. When you gave me and Jane water after our run. I honestly thought you were going to murder us."

"Well, I was going to." Sam screwed the cap back on his bottle. "I changed my mind when I found out you liked to bake."

"Baking saves lives."

"It does." Sam gestured toward Elena and Oliver, who'd left them to talk to Danny and Star. "So, what was the sticking around thing about?"

Tinka shrugged. "My parents and I had a chat...a fight...a chat-fight. They told me I had the option of going back to Florian's or staying here in North Pole with them, so we could work on our 'relationship.'"

"Maybe not a bad idea," Sam said.

"Maybe not. They're all of a sudden very interested

in my future baking career. That's why they came with me this morning to finish the cake. My dad's been gathering information on everything from your dad's friend's bakery in South Carolina to culinary institutes around the country." She shook her head. "They're so embarrassing."

"They care."

"Too much, sometimes." Tinka gestured toward the dance floor, where her mom and dad were dancing close. "I don't know what I'm gonna do. Based on how in-my-face they've been today, going back to Florian's isn't sounding too bad."

"They're excited. They'll calm down. You can ask them to calm down."

"And I think they might actually listen, if you can believe it." She sighed. "The thing with your dad's friend is a legit great opportunity, though."

"But there are other bakeries in the world."

"That's what Jane said."

"She's very wise."

Tinka played with his right cufflink. "If I stayed here, you and I would only be half a continent apart, and you wouldn't have to choose between coming to see me and visiting your family."

Sam's heart sped up as her hands tickled his wrist. "But that can't factor into your decision. You and I will work things out, no matter what." He reached into his pocket for a box he'd been carrying around all day. "Tinka—"

But then DJ Craig and his assistant Dinesh were calling for their attention. Matthew and Hakeem were about to cut the cake.

"Eek," Tinka squealed. She grabbed Sam's hand and dragged him toward the dance floor. "It's still standing," she whispered.

The cake was gorgeous. It was exactly like Hakeem's picture. Three tiers stood on top of pillars surrounding a bubbling fountain, and a wedding party of plastic figures lined a winding staircase down to the bottom tier. But the cheesy '70s vibe didn't distract at all from Tinka's flawless piping work. "Wow. You did that."

"We all did."

"No." He squeezed her hand. "Don't get all humble now. That cake would be a wreck without you."

Tinka gazed toward the dance floor, where a few couples were intertwined. Danny and Star were out there, plus Oliver and Elena, Jane and Brian, Karen and Eric. She turned to Sam. "You want to dance?"

"Yes, but first." He reached into his pocket for the jewelry box, which he passed to her. "Please do not throw this back at me again."

She flipped it over in her hand. "What's this?"

"Remember the night we…broke up?"

She winced.

"I tried to give you this. I had Maurice pick them up for me while we were out on the town."

She opened the box. In it were the rainbow quadrangle earrings they'd seen at Mrs. Claus's Closet that day.

"You said they'd match your dress. You were right."

"Sam." She handed the box to him while she put the earrings on.

"I figured they can be a thank you for making the cake, plus, you know, I just really like you and stuff." He blushed, shaking his head.

She squeezed his hand. "I just really like you and stuff, too."

"Now, will you please dance with me before someone else drags me away for a photo op?"

"You're such a big deal," she said, wrapping her arms around his neck and pressing her lips to his.

"Don't you forget it."

Epilogue

"I've never done this before." Tinka had barely slept all night in anticipation of what she and Sam were about to do today. She kept having nightmares about everything going horribly wrong.

"I know you haven't," Sam said. "But I have. Follow my lead."

"Go slow." She clenched her fists, digging her fingernails into her palms. Her entire body was tense. She needed a massage. Maybe they should do that instead.

He hugged her close, rubbing her back. "I promise, I will. Whatever you need."

"I mean it," she said, pushing him away and staring him down. "Like, if the sign says 'Slow,' go slow. I'm not winding up in another ditch."

"I won't let that happen to you. Now if a branch falls on the tracks or something, there's nothing I can do about it." He waved to some friend of his down Main Street, who was coming out of the barbershop.

"You'd better hope that doesn't happen."

Behind them, the door to Santabucks flew open and the rest of their crowd streamed out, carrying beverages. Jane handed

Sam and Tinka their black coffees. Karen, Harper, Matthew, and Hakeem had cold drinks. "Ready for this?" Jane asked.

"Ready is such a strong word," Tinka said.

Sam put his arm around her, kneading her shoulder, which did nothing to relieve the tension in her body. She touched the ring around her neck but that didn't help either. "She's going to do great," he said.

Matthew and Hakeem were leaving on their honeymoon tomorrow and it was Jane and Karen's last day in North Pole, so they were all going down Jingle Falls. All of them. Tinka was fairly certain this would be the end of her. At least she'd die happy.

Happy. In North Pole. Four short weeks ago, she'd been pretty sure she was living in actual hell, but now there was no place she'd rather be. She knew North Pole wasn't magic—the magic, if she could even call it that, was in finally being true to herself, though she'd never say those embarrassing words out loud—but it felt that way today.

In the hot, bright July sunlight, the group headed down Main Street toward their cars. The Christmas in July festival had ended on Sunday, and most of the tourists had gone home to their lives and jobs. North Pole was calm and quiet. Some people were at work. Others had abandoned Main Street for pools and beaches.

"I love it like this," Sam said.

"I kind of do, too," Tinka agreed. "It feels like being in school after hours."

As they walked past the bakery, Nancy Gold ran out and flagged them down. "Sam!" she cried. "Matthew! Harper!"

Their group stopped and waited for Nancy to catch up. She was wearing a lime green Cancun T-shirt that set off her new tan. "I want to apologize again. That mix up was unacceptable. I want to offer your family free birthday cakes for life. It's the least I can do."

"We have a new baker now." Sam nodded to Tinka.

"Yeah," Harper said. "Tinka made the cake. She saved the day after Dottie screwed everything up."

Nancy glanced at Tinka. "I heard you stepped up. Maggie Garland told me the cake was to die for."

Tinka grinned and Sam squeezed her hand.

"It was to die for," Sam said.

"Absolutely," added Hakeem.

Tinka nodded toward the store window, where Nancy had put up a sign. "I see you're looking for help." The idea had occurred to her the other night at the wedding. There were other bakeries. In fact, there was one right here in town, one that might be looking for a good, reliable, less vindictive worker.

Nancy frowned. "Well, I had to fire Dottie after this, didn't I? She'd had it coming for a while. I'm looking for help around the store. Not only that, but I'd like to have someone I can count on to pick up the slack, baking-wise. Dottie was never good for that." Her eyes widened at Tinka. "You're not interested, are you?"

"I might be," Tinka said. "I'm supposed to go back to school in South Carolina, but my parents kind of want me to stay here, and I kind of want to stay with them…maybe." She'd been thinking about it a lot. The three of them were finally talking, finally being honest with each other. How would it help matters if she up and left them in a few weeks? They needed time to heal together, and to get to know each other for real, all cards on the table.

"Well, if you do stick around, I think this job would be worth your while. I've been doing this a long time, and I need someone talented to assist me. You'd have free reign to try new things."

"What kinds of new things?" Tinka asked.

"Whatever you want. It's hard for me to stay on top of new trends when I'm always trying to keep up with filling my regular orders. I want to bring Sugarplum Sweets into the future, but I need help with that."

"Wow," Tinka said. "That sounds…kind of amazing."

"But if you do decide to go back to school, maybe in the summer, then. Or winter break." Nancy said good-bye, waved, and turned around.

Tinka stared hard at her back. The decision was obvious, wasn't it?

"Hey, Nancy!" she shouted. "I'll call you, okay?"

Nancy turned back, grinning. "Okay."

Sam and Tinka hopped into his truck, just the two of them. "Are you really doing this? Are you going to stay in North Pole?" He backed out of his parking spot.

"I don't know," Tinka said. "I kind of think maybe I am. Is that silly?"

Sam shook his head. "It's not silly. It's North Pole." He let that one sink in. "But you need to choose what's best for you."

She stared out the passenger's side window. The Christmas-themed stores flew by in a rush. "I'm not sure what's best. You'd like it if I stuck around, right?"

He shook his head. "Doesn't matter what I'd like. And if you're fishing for me to tell you what to do, not gonna happen. I am neutral. I'm Switzerland."

She squeezed his wrist. "You're a jerk."

At the top of Jingle Falls, the two of them met the rest of their group. "Are we doing this or what?" Harper had a hand on her hip.

Tinka's right leg was shaking hard like it was begging her to run the hell away from this foolishness. "We're doing it."

"Okay." Harper held up her sled. "Let's make it interesting. Whoever wipes out buys lunch at Mags's afterward."

"No one's going to wipe out." Sam glanced at Tinka as if he could see the words "wipe out" echoing through her head.

"Sure, sure," Matthew said. "But this is an added incentive

to stay on the track." He nodded toward the slide and Hakeem followed him over. Matthew went first, then his new husband. Harper followed, then Jane and Karen.

At last, only Tinka and Sam were left.

"You ready?" he asked.

She nodded, then said, "No."

"You can back out."

She drew in a deep breath, and let it out. "I'm doing this. We're doing it. Together." She stepped up to the slide attendant and handed him her sled. Sam got in first, then he held out a hand to help Tinka in. She got in front of him and sat down, nestled between his legs.

"I will go slow. I promise." He wrapped his arms around her, reached between her knees, and grabbed the throttle. The fact that he was holding her so tight in his strong, wonderful arms while breathing right next to her ear, almost made her forget about her impending doom. Almost. "Here we go," he whispered.

The ride started easy enough, slow and gradual. After a few seconds, she leaned into Sam, relaxing a bit.

"See?" he said. "This is fun!"

"It is!" She squinted into the sun, feeling the warm air whipping at her face. This was safe. This was fun. This was perfect.

Then it happened. A squirrel or a chipmunk or something crossed the track. Tinka screamed as her life flashed before her eyes. Sam pulled hard on the throttle to stop, but it was no use. Their sled tipped over and they skidded on the track. Tinka landed in a patch of grass and pinched herself to make sure she was alive. She was.

Sam jumped up immediately and ran to her. "Shit! Are you okay?" He helped her stand. "Please don't hold this over me. I was going slow—"

She brushed herself off. "I think I'm fine."

"Are you sure?" Sam examined her. Then, "Oh my God.

Your knee."

Tinka glanced at her right leg, the leg that had been warning her earlier with all its shaking. The crash had ripped a hole in her jeans, and her knee had been skinned raw. She hadn't felt the pain until she saw her injury, but now it hurt like hell. "Just a flesh wound," she said, hopping around to distract herself from the pain. "I'll survive. I'm Walter, remember?"

"If it makes you feel any better, I didn't escape this unscathed." Wincing from his own injury, Sam held up his forearm, which looked a lot like Tinka's knee.

She grimaced. "I guess we're paying for lunch." She glanced down at her leg again. Sam held out an arm, like he was ready to catch her if she fell. But she wouldn't. She gritted her teeth and attempted to smile up at him. It didn't go well. "I guess I'm a real North Poler now, huh?"

"You know, you didn't actually have to injure yourself," Sam said. "We would've let you stay anyway. I mean, Hakeem's scar-free and we still like him."

"I want to stay." Tinka focused on the sky where big, white, fluffy clouds floated across the expanse of blue. "I really do, not because of my parents." She glanced at him. "And, no, not because of you." Tinka's whole body warmed and even the pain subsided. "I think you've actually managed to convince me. This place is home."

Sam took her hand and nodded toward the slide. "You know there's only one way down from this point, unless you brought your rock climbing gear."

"I was afraid of that." She dragged the sled back onto the track and climbed in.

Sam got in behind Tinka and wrapped his arms around her. With wide eyes, she glanced back at him. "Don't let me go."

"Never," he said, giving her one last squeeze before pulling on the throttle and sending them hurtling the rest of the way down the slide.

Acknowledgments

Much love to Kate Brauning, Bethany Robison, the rest of the team at Entangled, and my agent, Beth Phelan.

I told Amy Henning, Rita Kerrigan, Annie Martinez, and Bridget Eaglin I'd thank them in a book someday, so here that is. Thank you, girls, for being such good friends for so many, many years. We all look great at our advanced age. I also want to throw a special shout out to Meg Kelly. Seeing my daughter make friends of her own reminds me of all the goofy stuff we used to do when we were kids and takes me back to when we were going to own our own Hallmark store. There's still time!

All the love and thanks to my family, especially John and my parents.

Everything I know about baking (and life, basically), I learned from America's Test Kitchen.

Thank you to you—yes, *you*!—for reading this book. You're the reason I do this. Also the fame, but mostly you.

About the Author

Julie Hammerle is the author of *The Sound of Us* (Entangled TEEN, 2016) and the North Pole, Minnesota YA romance series (Entangled Crush, 2017). She writes about TV and pop culture for the ChicagoNow blog, Hammervision, and lives in Chicago with her family. She enjoys reading, cooking, and watching all the television.

Discover more of Entangled Teen Crush's books...

THE PERFECTLY IMPERFECT MATCH
a Suttonville Sentinels novel by Kendra C. Highley

Pitcher Dylan Dennings has his future all mapped out: make the minors straight out of high school, work his way up the farm system, and get called up to the majors by the time he's twenty-three. The Plan has been his sole focus for years, and if making his dreams come true means instituting a strict "no girls" policy, so be it. Problem is, Dylan keeps running into Lucy Foster—needlepoint ninja, chicken advocate, and lover of mayhem. Every interaction sparks hotter than the last, but with Dylan's future on the line, he has to decide whether some rules are made to be broken...

TIED UP IN YOU
a novel by Erin Fletcher

Everyone says hotshot goalie Luke Jackson is God's gift to girls, but the only girl he *wants* is his best friend, Malina Hall. Problem is, one of his teammates is showing interest, and the guy has more in common with Malina than Jackson ever will. As her best friend, Jackson should get out of the way. But if there's one thing he's learned from hockey, it's to go for what you want, even if it means falling flat on your face. And he's definitely falling for Malina.

INCRIMINATING DATING
a novel by Rebekah Purdy

Ayla Hawkins wants to affect change in her high school by running for class president. But she'll need a miracle to win—enter Luke Pressler. If he can pose as her fake boyfriend, she's got the election in the bag. Luke can't believe he's been forced to pretend to date Ayla, but she turns out to be just the breath of fresh air he needed. Still, they come from different worlds, and when the election is over, their fauxmance will be, too.

CPSIA information can be obtained
at www.ICGtesting.com
Printed in the USA
BVOW06s2155150118
505351BV00001B/4/P